CARTOON NETWORK

STEVEN UNIVERSE

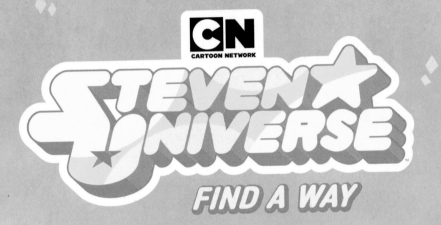

FIND A WAY

kaboom!

WWW.BOOM-STUDIOS.COM

STEVEN UNIVERSE ONGOING Volume Five, July 2019. Published by KaBOOM!, a division of Boom Entertainment, Inc. STEVEN UNIVERSE, CARTOON NETWORK, the logos, and all related characters and elements are trademarks of and © Cartoon Network. A WarnerMedia Company. All rights reserved. (S19) Originally published in single magazine form as STEVEN UNIVERSE ONGOING No. 17-20 © Cartoon Network. A WarnerMedia Company. All rights reserved. (S18) KaBOOM!™ and the KaBOOM! logo are trademarks of Boom Entertainment, Inc., registered in various countries and categories. All characters, events, and institutions depicted herein are fictional. Any similarity between any of the names, characters, persons, events, and/or institutions in this publication to actual names, characters, and persons, whether living or dead, events, and/or institutions is unintended and purely coincidental. KaBOOM! does not read or accept unsolicited submissions of ideas, stories, or artwork.

For information regarding the CPSIA on this printed material, call: (203) 595-363 and provide reference #RICH - 844881.

BOOM! Studios, 5670 Wilshire Boulevard, Suite 400, Los Angeles, CA 90036-5679. Printed in USA. First Printing.

ISBN: 978-1-68415-387-9, eISBN: 978-1-64144-370-8

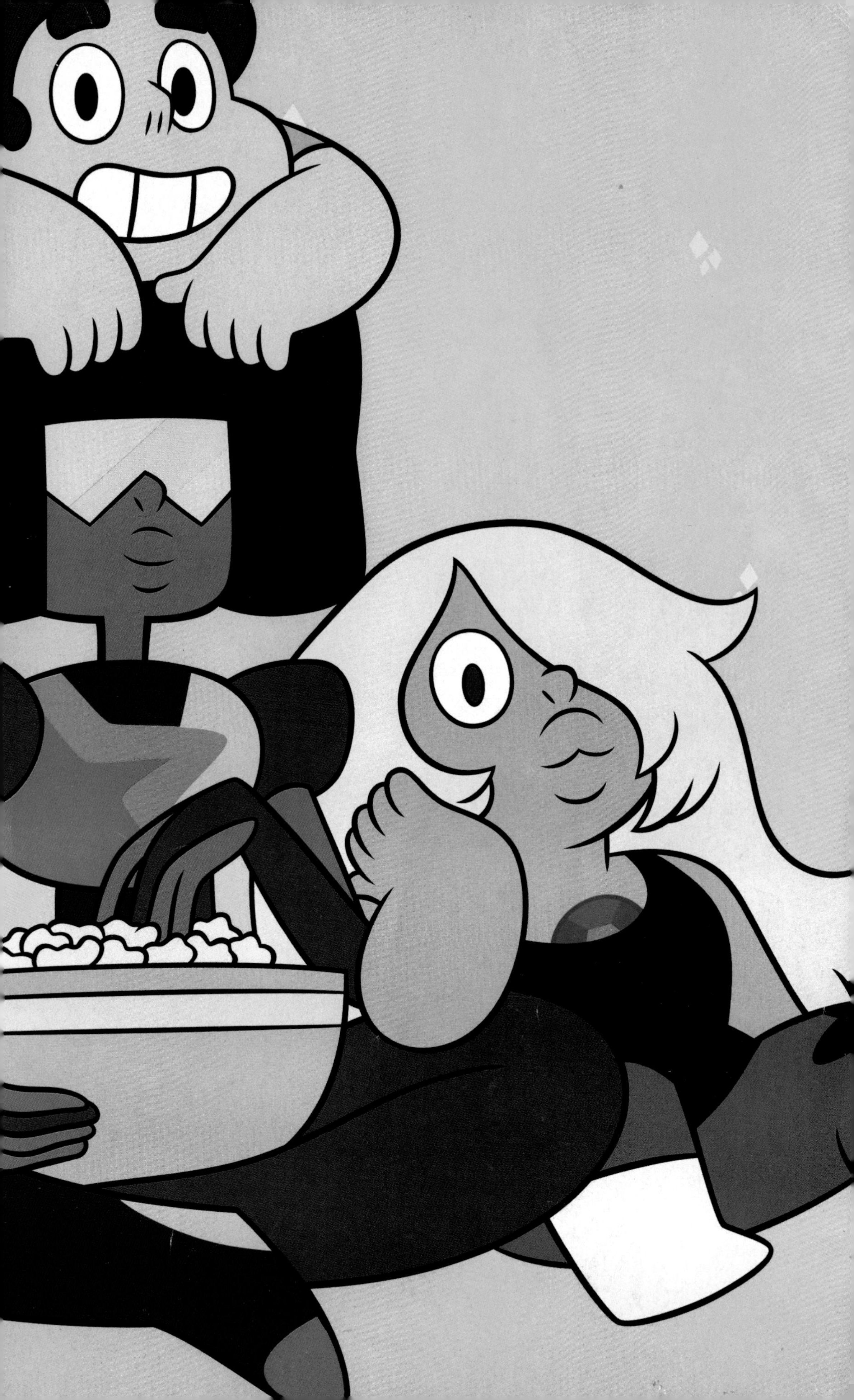

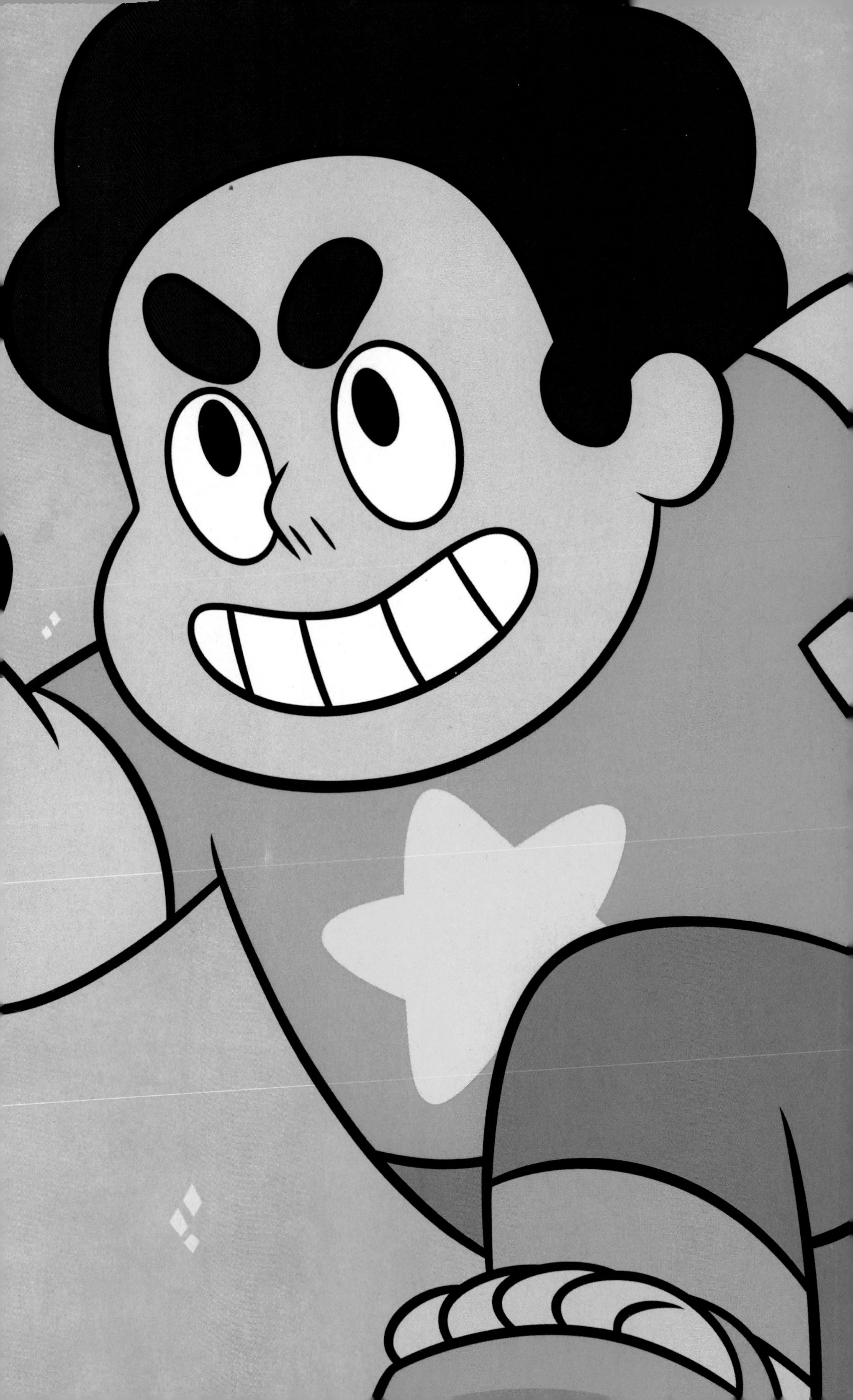

CARTOON NETWORK

STEVEN UNIVERSE

FIND A WAY

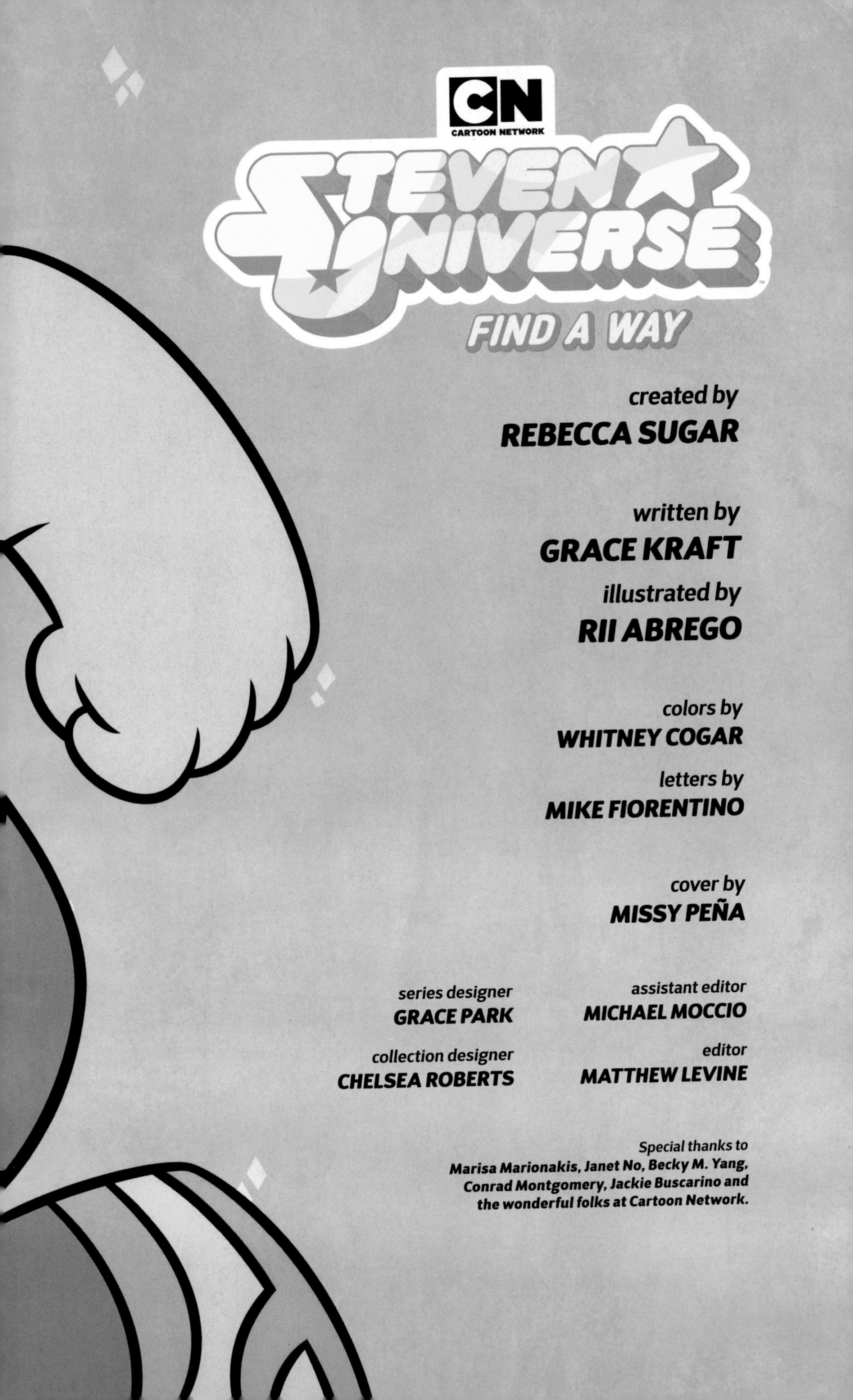

created by
REBECCA SUGAR

written by
GRACE KRAFT

illustrated by
RII ABREGO

colors by
WHITNEY COGAR

letters by
MIKE FIORENTINO

cover by
MISSY PEÑA

series designer
GRACE PARK

collection designer
CHELSEA ROBERTS

assistant editor
MICHAEL MOCCIO

editor
MATTHEW LEVINE

Special thanks to
Marisa Marionakis, Janet No, Becky M. Yang, Conrad Montgomery, Jackie Buscarino and the wonderful folks at Cartoon Network.

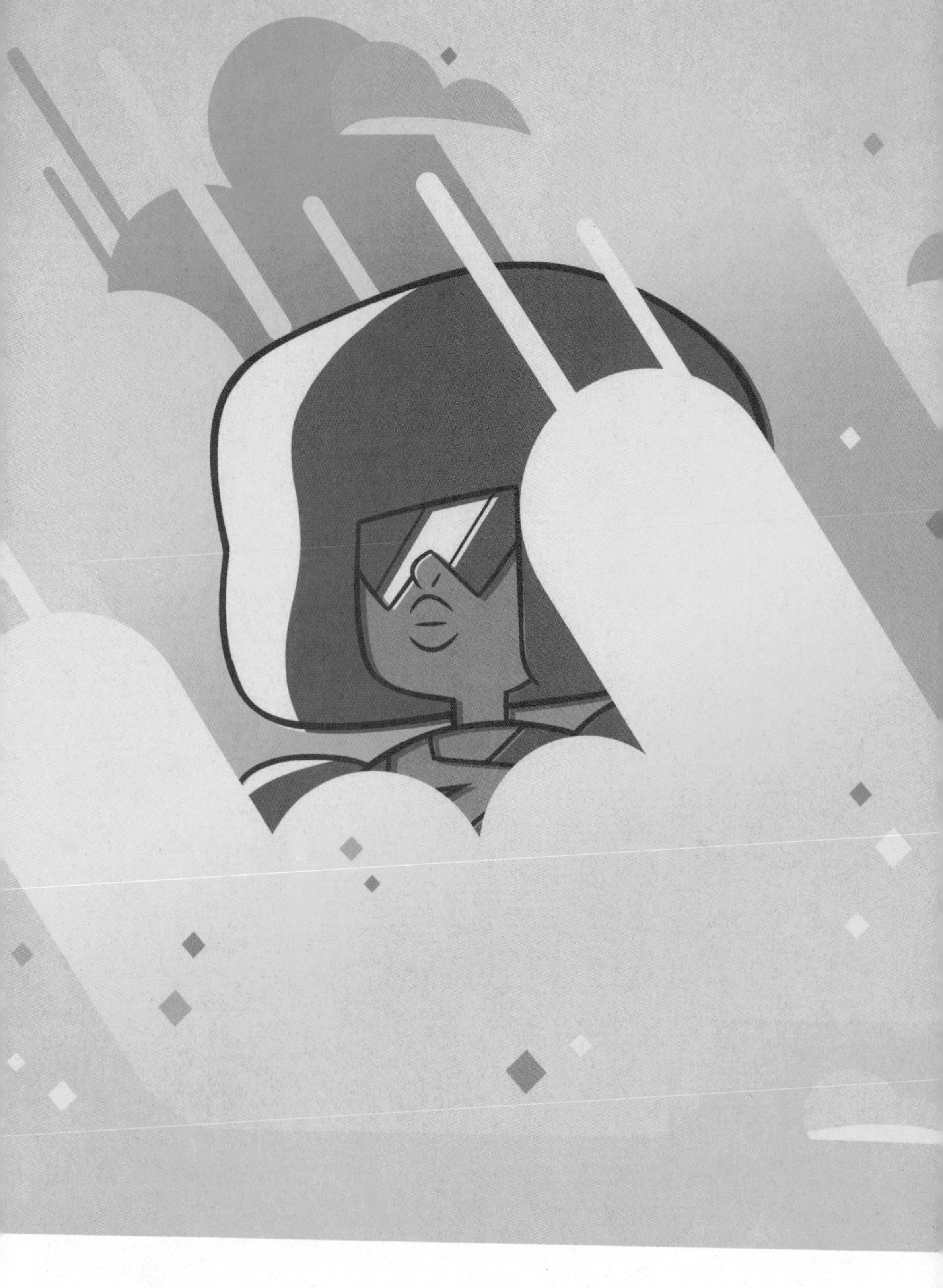

CHAPTER SEVENTEEN

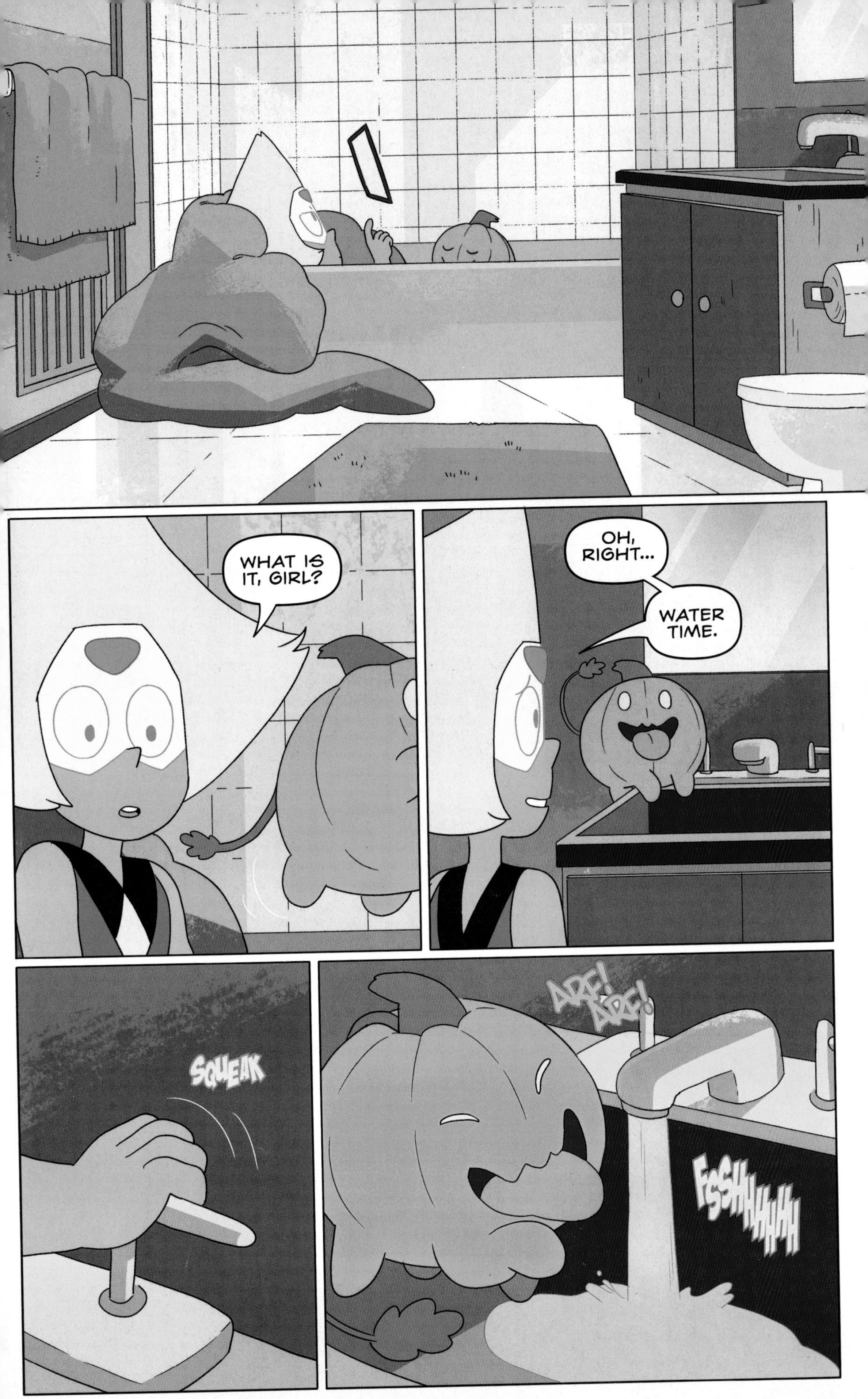
WHAT IS IT, GIRL?
OH, RIGHT...
WATER TIME.
SQUEAK
ARF! ARF!
FSSHHHHHHH

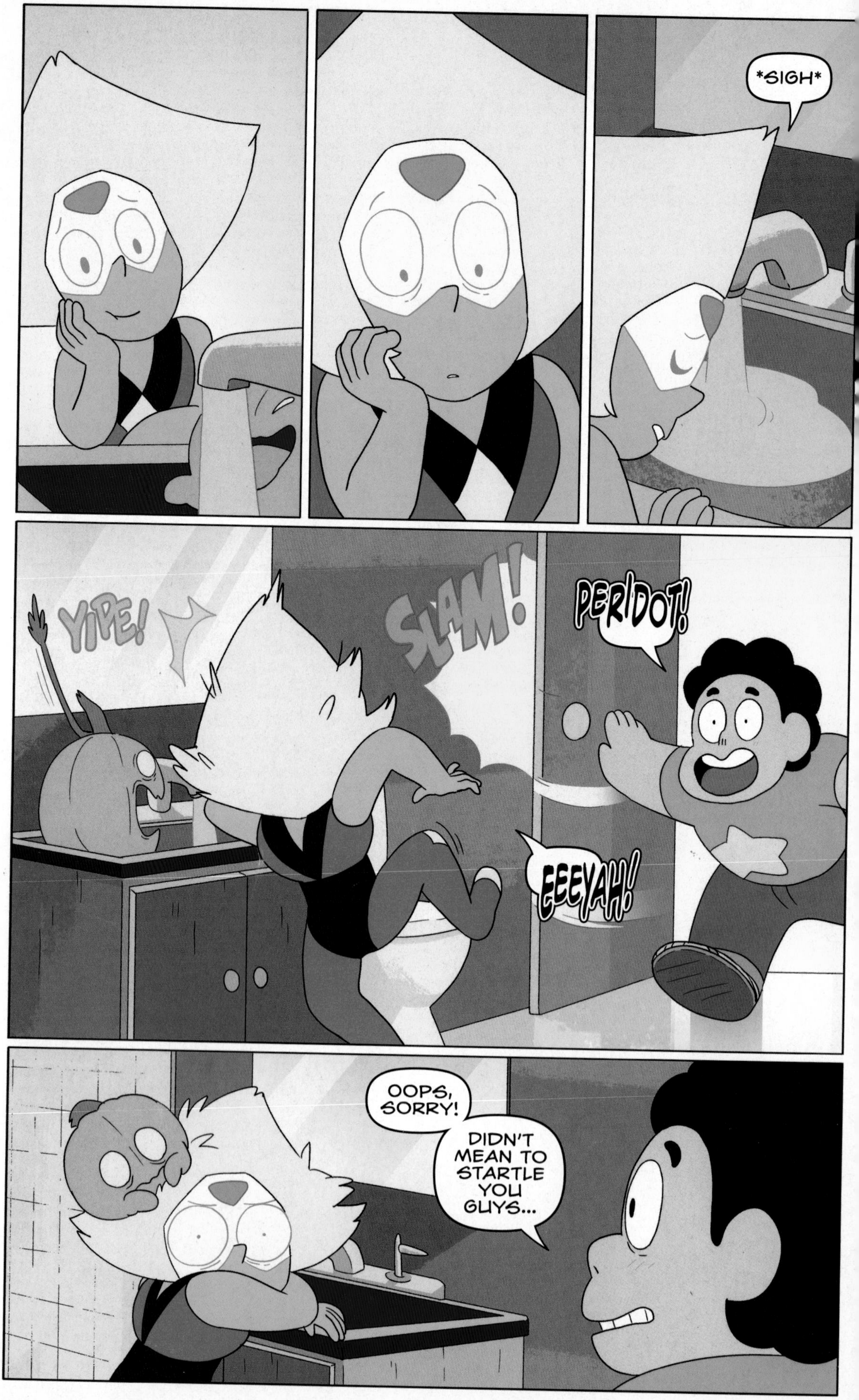
SIGH
YIPE!
SLAM!
PERIDOT!
EEEYAH!
OOPS, SORRY!
DIDN'T MEAN TO STARTLE YOU GUYS...

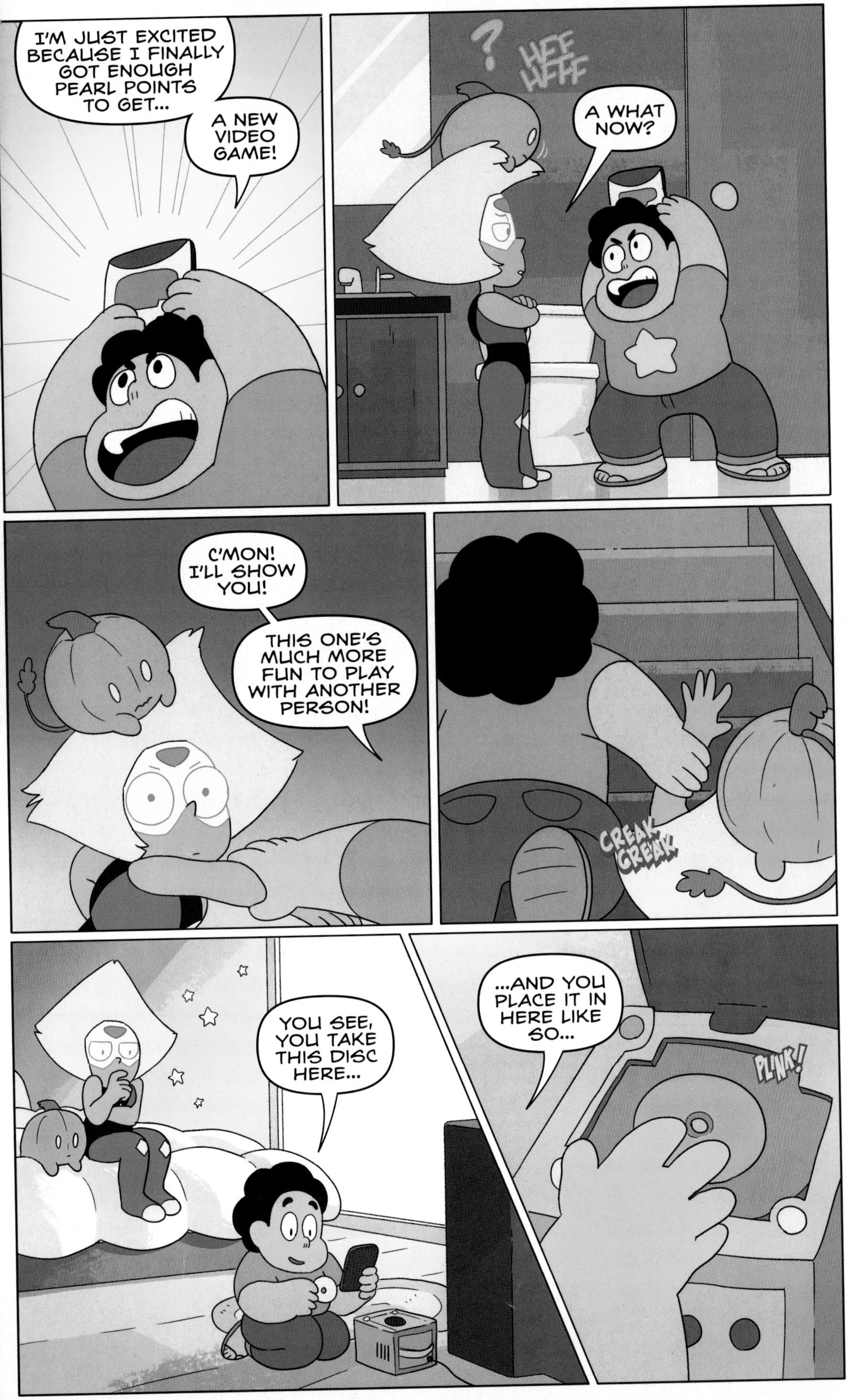

I'M JUST EXCITED BECAUSE I FINALLY GOT ENOUGH PEARL POINTS TO GET...
A NEW VIDEO GAME!
?
HFF HFFF
A WHAT NOW?
C'MON! I'LL SHOW YOU!
THIS ONE'S MUCH MORE FUN TO PLAY WITH ANOTHER PERSON!
CREAK CREAK
YOU SEE, YOU TAKE THIS DISC HERE...
...AND YOU PLACE IT IN HERE LIKE SO...
PLINK!

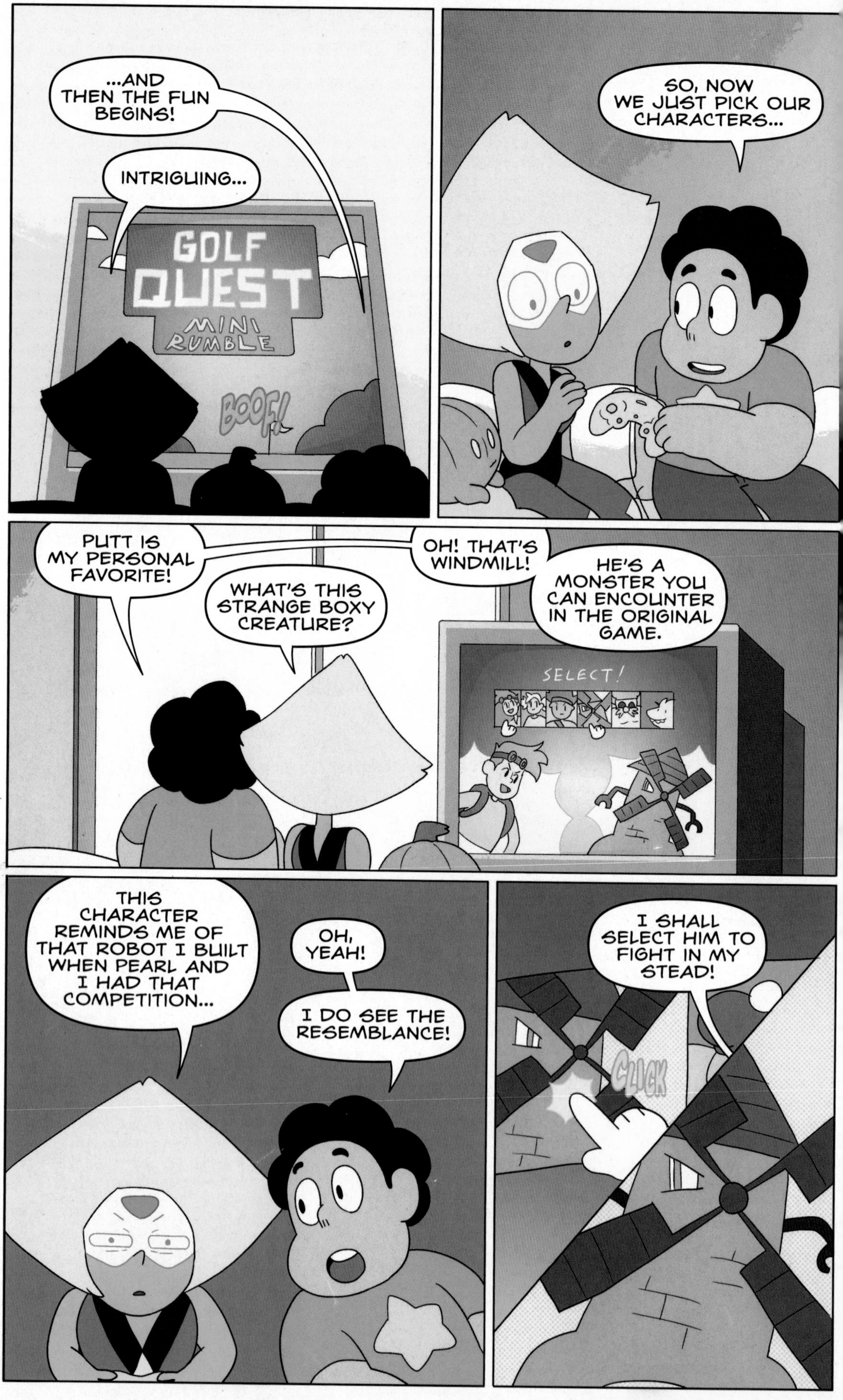
...AND THEN THE FUN BEGINS!
INTRIGUING...
GOLF QUEST MINI RUMBLE
BOOF!
SO, NOW WE JUST PICK OUR CHARACTERS...
PUTT IS MY PERSONAL FAVORITE!
WHAT'S THIS STRANGE BOXY CREATURE?
OH! THAT'S WINDMILL!
HE'S A MONSTER YOU CAN ENCOUNTER IN THE ORIGINAL GAME.
SELECT!
THIS CHARACTER REMINDS ME OF THAT ROBOT I BUILT WHEN PEARL AND I HAD THAT COMPETITION...
OH, YEAH!
I DO SEE THE RESEMBLANCE!
I SHALL SELECT HIM TO FIGHT IN MY STEAD!
CLICK

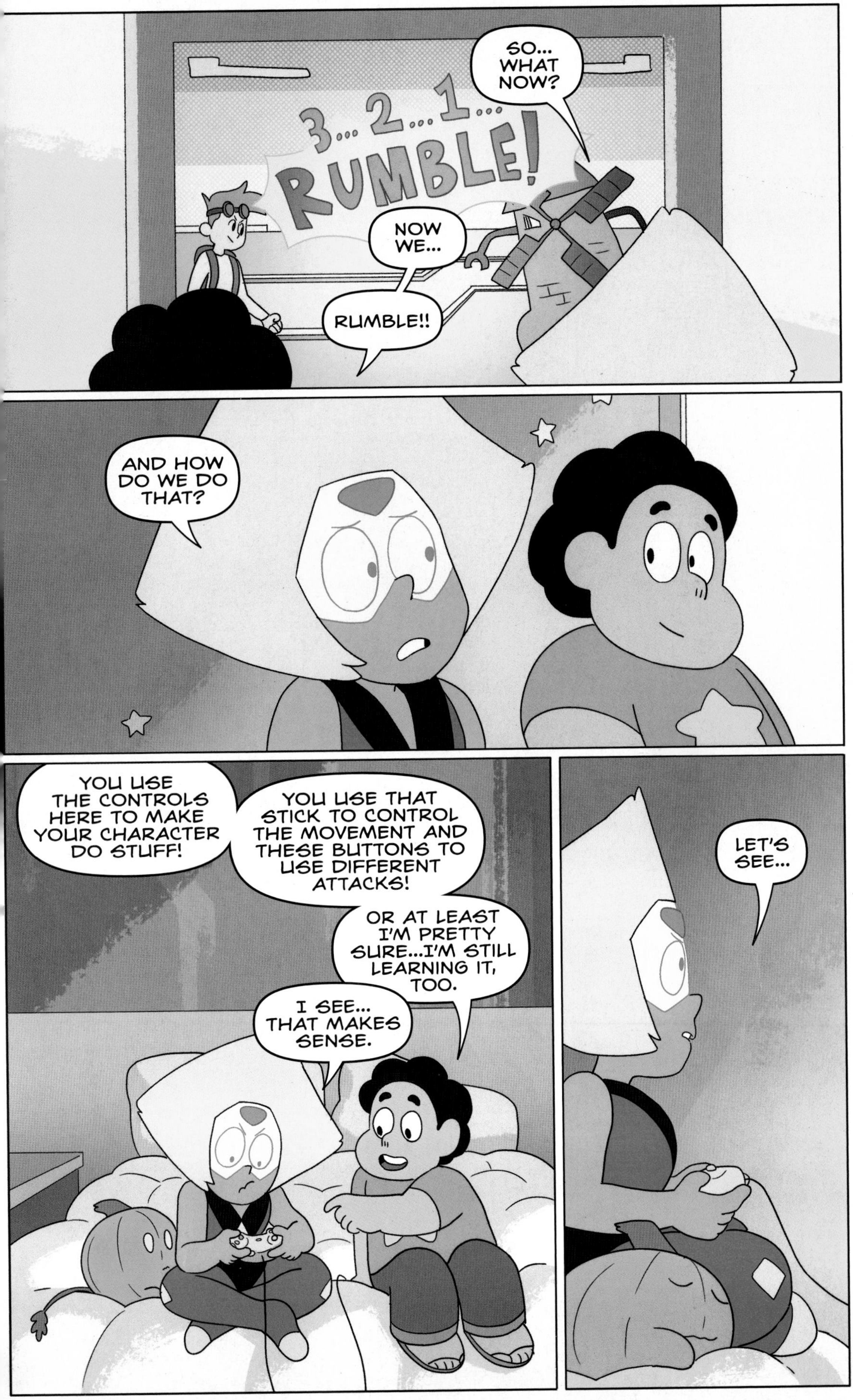
3... 2... 1...
RUMBLE!
SO... WHAT NOW?
NOW WE...
RUMBLE!!
AND HOW DO WE DO THAT?
YOU USE THE CONTROLS HERE TO MAKE YOUR CHARACTER DO STUFF!
YOU USE THAT STICK TO CONTROL THE MOVEMENT AND THESE BUTTONS TO USE DIFFERENT ATTACKS!
OR AT LEAST I'M PRETTY SURE...I'M STILL LEARNING IT, TOO.
I SEE... THAT MAKES SENSE.
LET'S SEE...

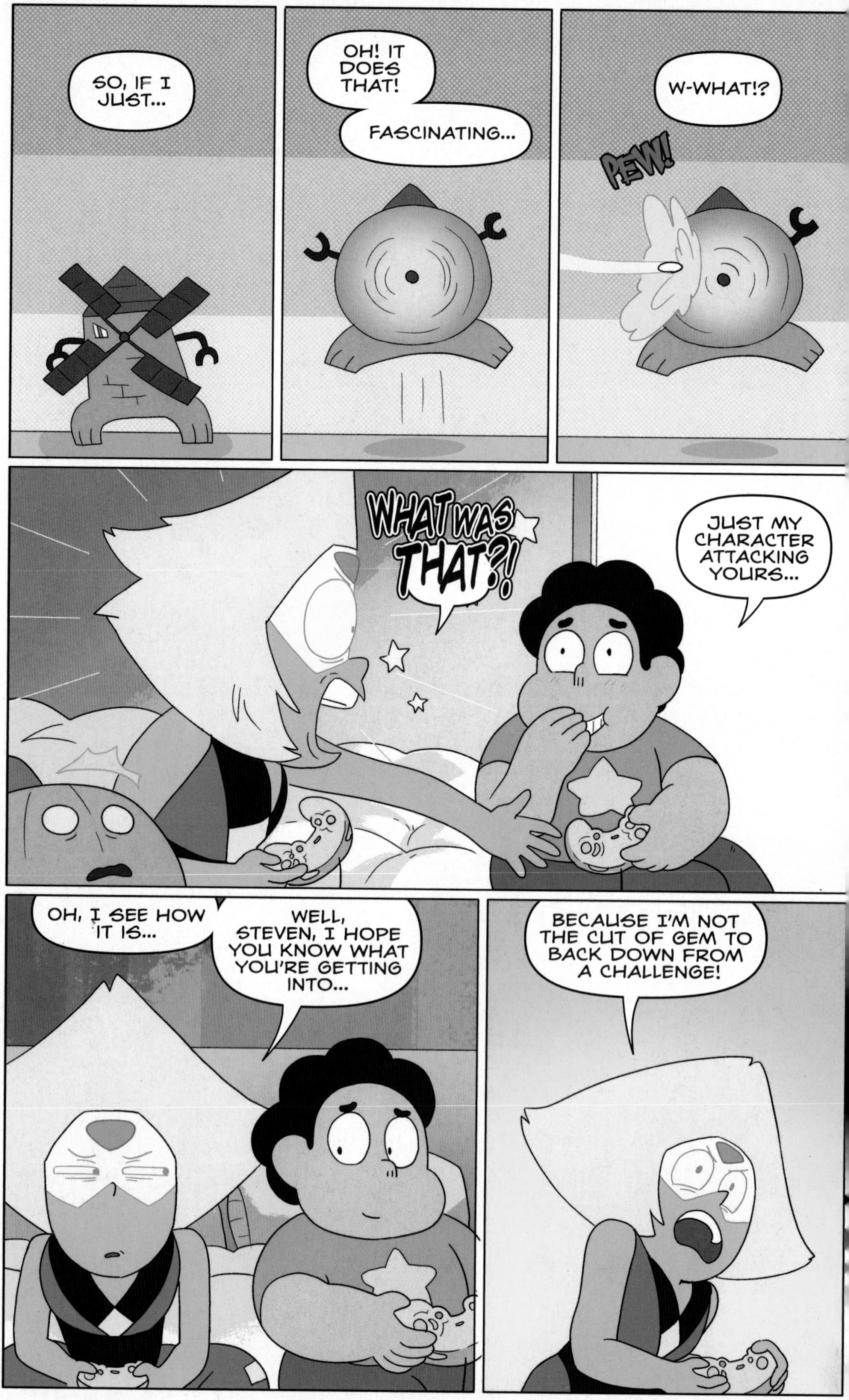
SO, IF I JUST...
OH! IT DOES THAT!
FASCINATING...
W-WHAT!?
PEW!
WHAT WAS THAT?!
JUST MY CHARACTER ATTACKING YOURS...
OH, I SEE HOW IT IS...
WELL, STEVEN, I HOPE YOU KNOW WHAT YOU'RE GETTING INTO...
BECAUSE I'M NOT THE CUT OF GEM TO BACK DOWN FROM A CHALLENGE!

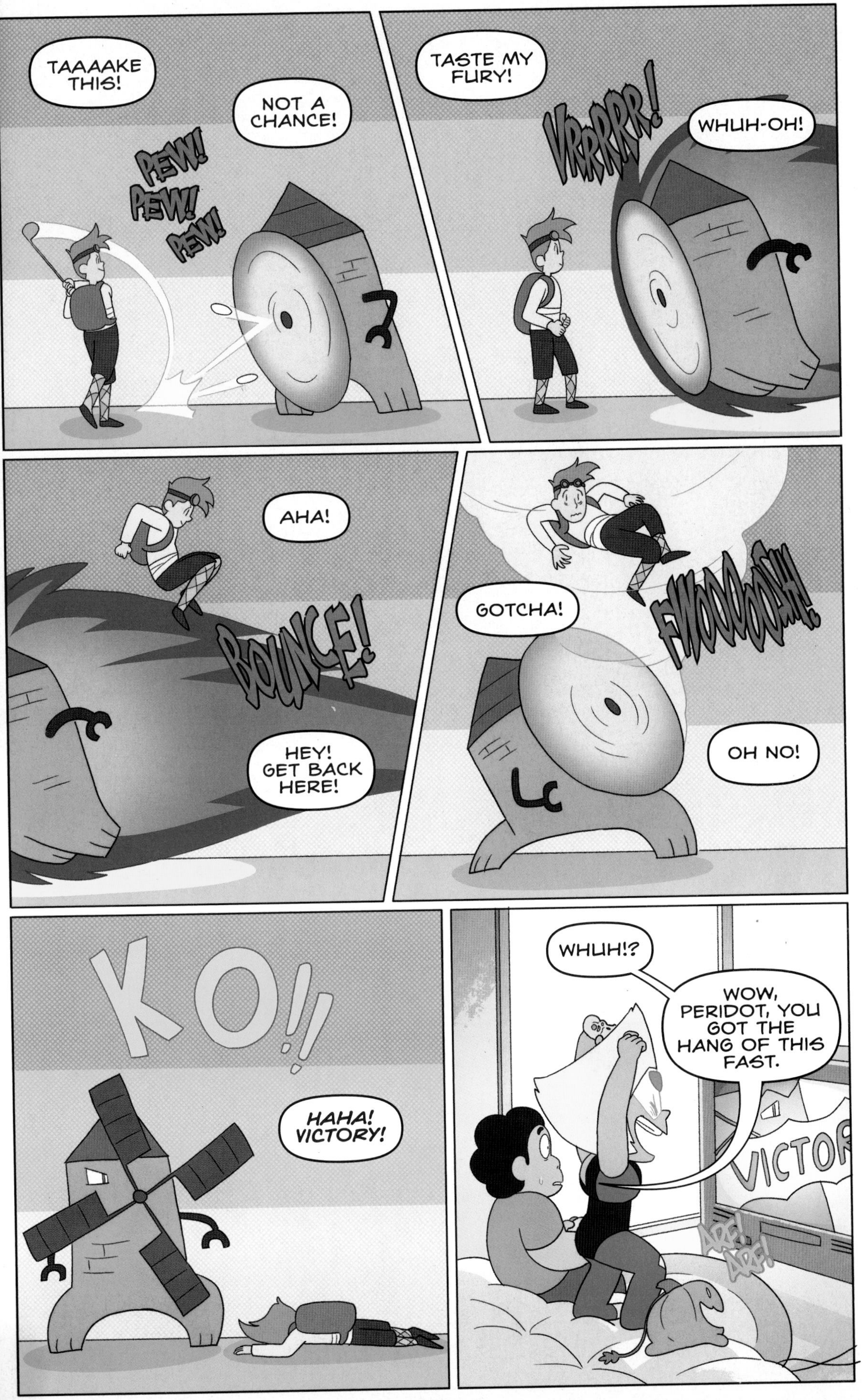
TAAAAKE THIS!
NOT A CHANCE!
PEW! PEW! PEW!
TASTE MY FURY!
VRRRRR!
WHUH-OH!
AHA!
BOUNCE!
HEY! GET BACK HERE!
GOTCHA!
FWOOOOSH!
OH NO!
KO!!
HAHA! VICTORY!
WHUH!?
WOW, PERIDOT, YOU GOT THE HANG OF THIS FAST.
VICTOR
ARF! ARF!

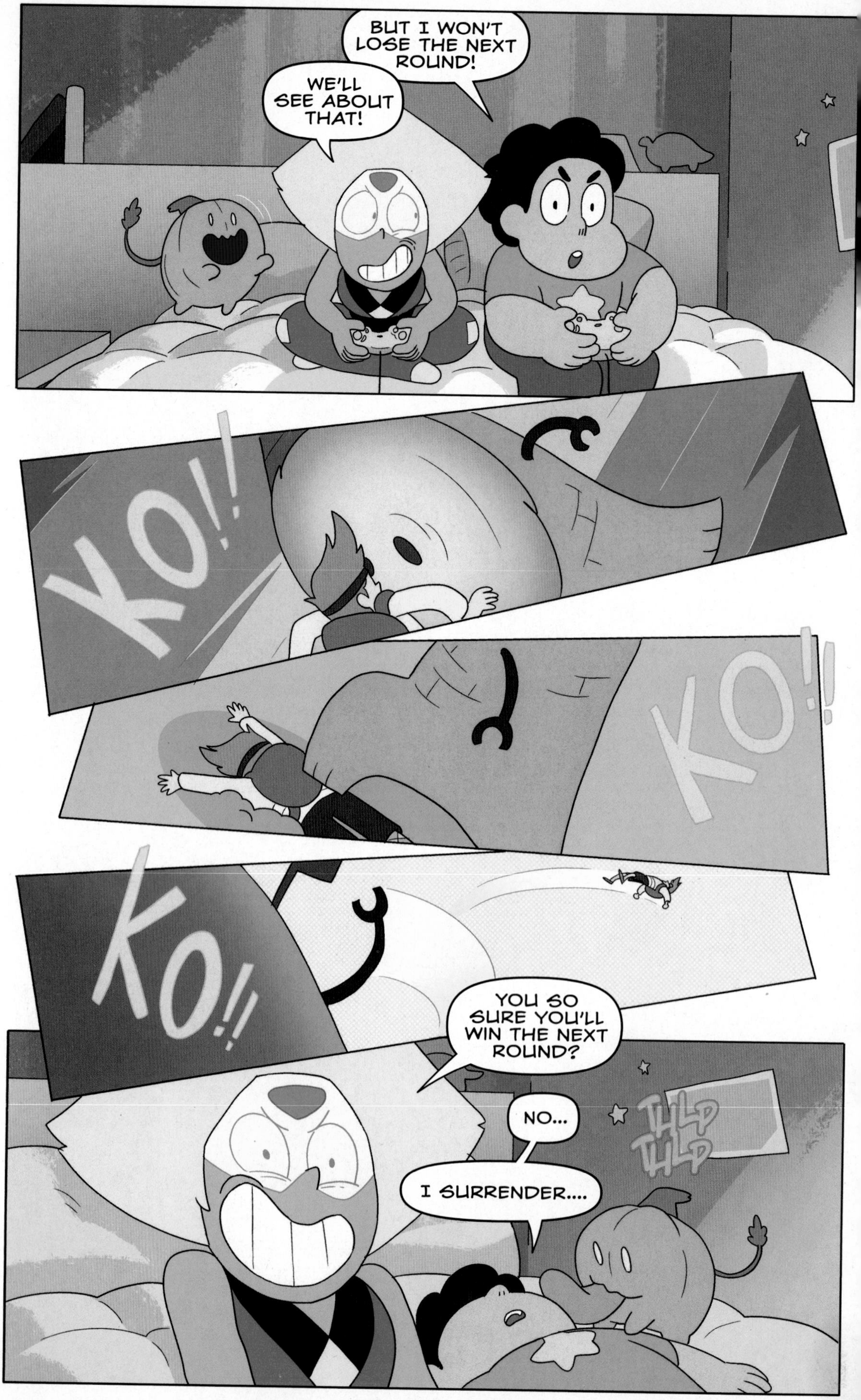
BUT I WON'T LOSE THE NEXT ROUND!
WE'LL SEE ABOUT THAT!
KO!!
KO!!
KO!!
YOU SO SURE YOU'LL WIN THE NEXT ROUND?
NO...
I SURRENDER....
THLP THLP

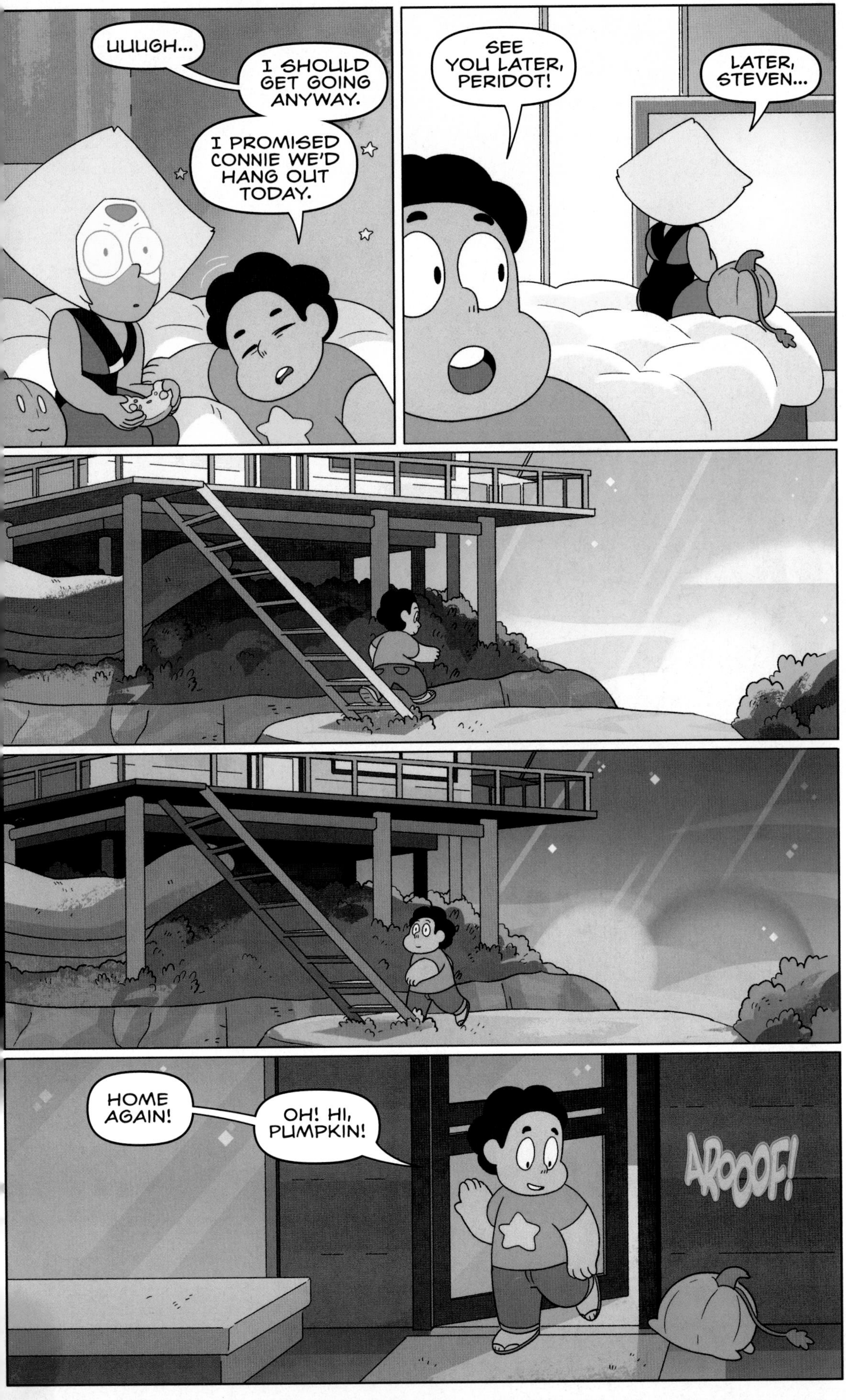
UUUGH...
I SHOULD GET GOING ANYWAY.
I PROMISED CONNIE WE'D HANG OUT TODAY.
SEE YOU LATER, PERIDOT!
LATER, STEVEN...
HOME AGAIN!
OH! HI, PUMPKIN!
AROOOF!

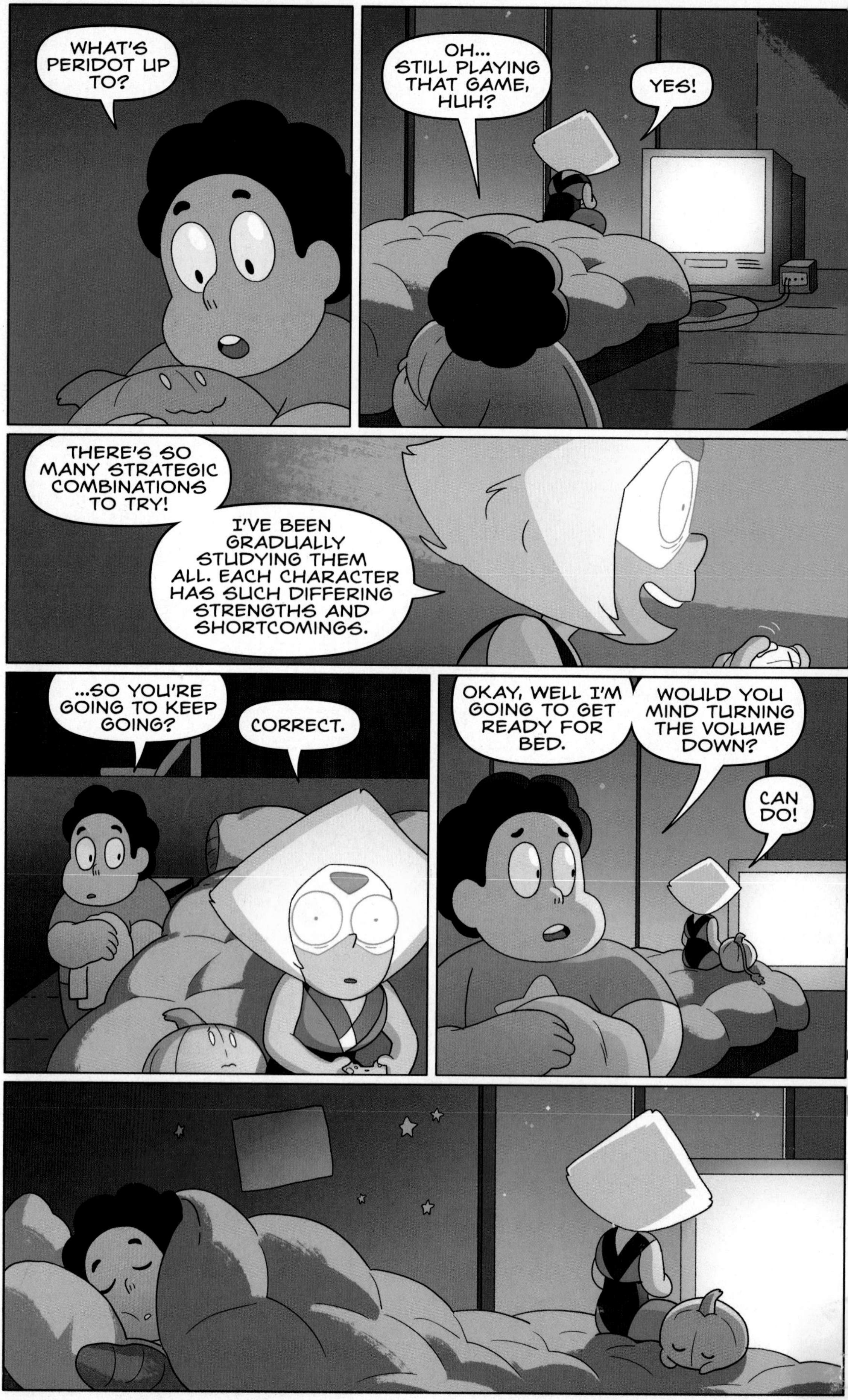
WHAT'S PERIDOT UP TO?
OH... STILL PLAYING THAT GAME, HUH?
YES!
THERE'S SO MANY STRATEGIC COMBINATIONS TO TRY!
I'VE BEEN GRADUALLY STUDYING THEM ALL. EACH CHARACTER HAS SUCH DIFFERING STRENGTHS AND SHORTCOMINGS.
...SO YOU'RE GOING TO KEEP GOING?
CORRECT.
OKAY, WELL I'M GOING TO GET READY FOR BED.
WOULD YOU MIND TURNING THE VOLUME DOWN?
CAN DO!

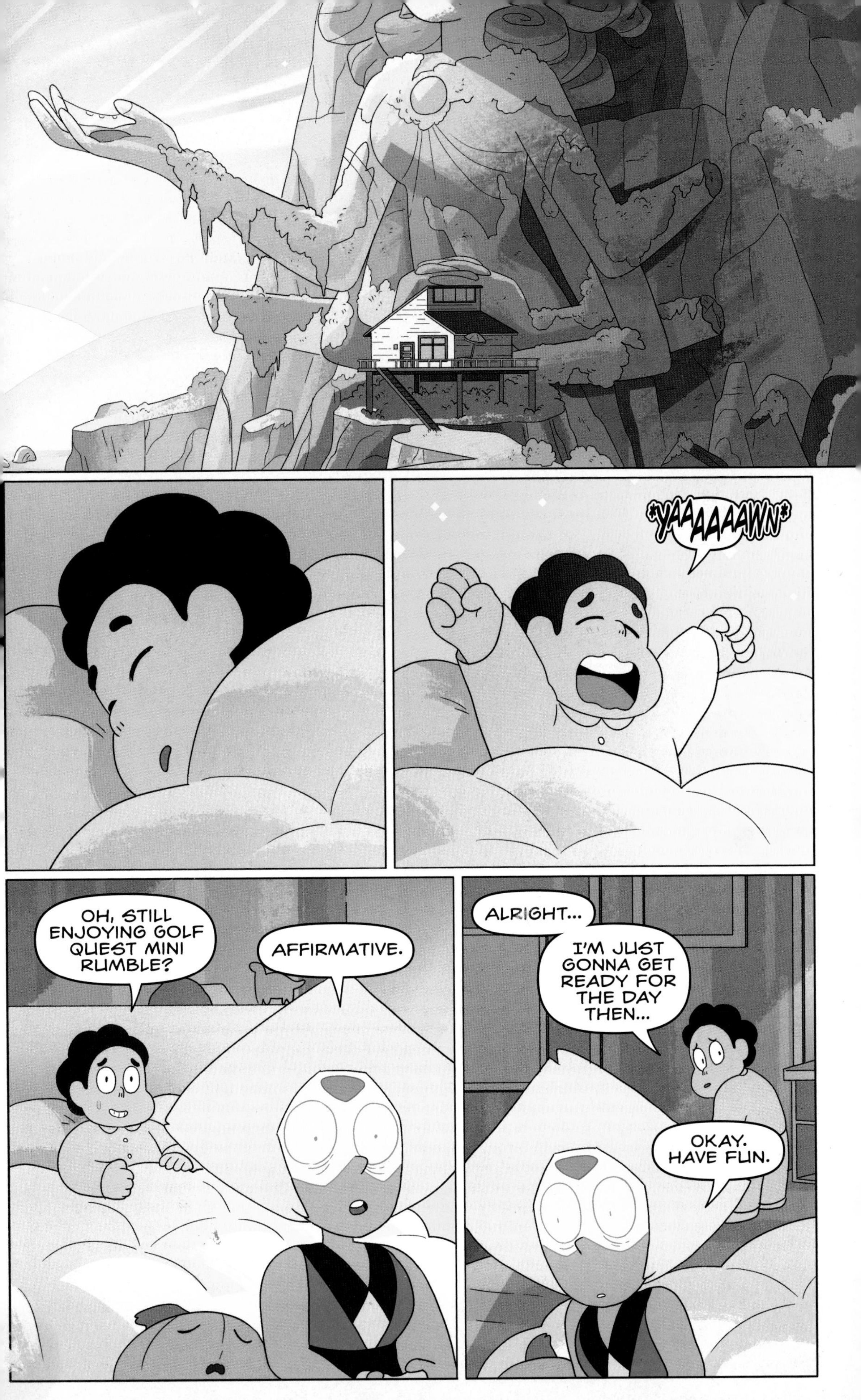
YAAAAAAWN
OH, STILL ENJOYING GOLF QUEST MINI RUMBLE?
AFFIRMATIVE.
ALRIGHT...
I'M JUST GONNA GET READY FOR THE DAY THEN...
OKAY. HAVE FUN.

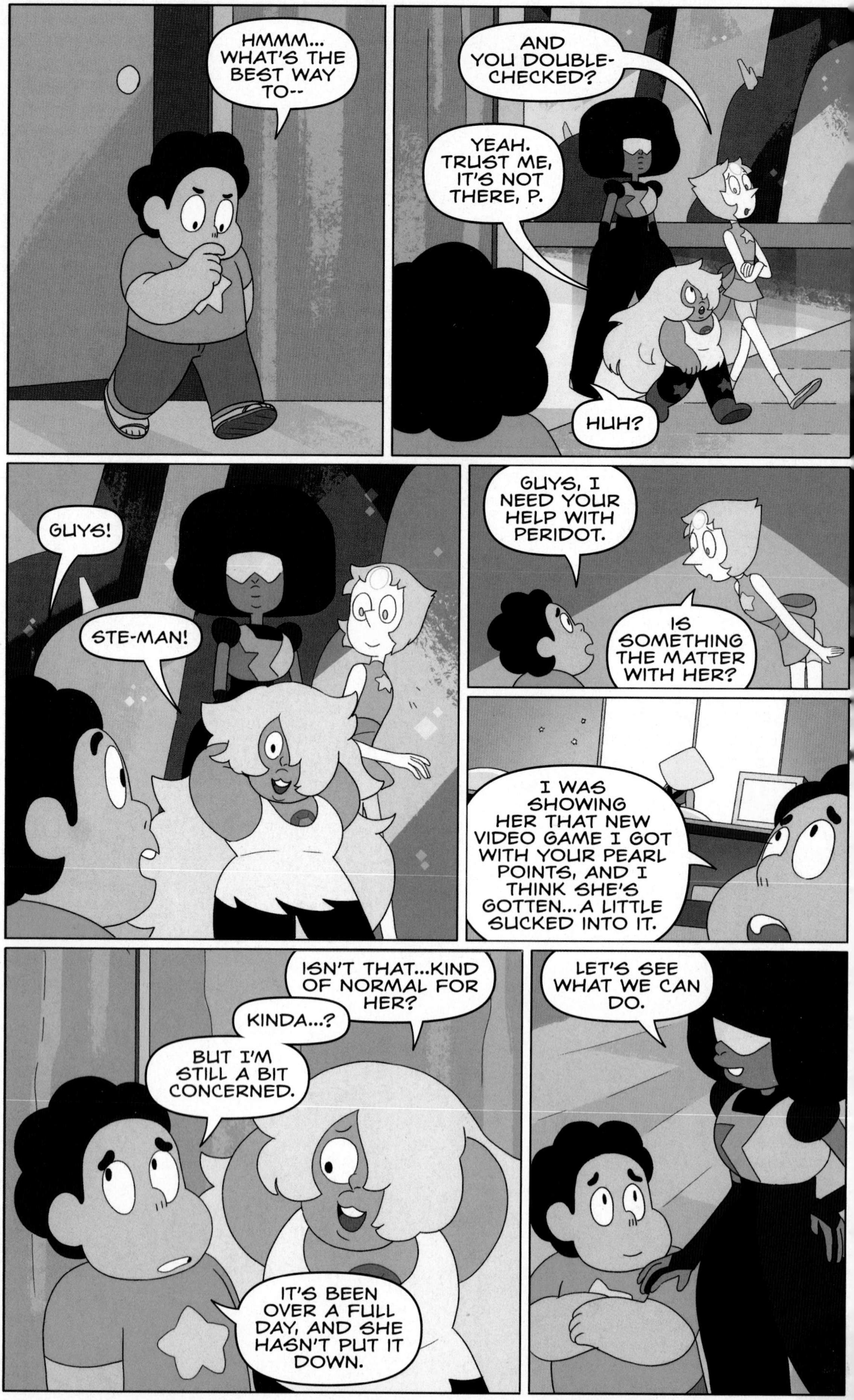
HMMM... WHAT'S THE BEST WAY TO--
AND YOU DOUBLE-CHECKED?
YEAH. TRUST ME, IT'S NOT THERE, P.
HUH?
GUYS!
STE-MAN!
GUYS, I NEED YOUR HELP WITH PERIDOT.
IS SOMETHING THE MATTER WITH HER?
I WAS SHOWING HER THAT NEW VIDEO GAME I GOT WITH YOUR PEARL POINTS, AND I THINK SHE'S GOTTEN...A LITTLE SUCKED INTO IT.
ISN'T THAT...KIND OF NORMAL FOR HER?
KINDA...?
BUT I'M STILL A BIT CONCERNED.
IT'S BEEN OVER A FULL DAY, AND SHE HASN'T PUT IT DOWN.
LET'S SEE WHAT WE CAN DO.

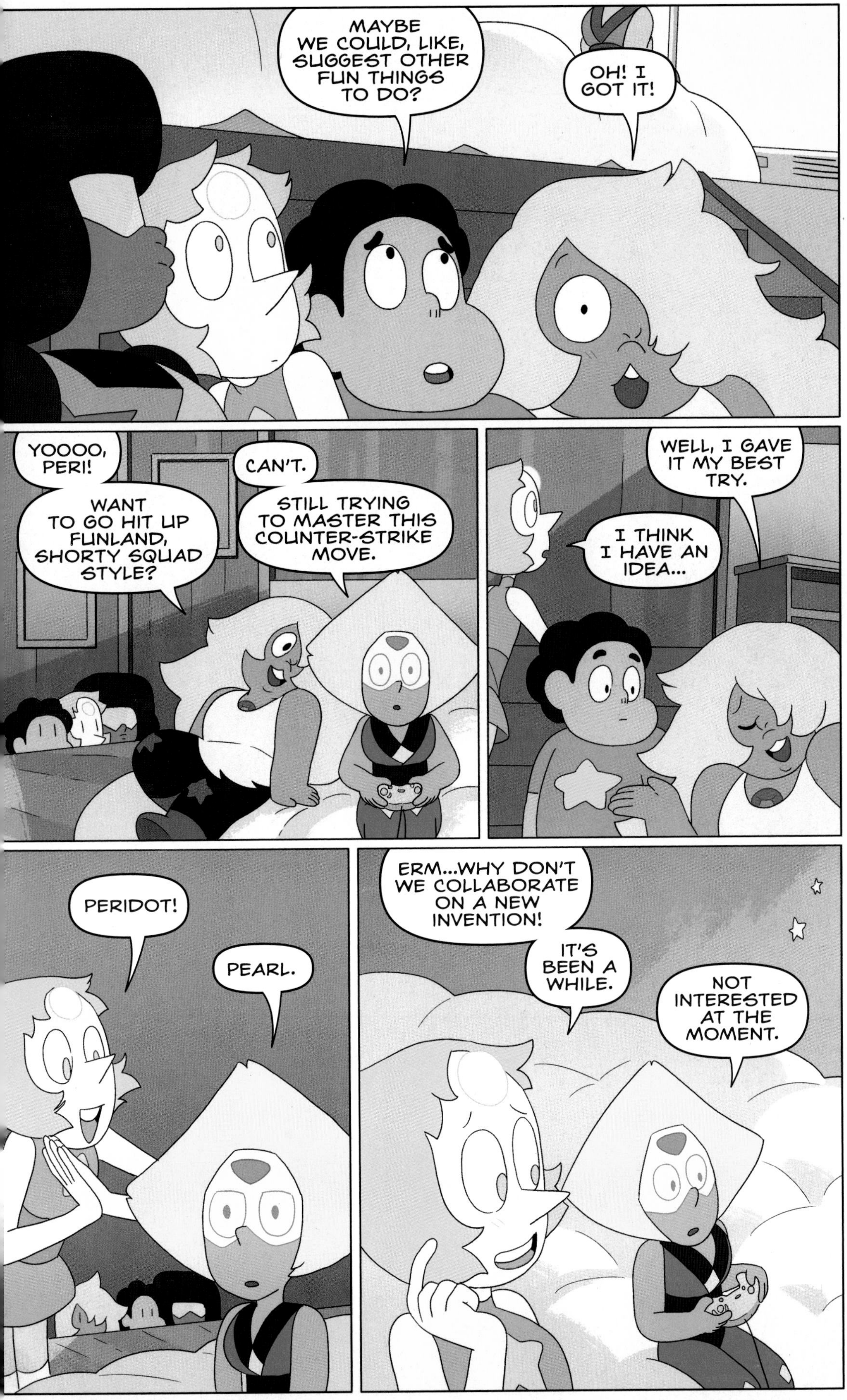
MAYBE WE COULD, LIKE, SUGGEST OTHER FUN THINGS TO DO?
OH! I GOT IT!
YOOOO, PERI!
WANT TO GO HIT UP FUNLAND, SHORTY SQUAD STYLE?
CAN'T.
STILL TRYING TO MASTER THIS COUNTER-STRIKE MOVE.
WELL, I GAVE IT MY BEST TRY.
I THINK I HAVE AN IDEA...
PERIDOT!
PEARL.
ERM...WHY DON'T WE COLLABORATE ON A NEW INVENTION!
IT'S BEEN A WHILE.
NOT INTERESTED AT THE MOMENT.

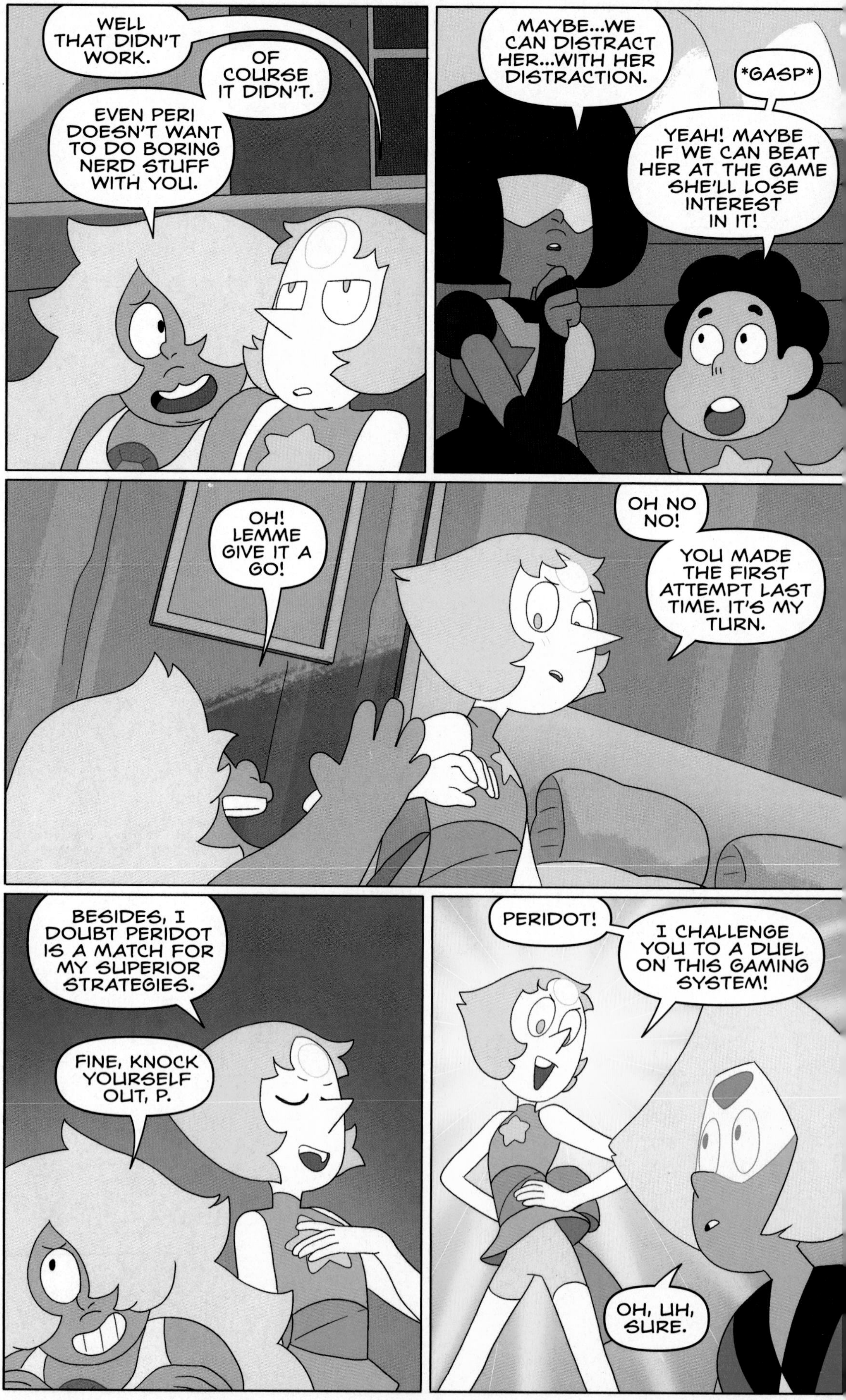
WELL THAT DIDN'T WORK.
OF COURSE IT DIDN'T.
EVEN PERI DOESN'T WANT TO DO BORING NERD STUFF WITH YOU.
MAYBE...WE CAN DISTRACT HER...WITH HER DISTRACTION.
GASP
YEAH! MAYBE IF WE CAN BEAT HER AT THE GAME SHE'LL LOSE INTEREST IN IT!
OH! LEMME GIVE IT A GO!
OH NO NO!
YOU MADE THE FIRST ATTEMPT LAST TIME. IT'S MY TURN.
BESIDES, I DOUBT PERIDOT IS A MATCH FOR MY SUPERIOR STRATEGIES.
FINE, KNOCK YOURSELF OUT, P.
PERIDOT!
I CHALLENGE YOU TO A DUEL ON THIS GAMING SYSTEM!
OH, UH, SURE.

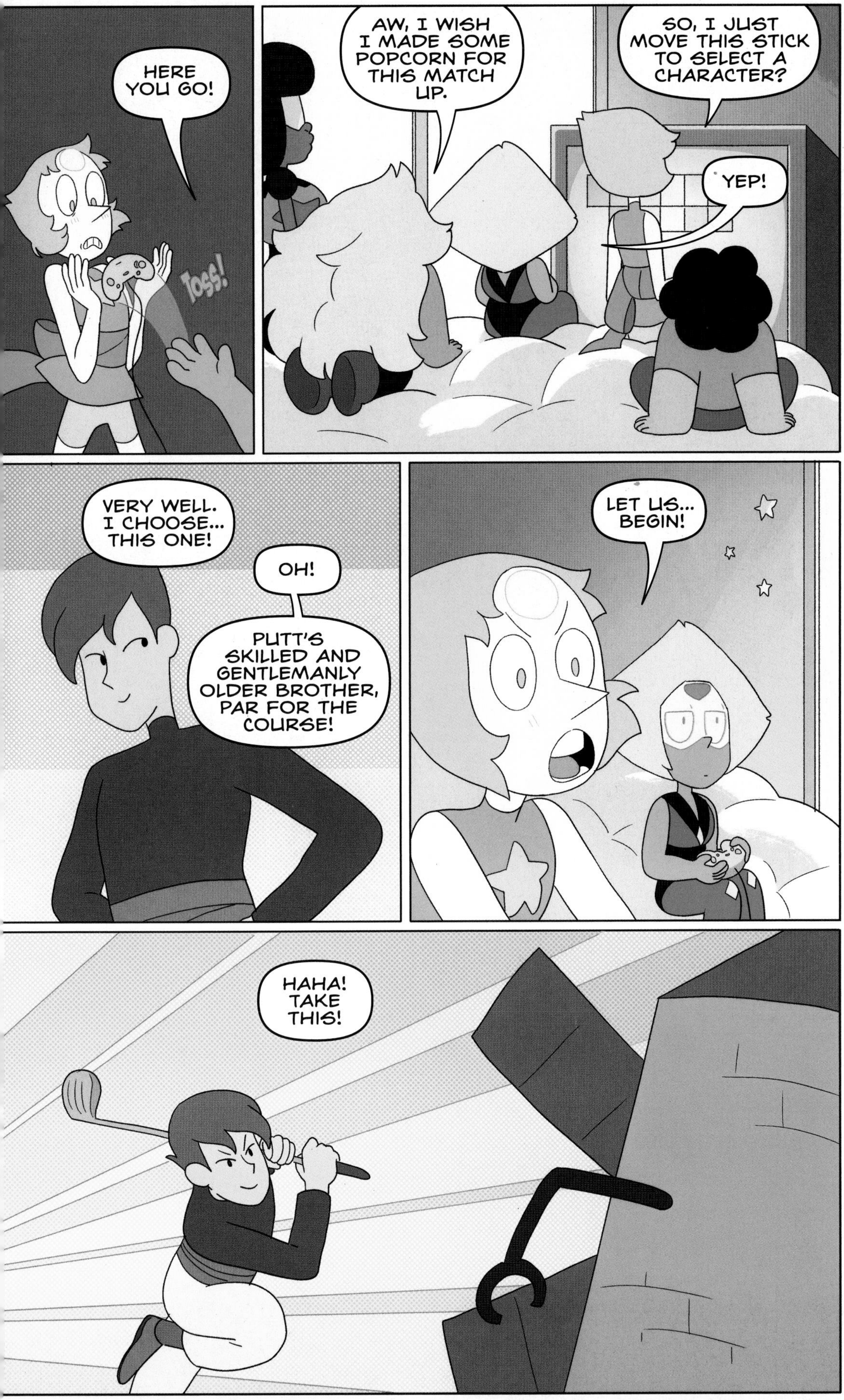
HERE YOU GO!
TOSS!
AW, I WISH I MADE SOME POPCORN FOR THIS MATCH UP.
SO, I JUST MOVE THIS STICK TO SELECT A CHARACTER?
YEP!
VERY WELL. I CHOOSE... THIS ONE!
OH!
PUTT'S SKILLED AND GENTLEMANLY OLDER BROTHER, PAR FOR THE COURSE!
LET US... BEGIN!
HAHA! TAKE THIS!

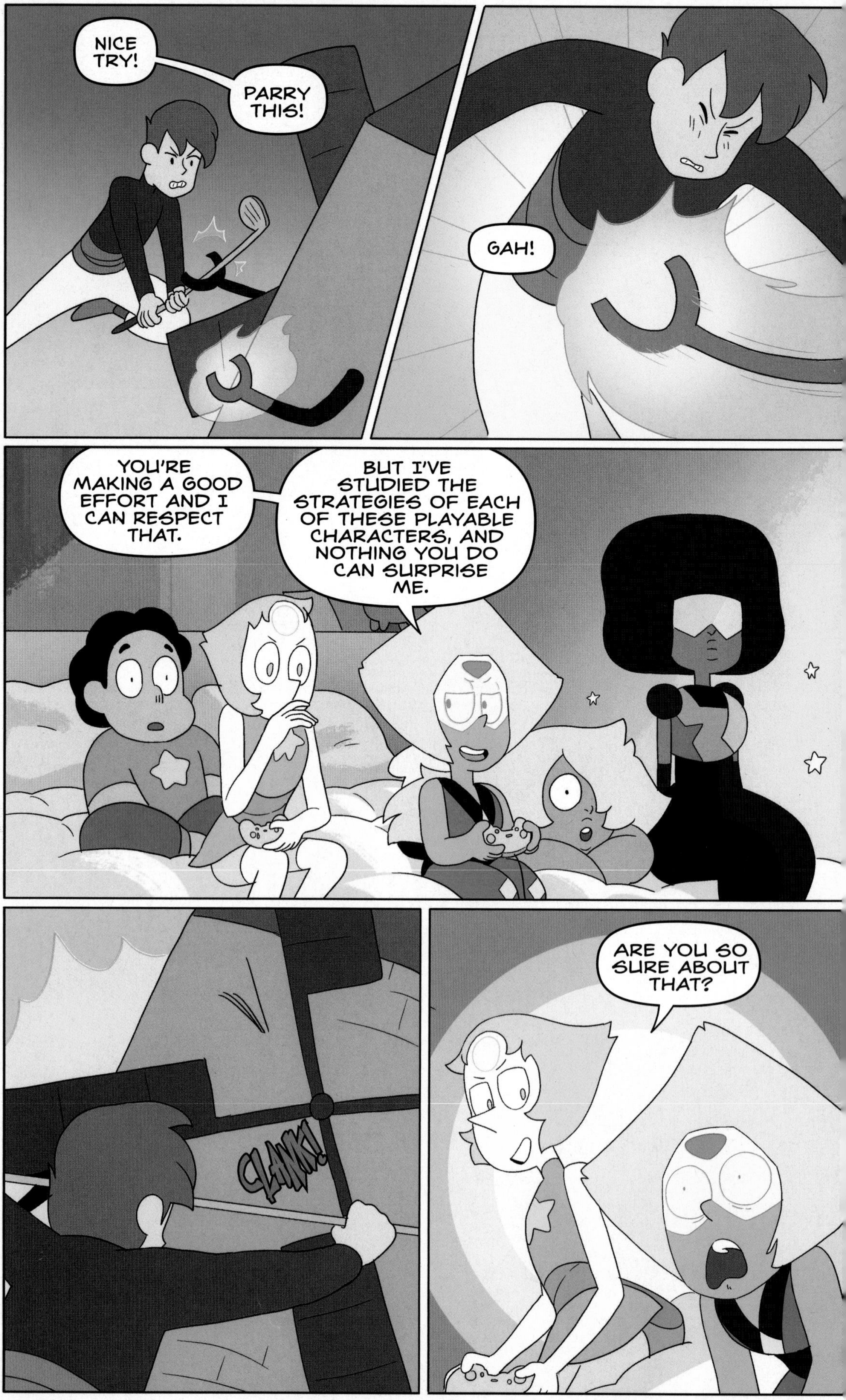
NICE TRY!
PARRY THIS!
GAH!
YOU'RE MAKING A GOOD EFFORT AND I CAN RESPECT THAT.
BUT I'VE STUDIED THE STRATEGIES OF EACH OF THESE PLAYABLE CHARACTERS, AND NOTHING YOU DO CAN SURPRISE ME.
CLANK!
ARE YOU SO SURE ABOUT THAT?

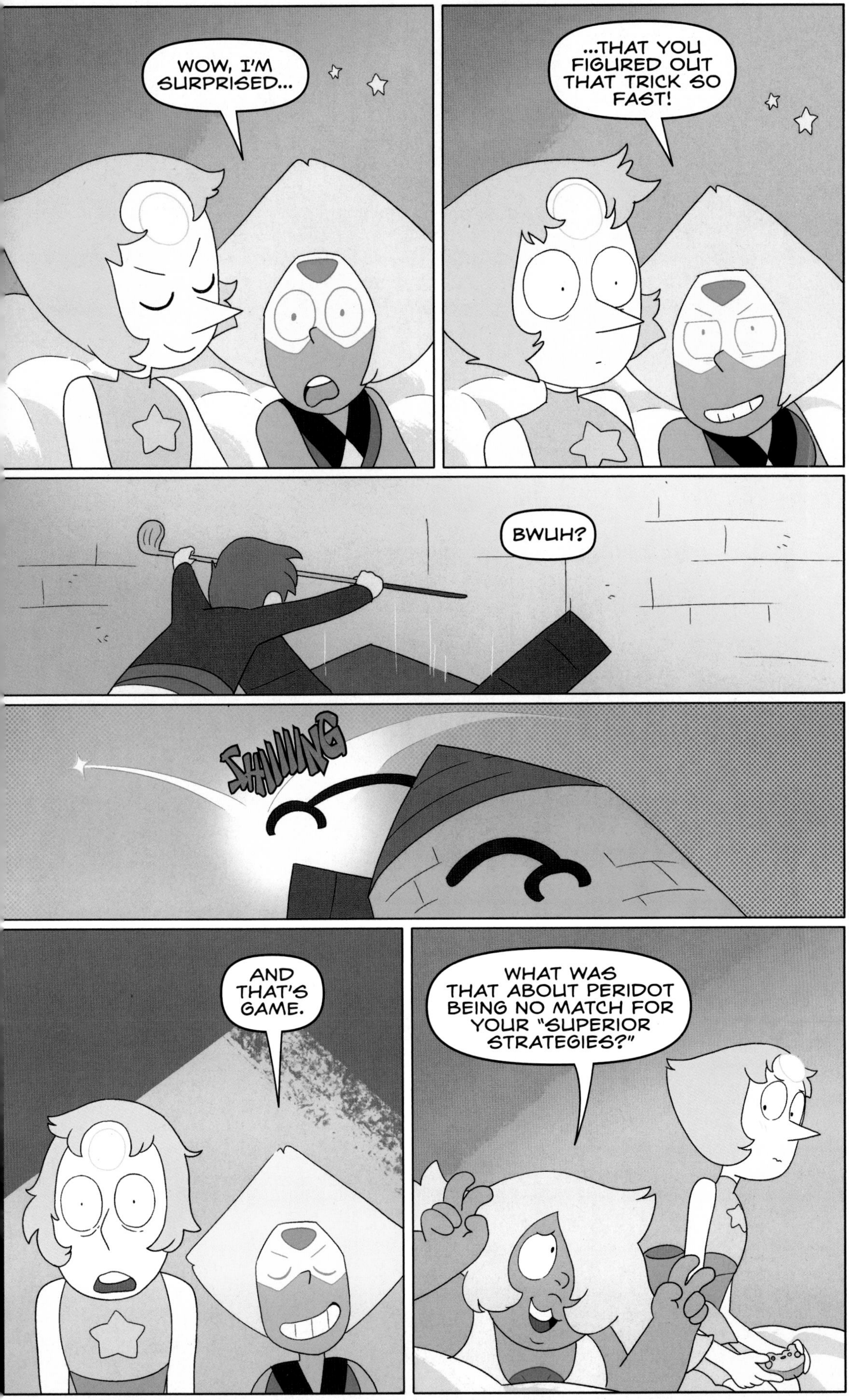
WOW, I'M SURPRISED...
...THAT YOU FIGURED OUT THAT TRICK SO FAST!
BWUH?
SHWING
AND THAT'S GAME.
WHAT WAS THAT ABOUT PERIDOT BEING NO MATCH FOR YOUR "SUPERIOR STRATEGIES?"

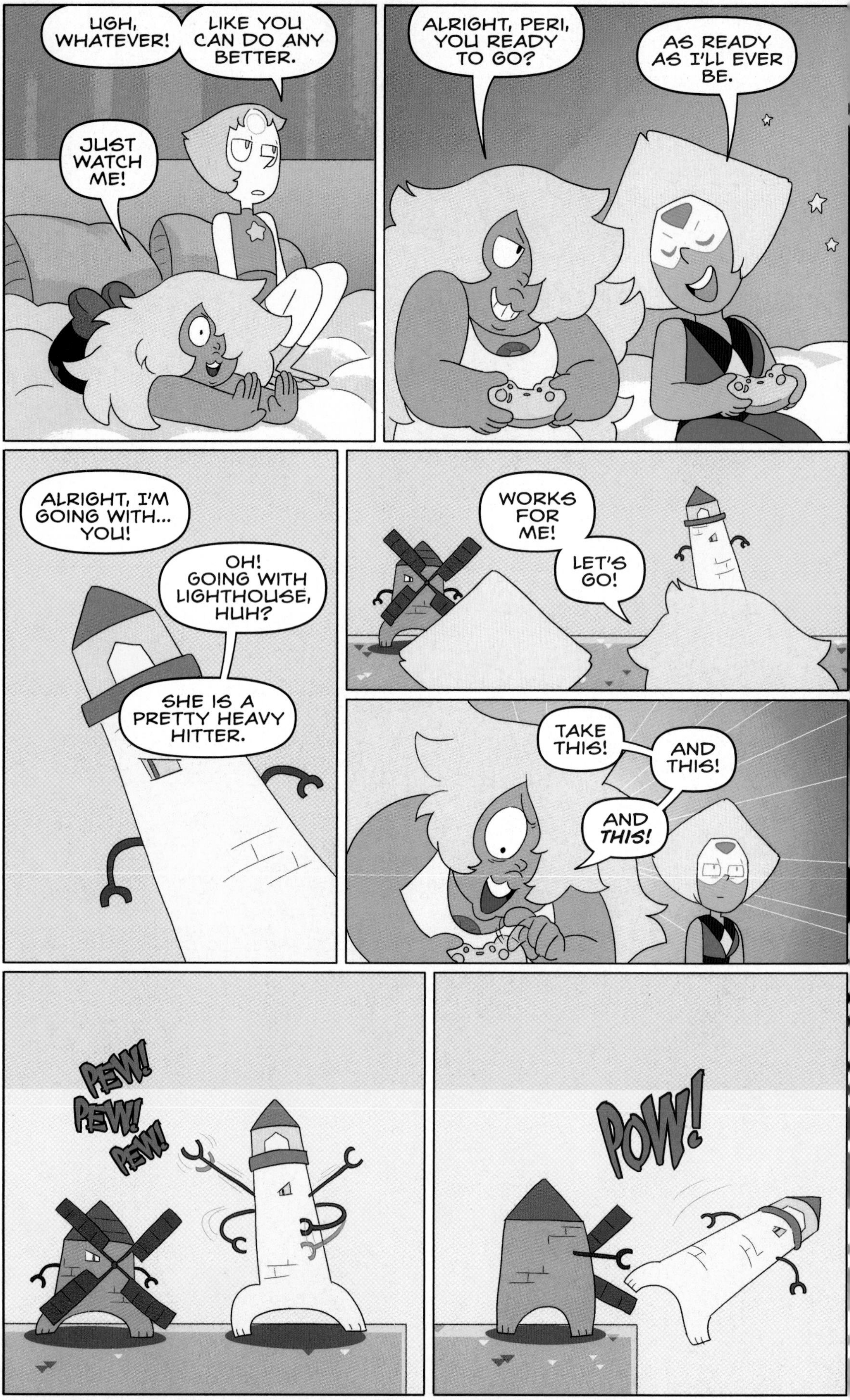
UGH, WHATEVER!
LIKE YOU CAN DO ANY BETTER.
JUST WATCH ME!
ALRIGHT, PERI, YOU READY TO GO?
AS READY AS I'LL EVER BE.
ALRIGHT, I'M GOING WITH... YOU!
OH! GOING WITH LIGHTHOUSE, HUH?
SHE IS A PRETTY HEAVY HITTER.
WORKS FOR ME!
LET'S GO!
TAKE THIS!
AND THIS!
AND *THIS!*
PEW! PEW! PEW!
POW!

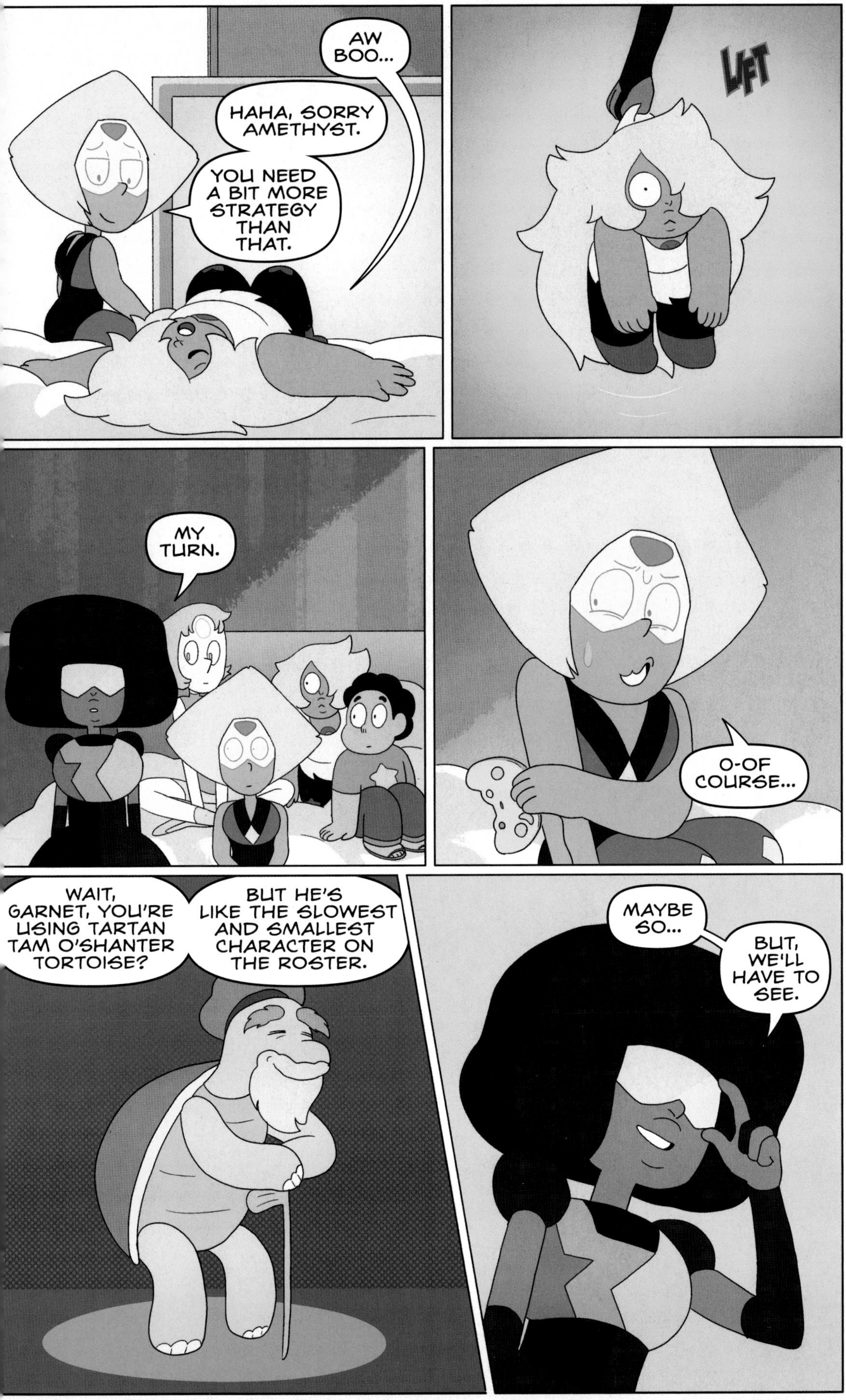
AW BOO...
HAHA, SORRY AMETHYST.
YOU NEED A BIT MORE STRATEGY THAN THAT.
LIFT
MY TURN.
O-OF COURSE...
WAIT, GARNET, YOU'RE USING TARTAN TAM O'SHANTER TORTOISE?
BUT HE'S LIKE THE SLOWEST AND SMALLEST CHARACTER ON THE ROSTER.
MAYBE SO...
BUT, WE'LL HAVE TO SEE.

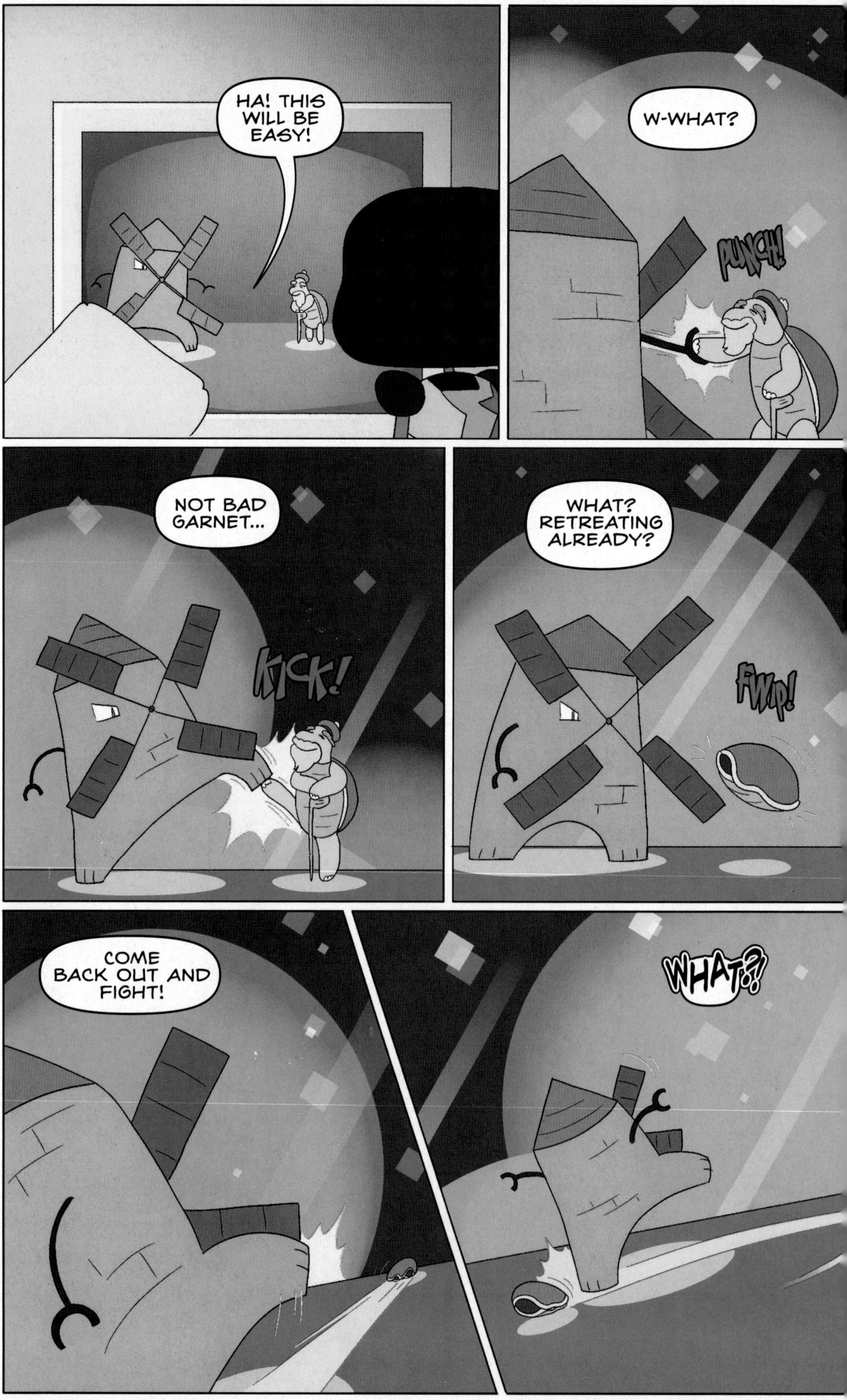
HA! THIS WILL BE EASY!
W-WHAT?
PUNCH!
NOT BAD GARNET...
KICK!
WHAT? RETREATING ALREADY?
FWIP!
COME BACK OUT AND FIGHT!
WHAT?!

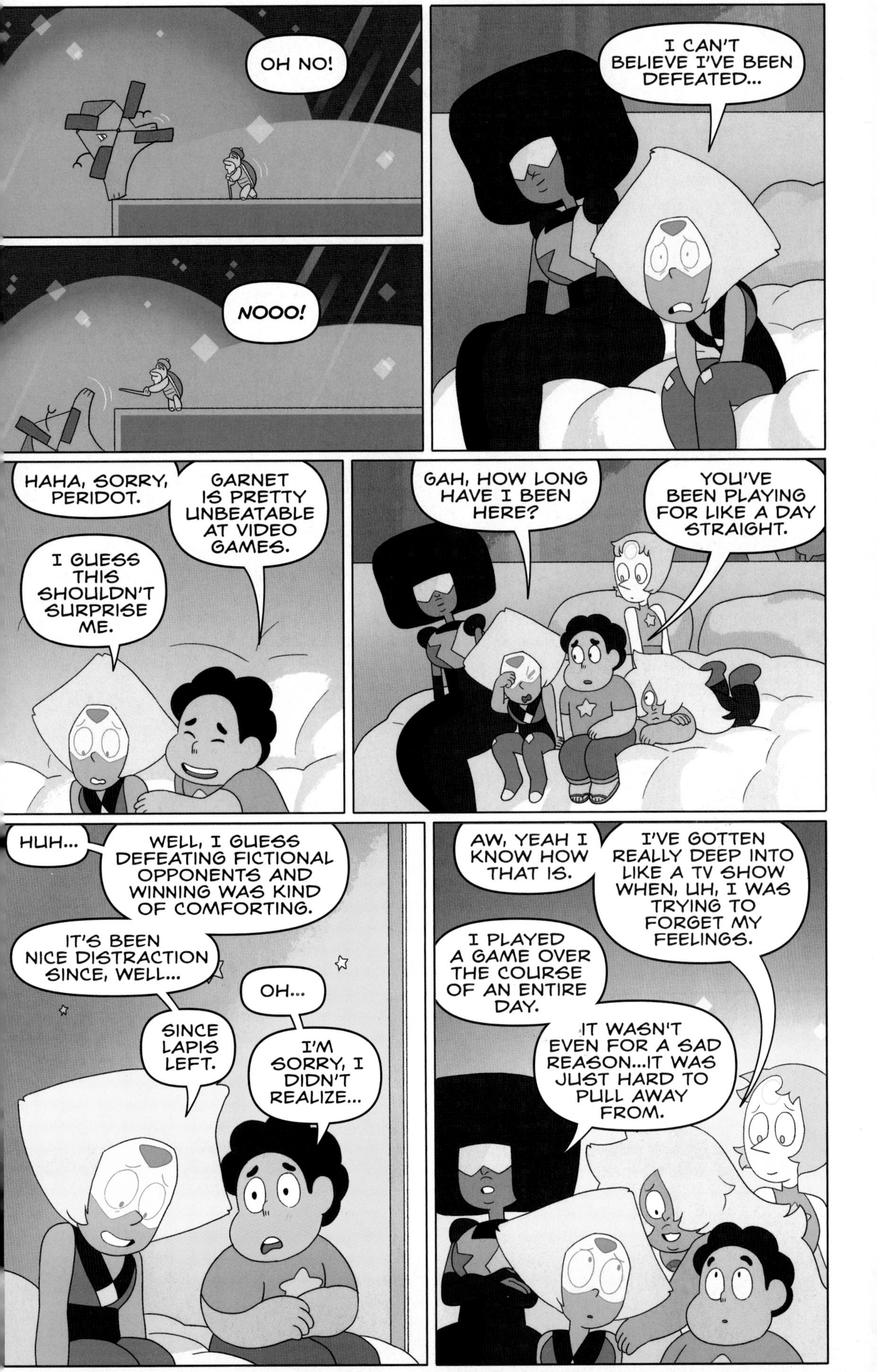
OH NO!
I CAN'T BELIEVE I'VE BEEN DEFEATED...
NOOO!
HAHA, SORRY, PERIDOT.
GARNET IS PRETTY UNBEATABLE AT VIDEO GAMES.
I GUESS THIS SHOULDN'T SURPRISE ME.
GAH, HOW LONG HAVE I BEEN HERE?
YOU'VE BEEN PLAYING FOR LIKE A DAY STRAIGHT.
HUH...
WELL, I GUESS DEFEATING FICTIONAL OPPONENTS AND WINNING WAS KIND OF COMFORTING.
IT'S BEEN NICE DISTRACTION SINCE, WELL...
SINCE LAPIS LEFT.
OH...
I'M SORRY, I DIDN'T REALIZE...
AW, YEAH I KNOW HOW THAT IS.
I'VE GOTTEN REALLY DEEP INTO LIKE A TV SHOW WHEN, UH, I WAS TRYING TO FORGET MY FEELINGS.
I PLAYED A GAME OVER THE COURSE OF AN ENTIRE DAY.
IT WASN'T EVEN FOR A SAD REASON...IT WAS JUST HARD TO PULL AWAY FROM.

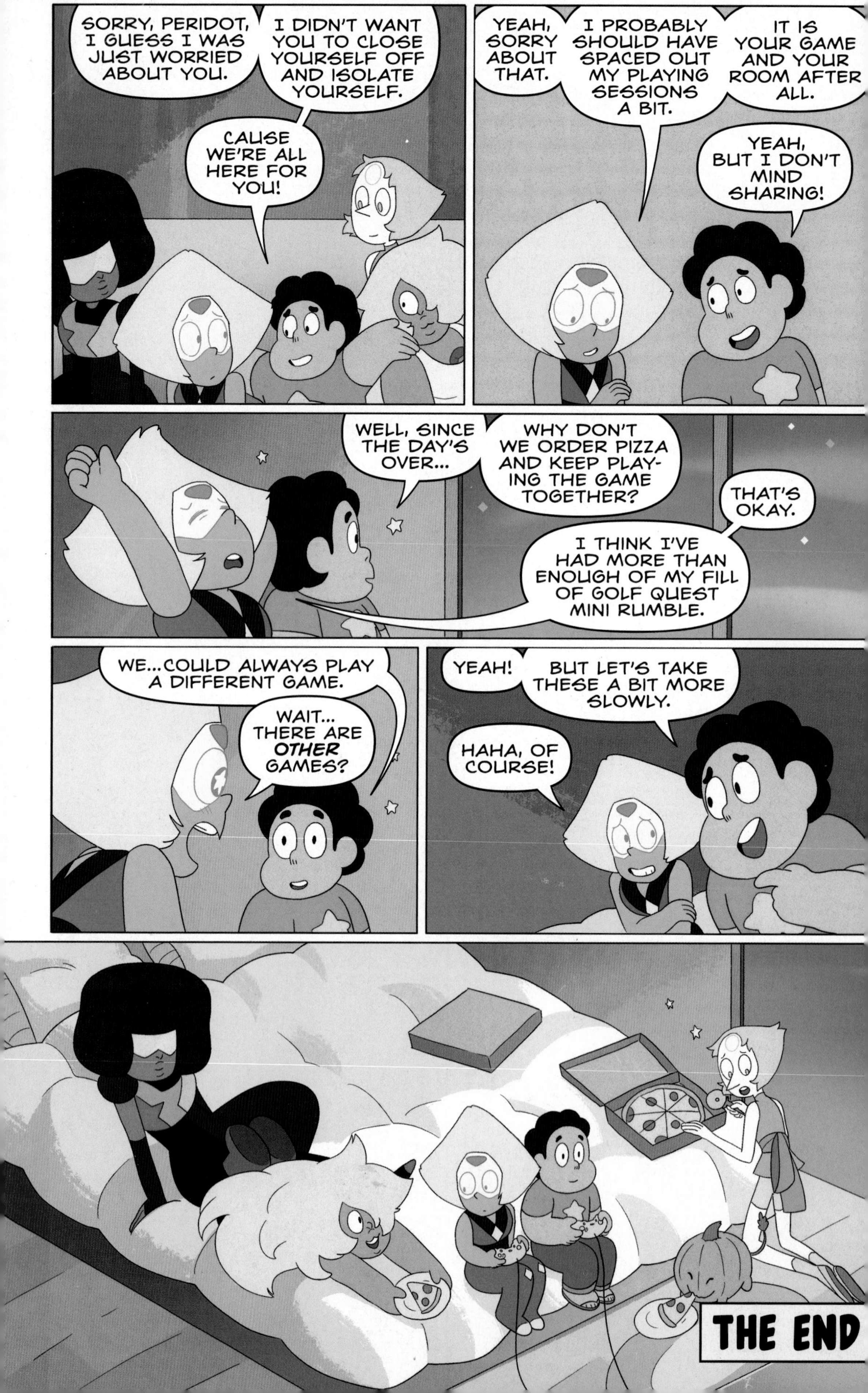
SORRY, PERIDOT, I GUESS I WAS JUST WORRIED ABOUT YOU.
I DIDN'T WANT YOU TO CLOSE YOURSELF OFF AND ISOLATE YOURSELF.
CAUSE WE'RE ALL HERE FOR YOU!
YEAH, SORRY ABOUT THAT.
I PROBABLY SHOULD HAVE SPACED OUT MY PLAYING SESSIONS A BIT.
IT IS YOUR GAME AND YOUR ROOM AFTER ALL.
YEAH, BUT I DON'T MIND SHARING!
WELL, SINCE THE DAY'S OVER...
WHY DON'T WE ORDER PIZZA AND KEEP PLAYING THE GAME TOGETHER?
THAT'S OKAY.
I THINK I'VE HAD MORE THAN ENOUGH OF MY FILL OF GOLF QUEST MINI RUMBLE.
WE...COULD ALWAYS PLAY A DIFFERENT GAME.
WAIT... THERE ARE *OTHER* GAMES?
YEAH!
BUT LET'S TAKE THESE A BIT MORE SLOWLY.
HAHA, OF COURSE!
THE END

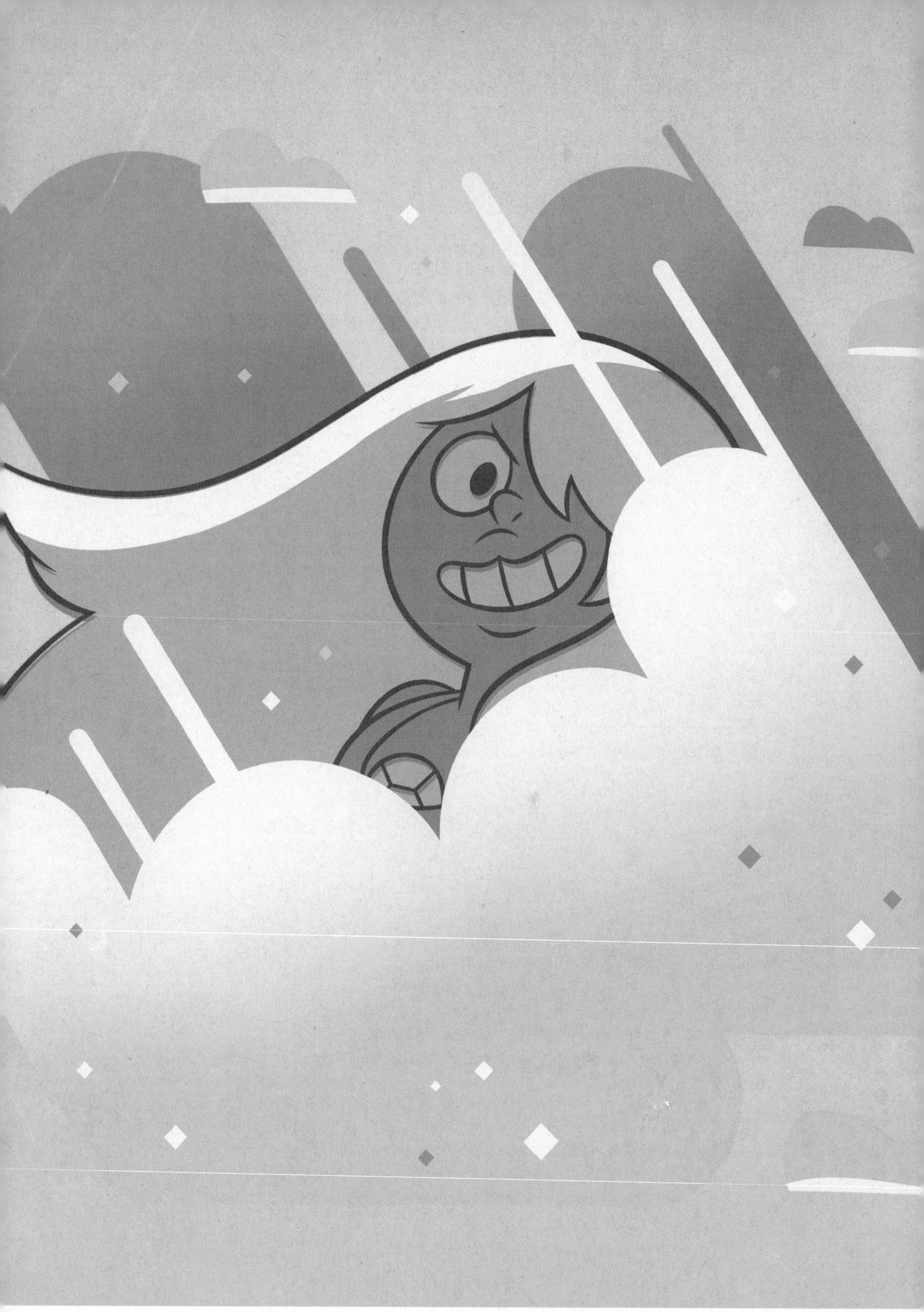

CHAPTER EIGHTEEN

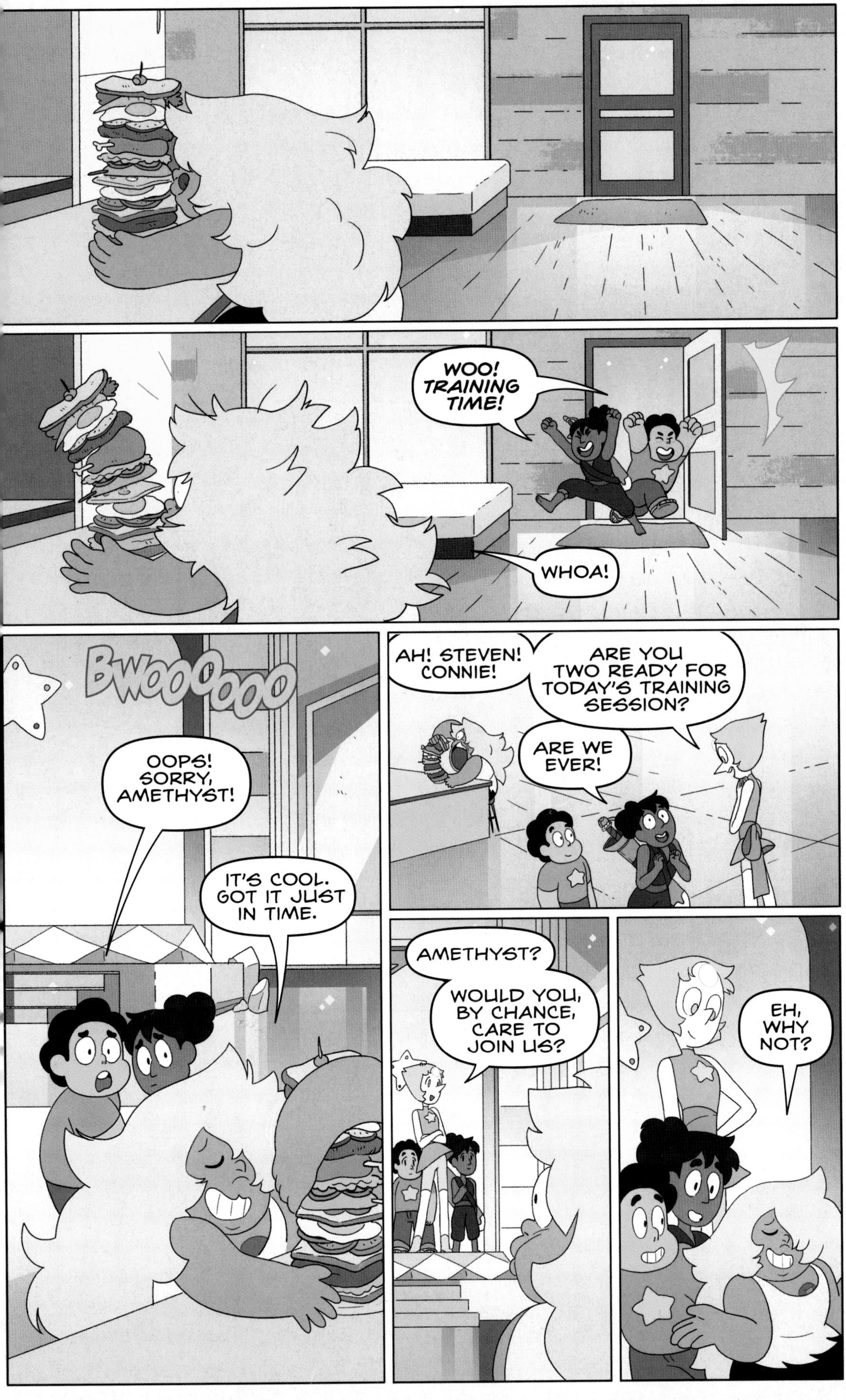

WOO! TRAINING TIME!
WHOA!
BWOOOOOO
OOPS! SORRY, AMETHYST!
IT'S COOL. GOT IT JUST IN TIME.
AH! STEVEN! CONNIE!
ARE YOU TWO READY FOR TODAY'S TRAINING SESSION?
ARE WE EVER!
AMETHYST?
WOULD YOU, BY CHANCE, CARE TO JOIN US?
EH, WHY NOT?

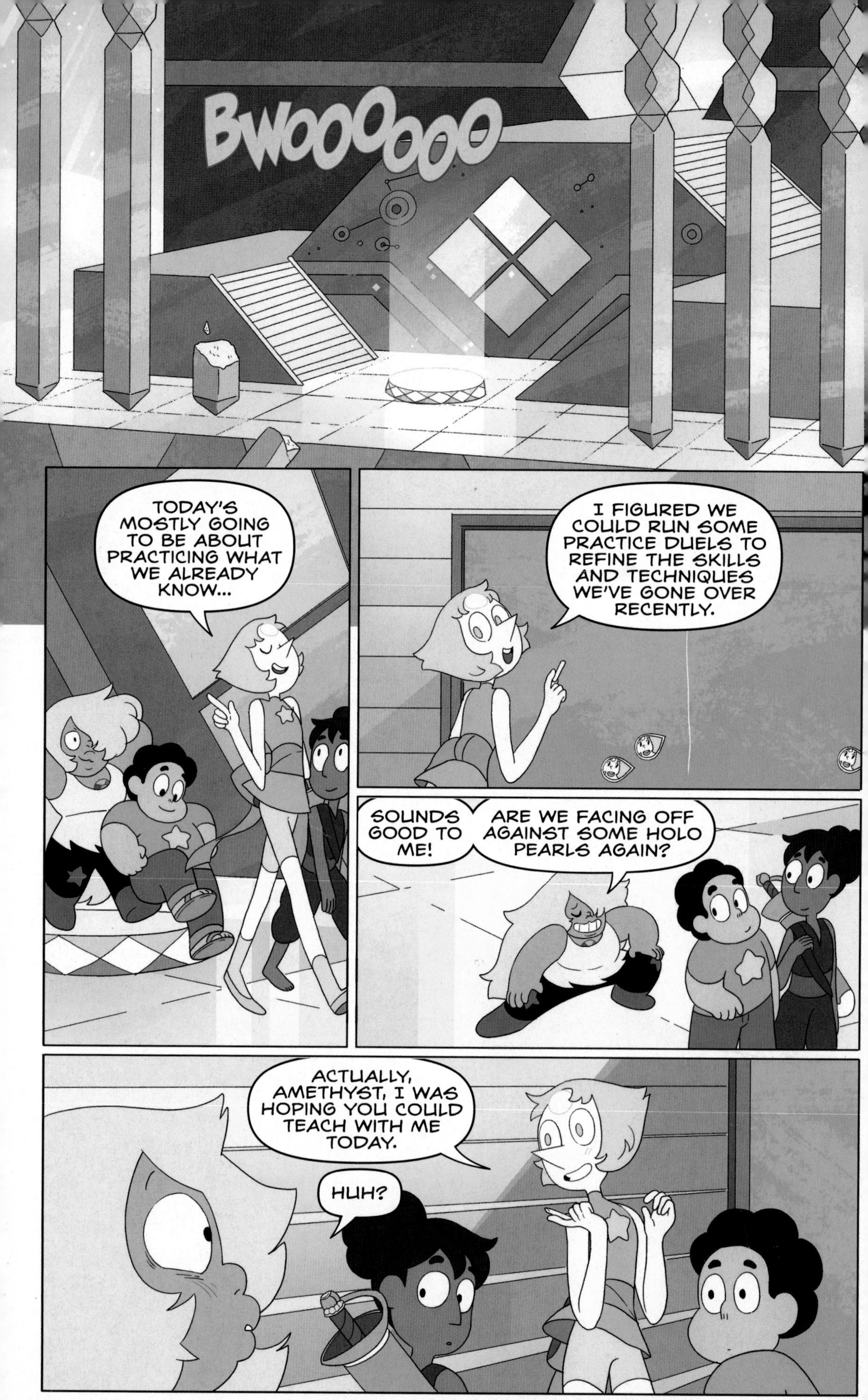
BWOOOOOO
TODAY'S MOSTLY GOING TO BE ABOUT PRACTICING WHAT WE ALREADY KNOW...
I FIGURED WE COULD RUN SOME PRACTICE DUELS TO REFINE THE SKILLS AND TECHNIQUES WE'VE GONE OVER RECENTLY.
SOUNDS GOOD TO ME!
ARE WE FACING OFF AGAINST SOME HOLO PEARLS AGAIN?
ACTUALLY, AMETHYST, I WAS HOPING YOU COULD TEACH WITH ME TODAY.
HUH?

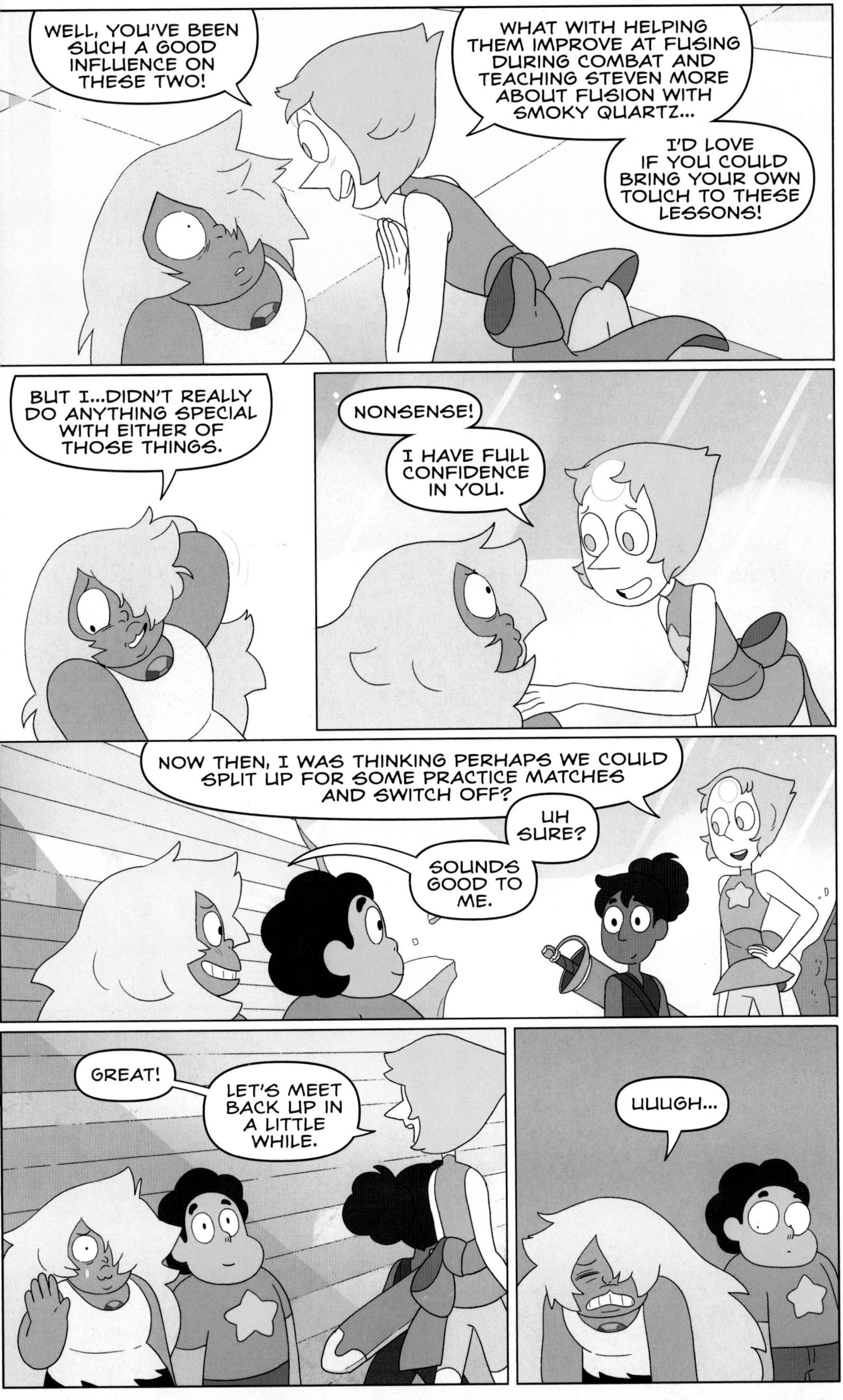
WELL, YOU'VE BEEN SUCH A GOOD INFLUENCE ON THESE TWO!
WHAT WITH HELPING THEM IMPROVE AT FUSING DURING COMBAT AND TEACHING STEVEN MORE ABOUT FUSION WITH SMOKY QUARTZ...
I'D LOVE IF YOU COULD BRING YOUR OWN TOUCH TO THESE LESSONS!
BUT I...DIDN'T REALLY DO ANYTHING SPECIAL WITH EITHER OF THOSE THINGS.
NONSENSE!
I HAVE FULL CONFIDENCE IN YOU.
NOW THEN, I WAS THINKING PERHAPS WE COULD SPLIT UP FOR SOME PRACTICE MATCHES AND SWITCH OFF?
UH SURE?
SOUNDS GOOD TO ME.
GREAT!
LET'S MEET BACK UP IN A LITTLE WHILE.
UUUGH...

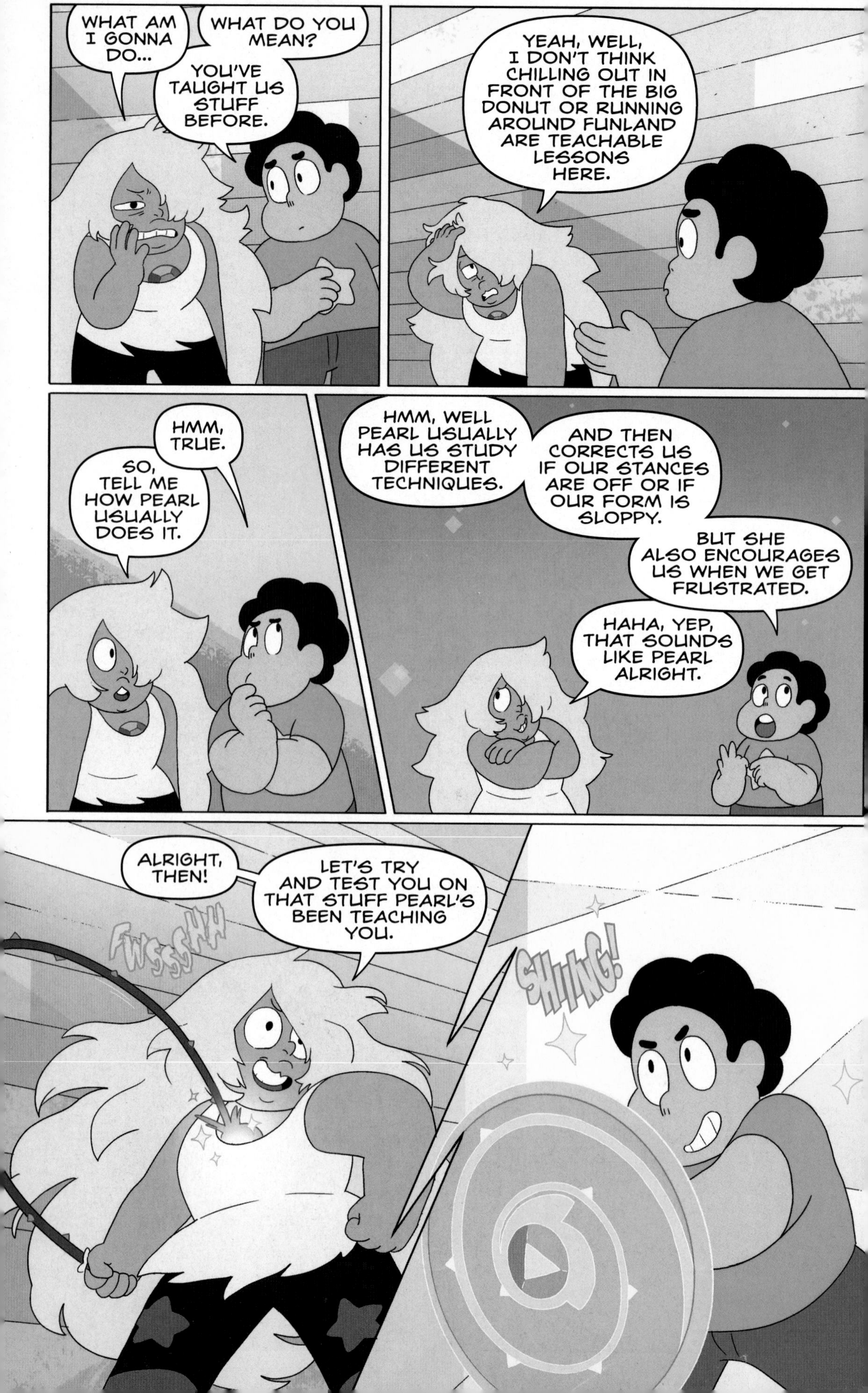
WHAT AM I GONNA DO...
WHAT DO YOU MEAN?
YOU'VE TAUGHT US STUFF BEFORE.
YEAH, WELL, I DON'T THINK CHILLING OUT IN FRONT OF THE BIG DONUT OR RUNNING AROUND FUNLAND ARE TEACHABLE LESSONS HERE.
HMM, TRUE.
SO, TELL ME HOW PEARL USUALLY DOES IT.
HMM, WELL PEARL USUALLY HAS US STUDY DIFFERENT TECHNIQUES.
AND THEN CORRECTS US IF OUR STANCES ARE OFF OR IF OUR FORM IS SLOPPY.
BUT SHE ALSO ENCOURAGES US WHEN WE GET FRUSTRATED.
HAHA, YEP, THAT SOUNDS LIKE PEARL ALRIGHT.
ALRIGHT, THEN!
LET'S TRY AND TEST YOU ON THAT STUFF PEARL'S BEEN TEACHING YOU.
FWSSSHH
SHIING!

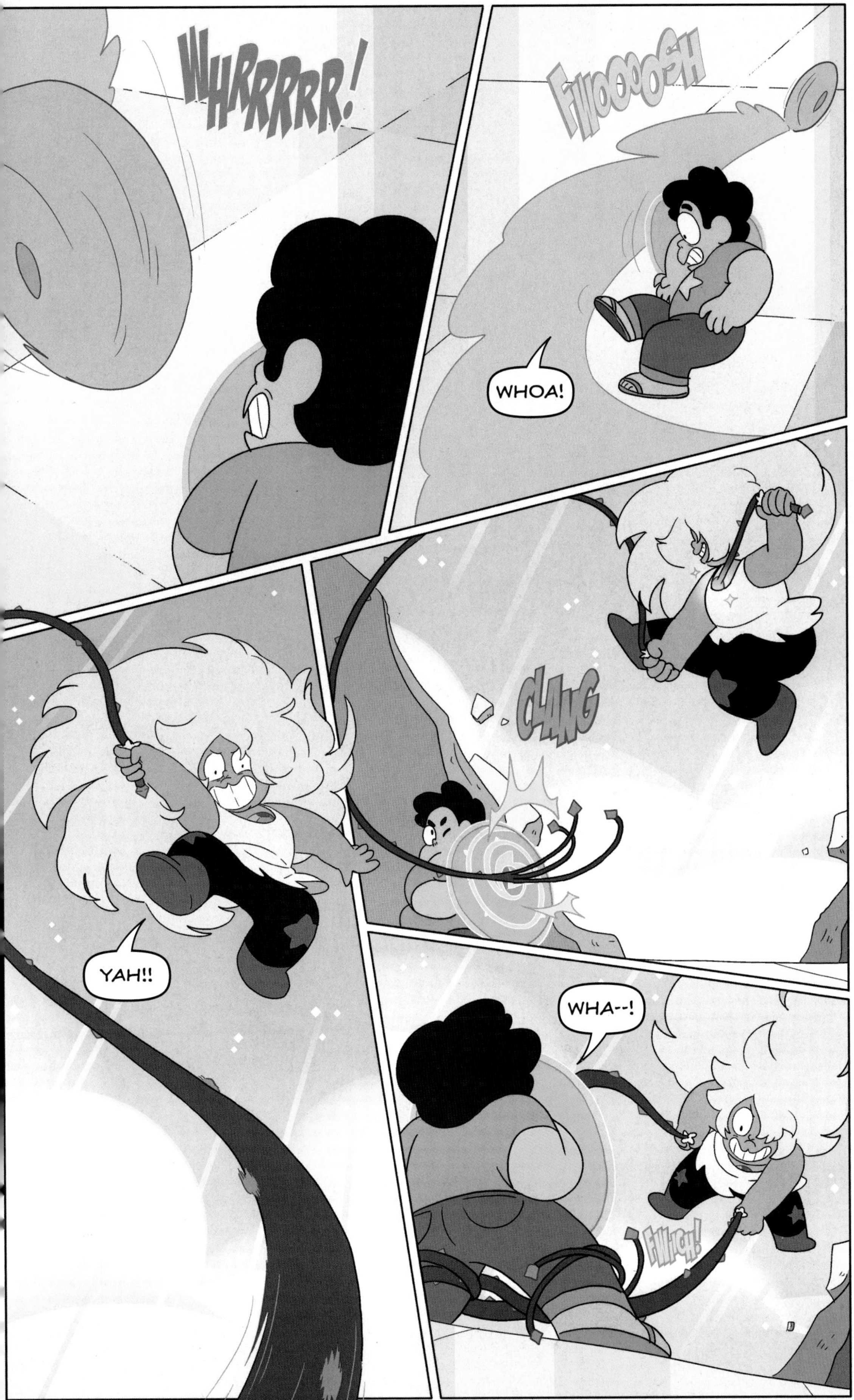
WHRRRRR!
FWOOOOSH
WHOA!
YAH!!
CLANG
WHA--!
FWICH!

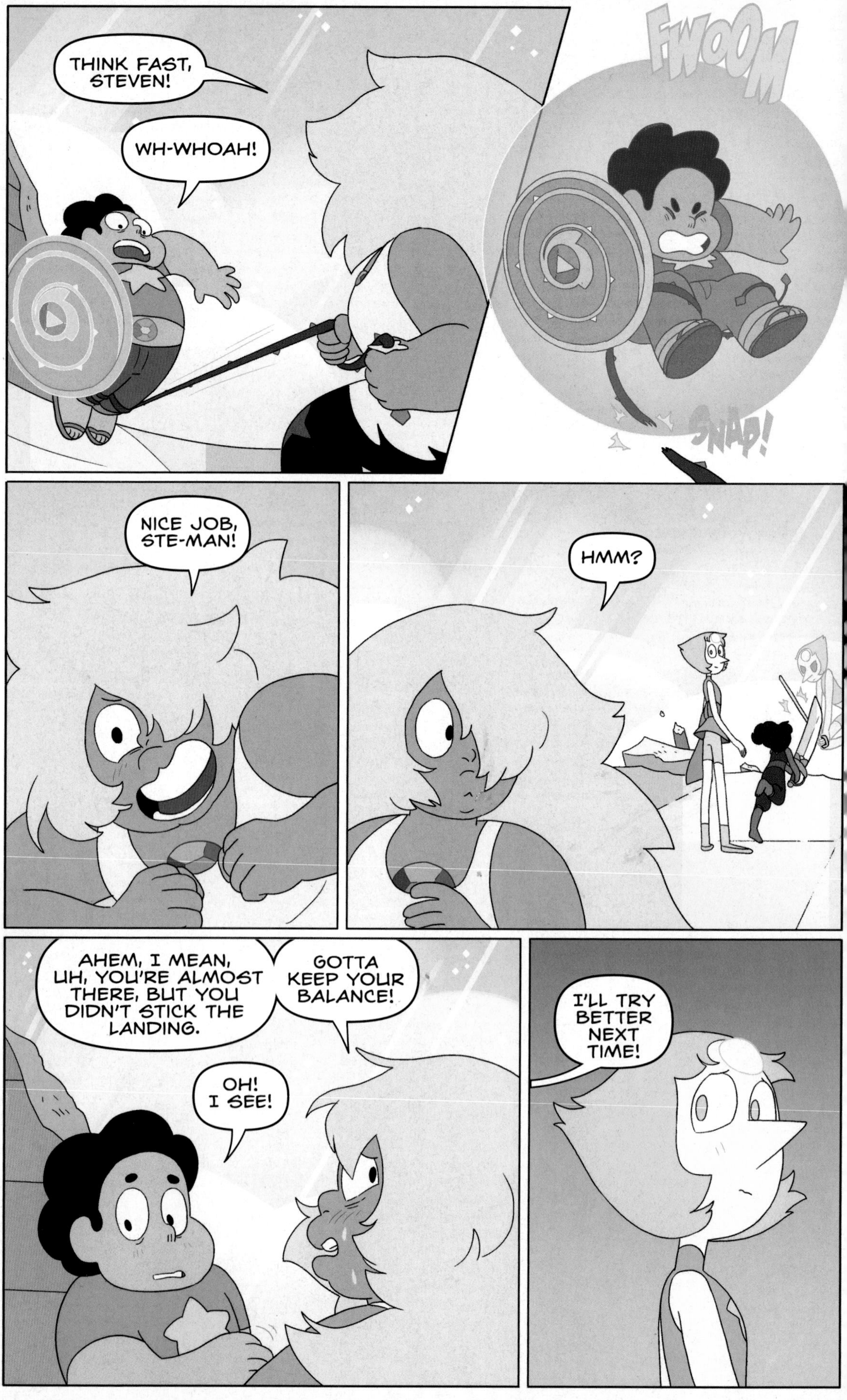
THINK FAST, STEVEN!
WH-WHOAH!
FWOOM
SNAP!
NICE JOB, STE-MAN!
HMM?
AHEM, I MEAN, UH, YOU'RE ALMOST THERE, BUT YOU DIDN'T STICK THE LANDING.
GOTTA KEEP YOUR BALANCE!
OH! I SEE!
I'LL TRY BETTER NEXT TIME!

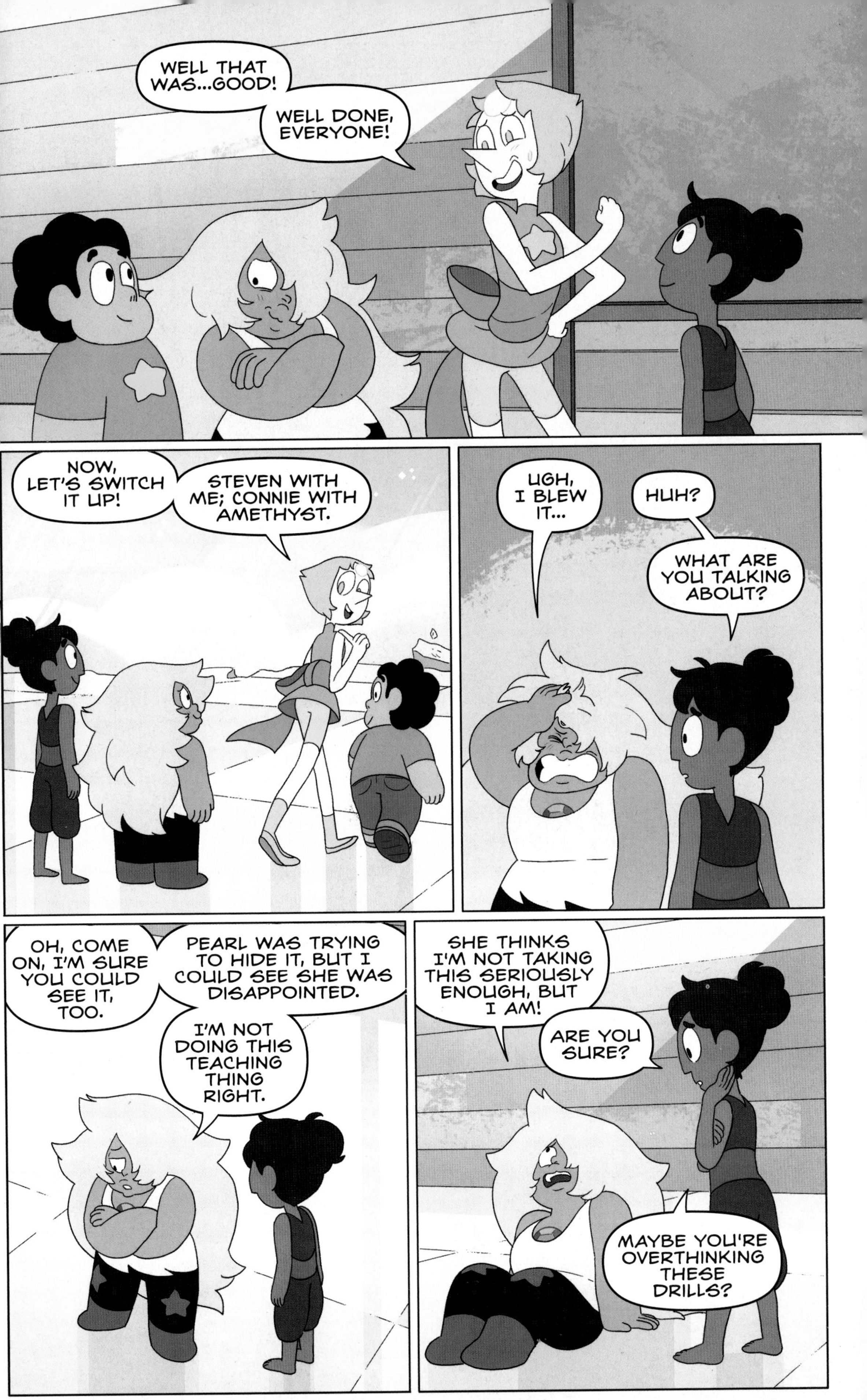
WELL THAT WAS...GOOD!
WELL DONE, EVERYONE!
NOW, LET'S SWITCH IT UP!
STEVEN WITH ME; CONNIE WITH AMETHYST.
UGH, I BLEW IT...
HUH?
WHAT ARE YOU TALKING ABOUT?
OH, COME ON, I'M SURE YOU COULD SEE IT, TOO.
PEARL WAS TRYING TO HIDE IT, BUT I COULD SEE SHE WAS DISAPPOINTED.
I'M NOT DOING THIS TEACHING THING RIGHT.
SHE THINKS I'M NOT TAKING THIS SERIOUSLY ENOUGH, BUT I AM!
ARE YOU SURE?
MAYBE YOU'RE OVERTHINKING THESE DRILLS?

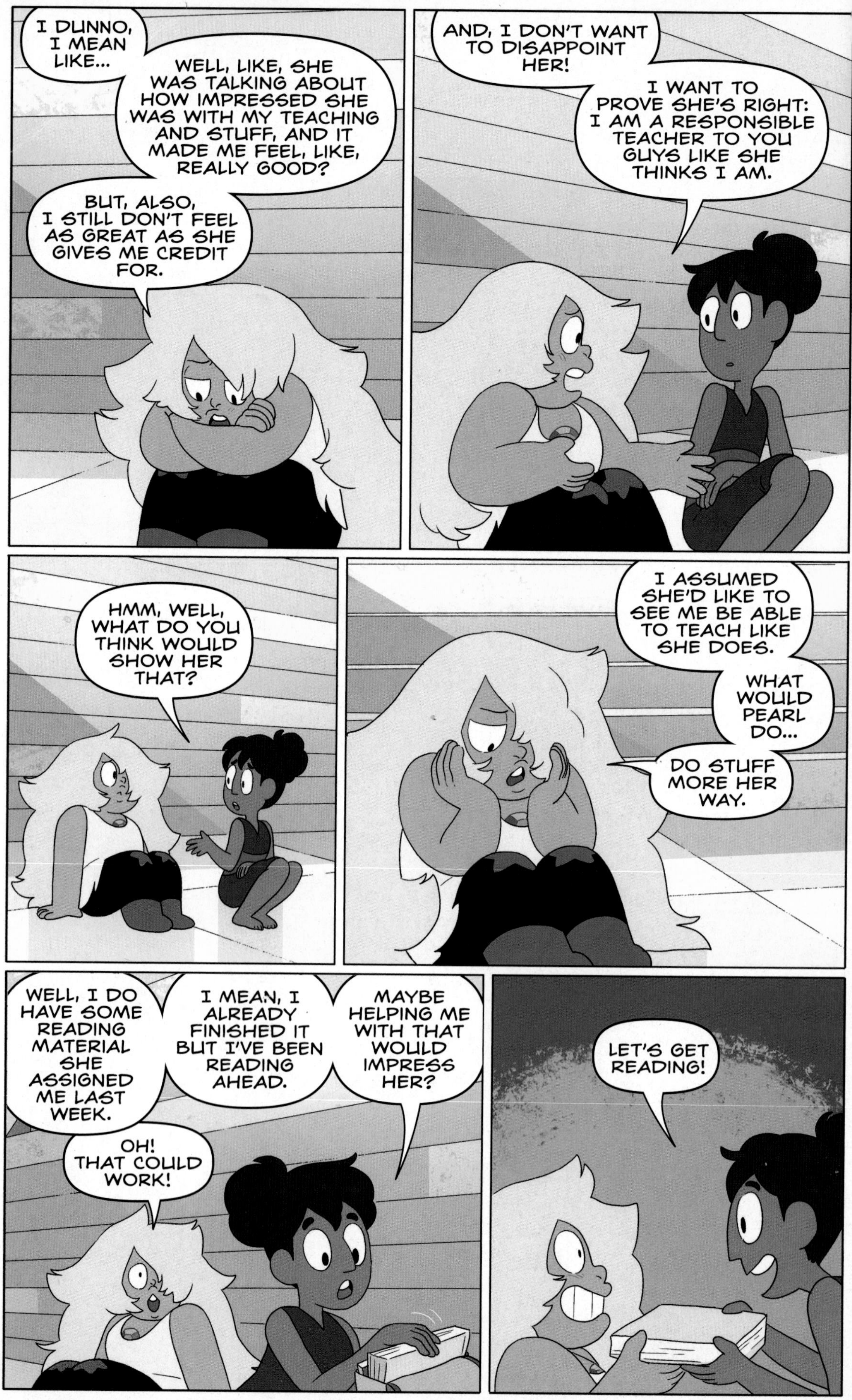
I DUNNO, I MEAN LIKE...
WELL, LIKE, SHE WAS TALKING ABOUT HOW IMPRESSED SHE WAS WITH MY TEACHING AND STUFF, AND IT MADE ME FEEL, LIKE, REALLY GOOD?
BUT, ALSO, I STILL DON'T FEEL AS GREAT AS SHE GIVES ME CREDIT FOR.
AND, I DON'T WANT TO DISAPPOINT HER!
I WANT TO PROVE SHE'S RIGHT: I AM A RESPONSIBLE TEACHER TO YOU GUYS LIKE SHE THINKS I AM.
HMM, WELL, WHAT DO YOU THINK WOULD SHOW HER THAT?
I ASSUMED SHE'D LIKE TO SEE ME BE ABLE TO TEACH LIKE SHE DOES.
WHAT WOULD PEARL DO...
DO STUFF MORE HER WAY.
WELL, I DO HAVE SOME READING MATERIAL SHE ASSIGNED ME LAST WEEK.
I MEAN, I ALREADY FINISHED IT BUT I'VE BEEN READING AHEAD.
MAYBE HELPING ME WITH THAT WOULD IMPRESS HER?
OH! THAT COULD WORK!
LET'S GET READING!

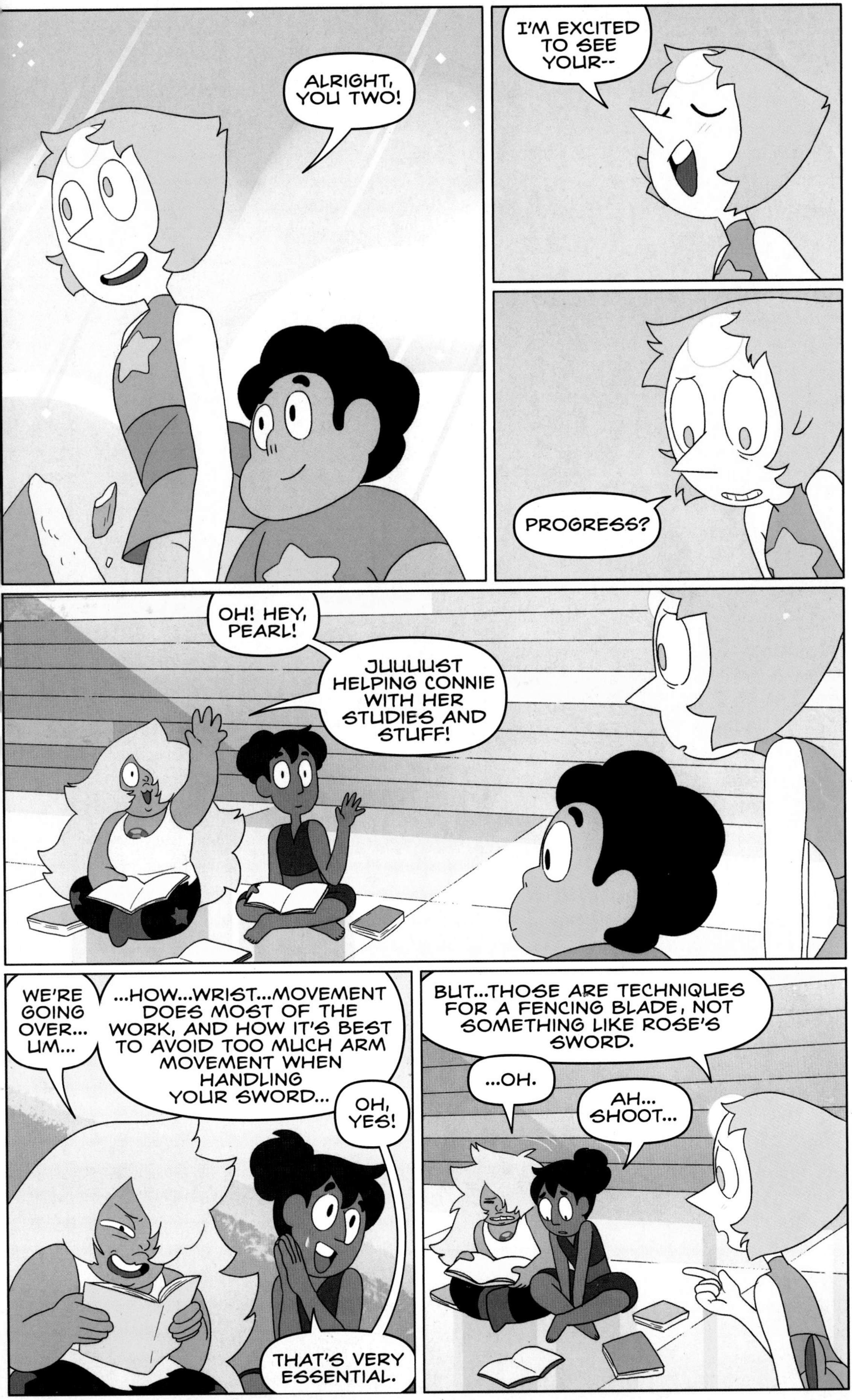
ALRIGHT, YOU TWO!
I'M EXCITED TO SEE YOUR--
PROGRESS?
OH! HEY, PEARL!
JUUUUST HELPING CONNIE WITH HER STUDIES AND STUFF!
WE'RE GOING OVER... UM...
...HOW...WRIST...MOVEMENT DOES MOST OF THE WORK, AND HOW IT'S BEST TO AVOID TOO MUCH ARM MOVEMENT WHEN HANDLING YOUR SWORD...
OH, YES!
THAT'S VERY ESSENTIAL.
BUT...THOSE ARE TECHNIQUES FOR A FENCING BLADE, NOT SOMETHING LIKE ROSE'S SWORD.
...OH.
AH... SHOOT...

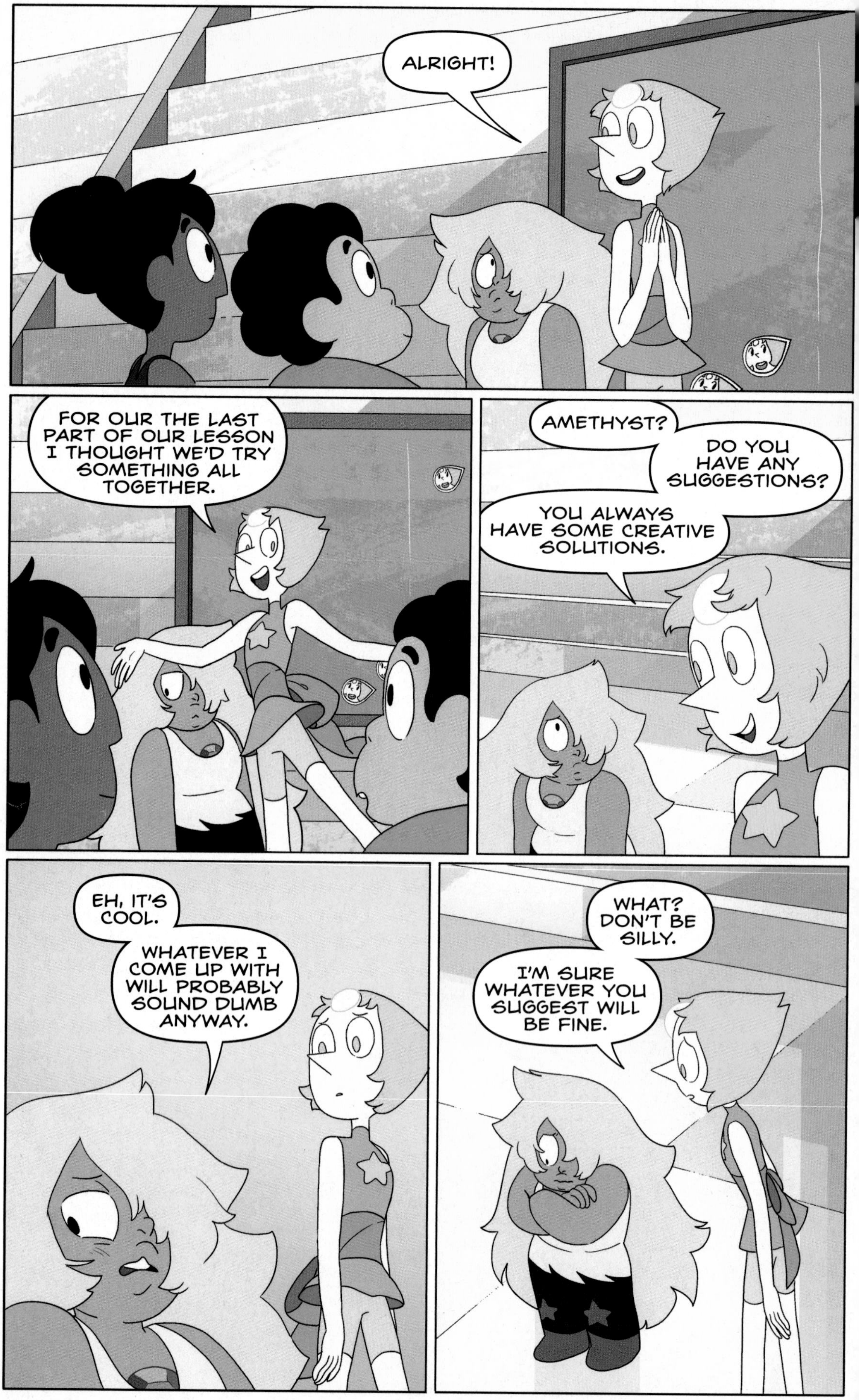

ALRIGHT!
FOR OUR THE LAST PART OF OUR LESSON I THOUGHT WE'D TRY SOMETHING ALL TOGETHER.
AMETHYST?
DO YOU HAVE ANY SUGGESTIONS?
YOU ALWAYS HAVE SOME CREATIVE SOLUTIONS.
EH, IT'S COOL.
WHATEVER I COME UP WITH WILL PROBABLY SOUND DUMB ANYWAY.
WHAT? DON'T BE SILLY.
I'M SURE WHATEVER YOU SUGGEST WILL BE FINE.

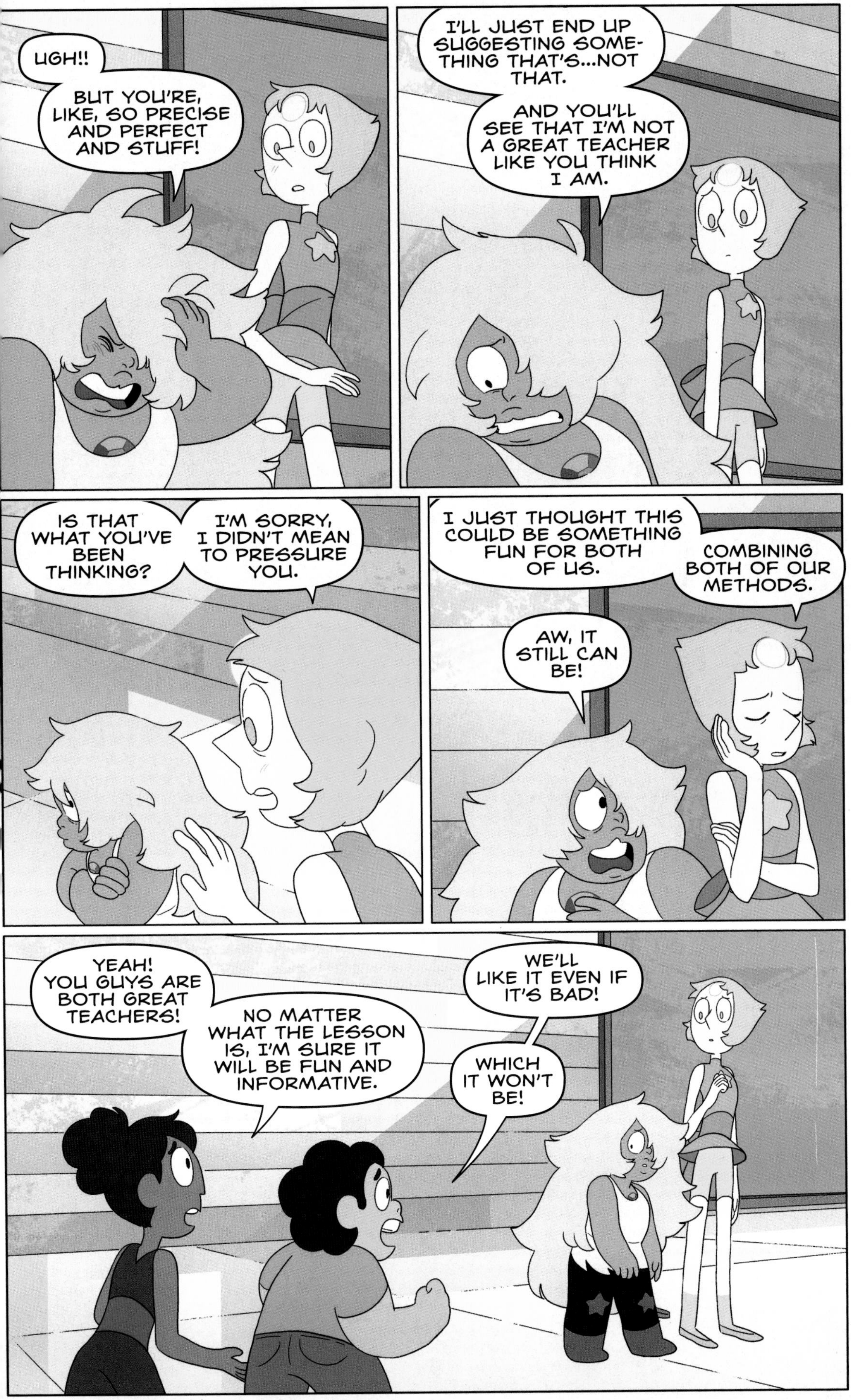
UGH!!
BUT YOU'RE, LIKE, SO PRECISE AND PERFECT AND STUFF!
I'LL JUST END UP SUGGESTING SOME-THING THAT'S...NOT THAT.
AND YOU'LL SEE THAT I'M NOT A GREAT TEACHER LIKE YOU THINK I AM.
IS THAT WHAT YOU'VE BEEN THINKING?
I'M SORRY, I DIDN'T MEAN TO PRESSURE YOU.
I JUST THOUGHT THIS COULD BE SOMETHING FUN FOR BOTH OF US.
COMBINING BOTH OF OUR METHODS.
AW, IT STILL CAN BE!
YEAH! YOU GUYS ARE BOTH GREAT TEACHERS!
NO MATTER WHAT THE LESSON IS, I'M SURE IT WILL BE FUN AND INFORMATIVE.
WE'LL LIKE IT EVEN IF IT'S BAD!
WHICH IT WON'T BE!

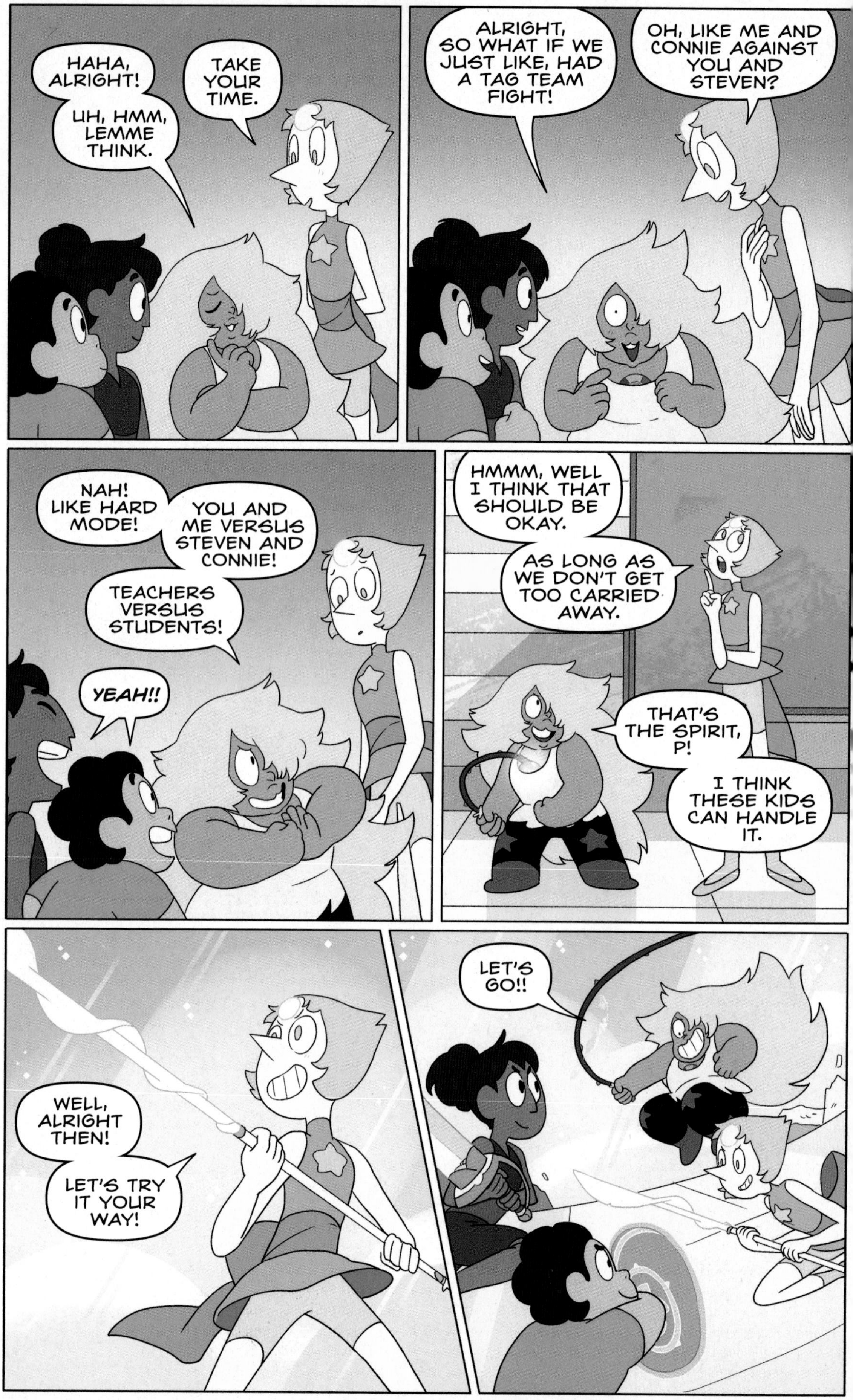
HAHA, ALRIGHT!
UH, HMM, LEMME THINK.
TAKE YOUR TIME.
ALRIGHT, SO WHAT IF WE JUST LIKE, HAD A TAG TEAM FIGHT!
OH, LIKE ME AND CONNIE AGAINST YOU AND STEVEN?
NAH! LIKE HARD MODE!
YOU AND ME VERSUS STEVEN AND CONNIE!
TEACHERS VERSUS STUDENTS!
YEAH!!
HMMM, WELL I THINK THAT SHOULD BE OKAY.
AS LONG AS WE DON'T GET TOO CARRIED AWAY.
THAT'S THE SPIRIT, P!
I THINK THESE KIDS CAN HANDLE IT.
WELL, ALRIGHT THEN!
LET'S TRY IT YOUR WAY!
LET'S GO!!

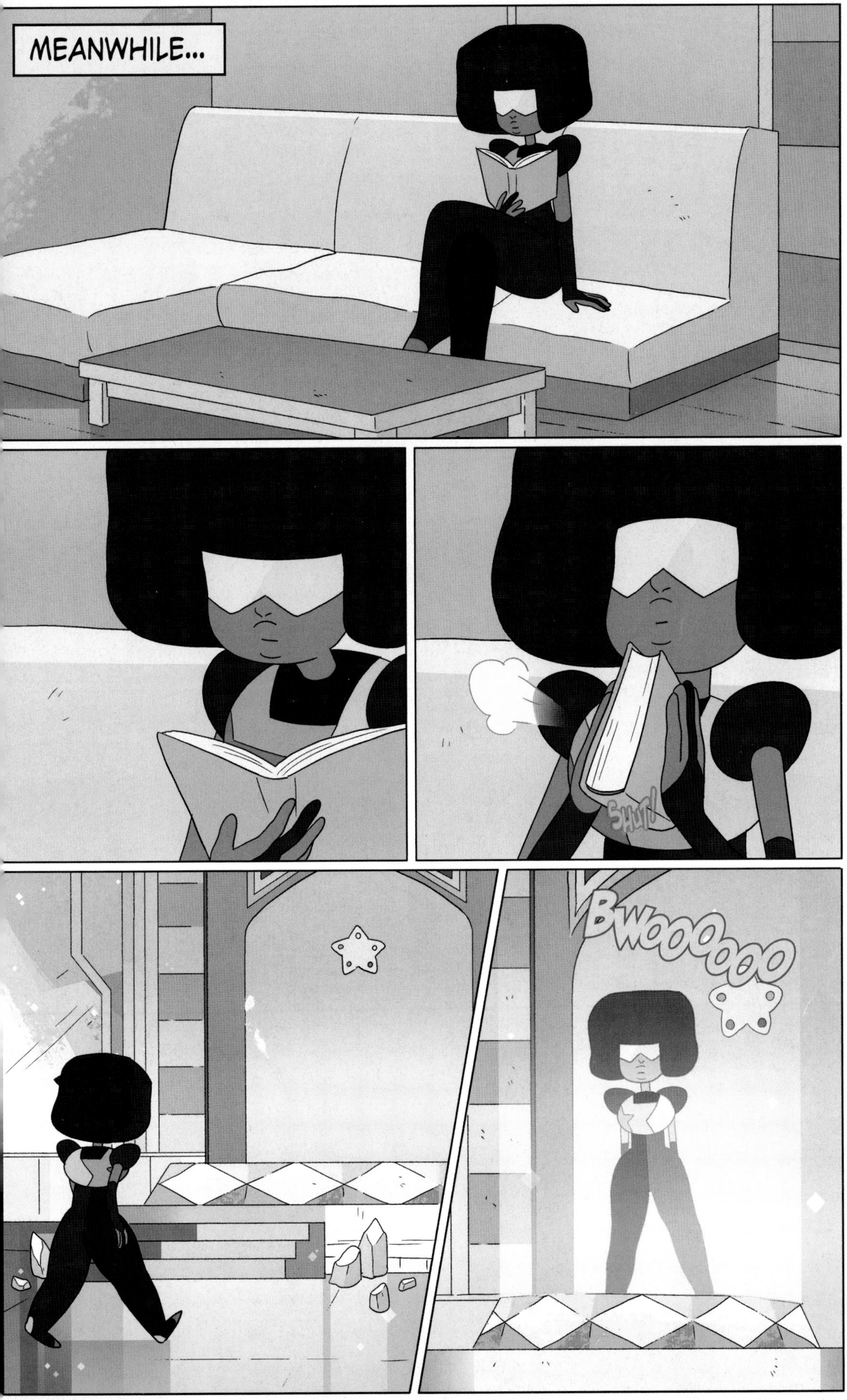
MEANWHILE...
SHUT!
BWOOOOOO

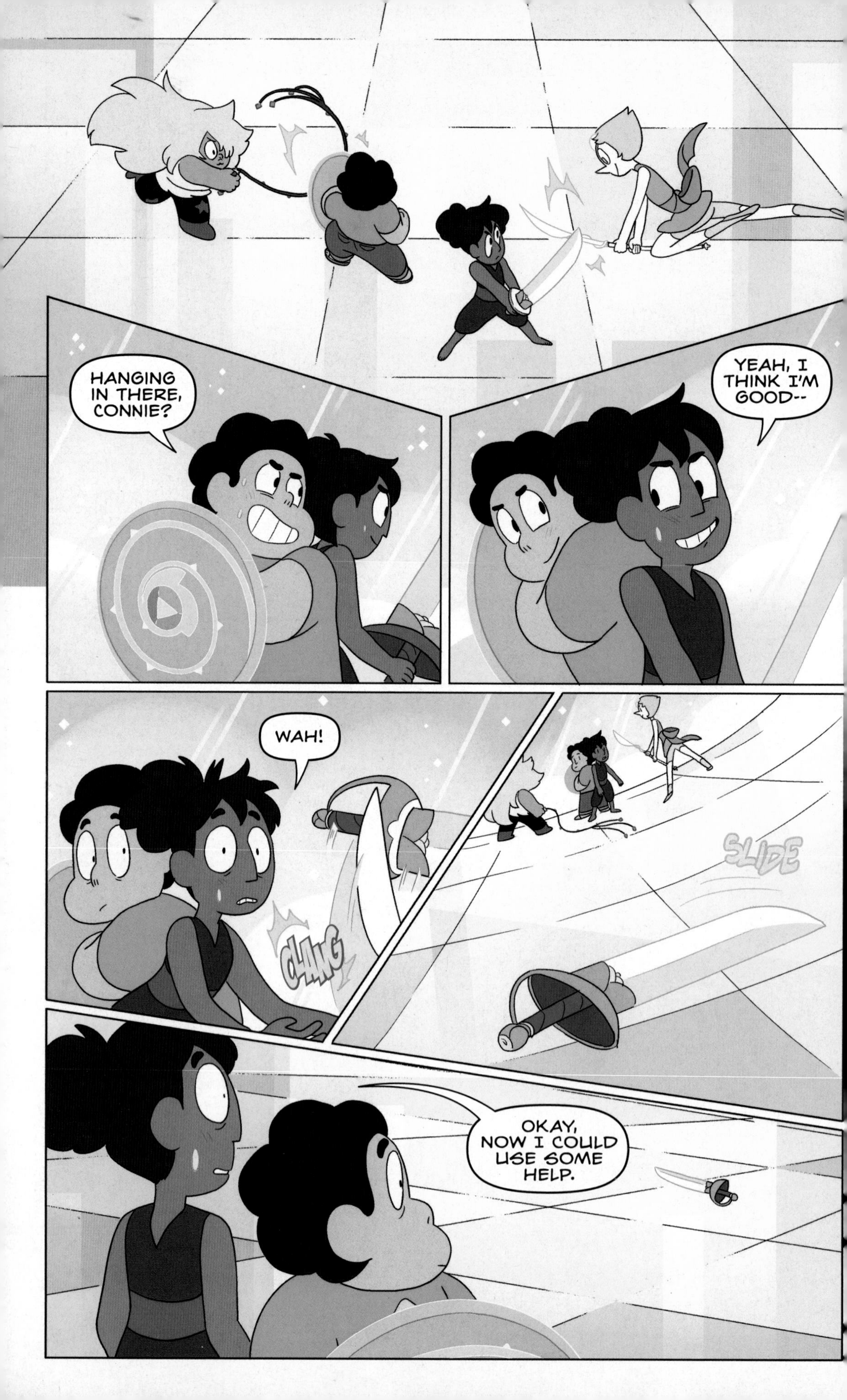
HANGING IN THERE, CONNIE?
YEAH, I THINK I'M GOOD--
WAH!
CLANG
SLIDE
OKAY, NOW I COULD USE SOME HELP.

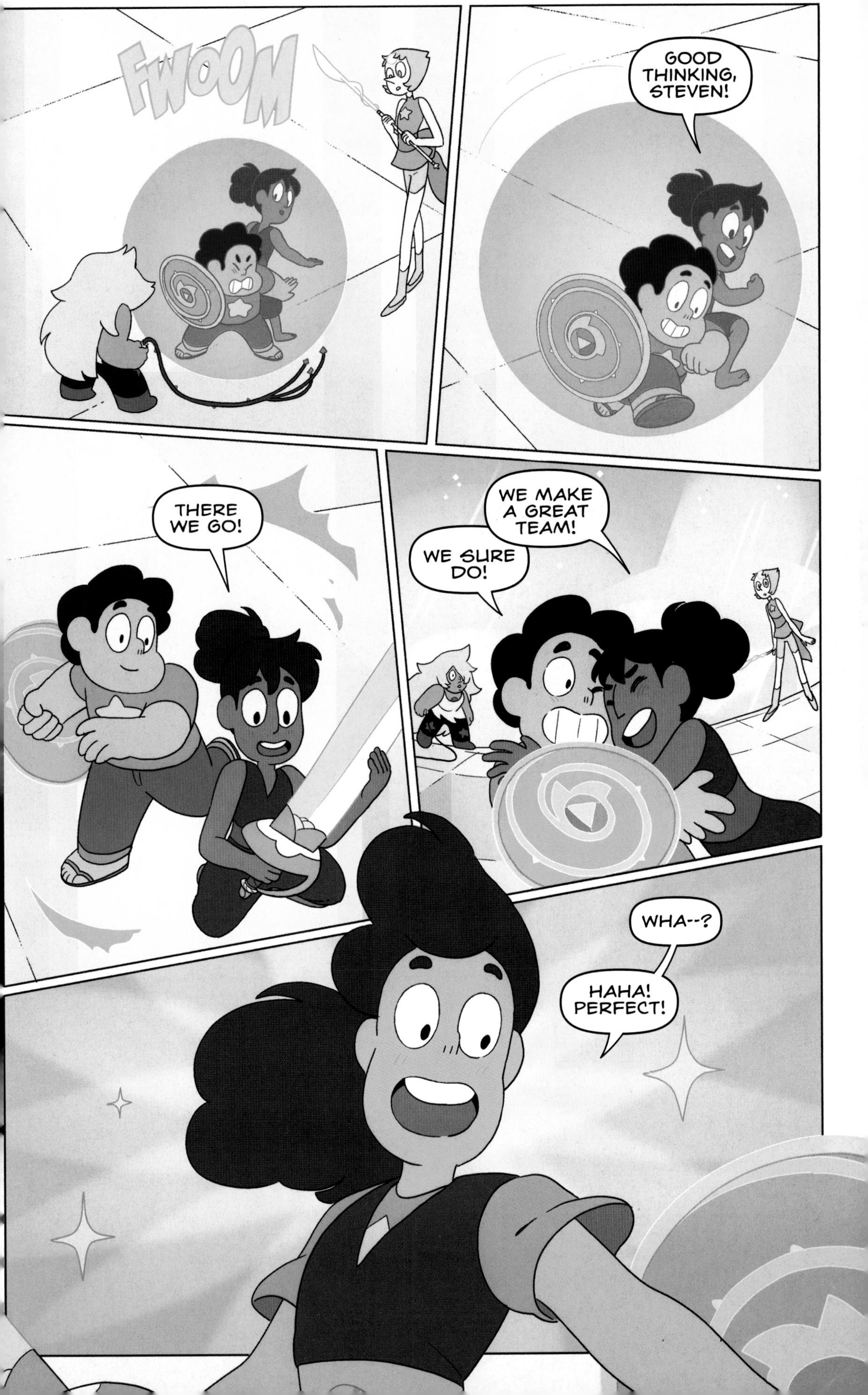
FWOOM
GOOD THINKING, STEVEN!
THERE WE GO!
WE MAKE A GREAT TEAM!
WE SURE DO!
WHA--?
HAHA! PERFECT!

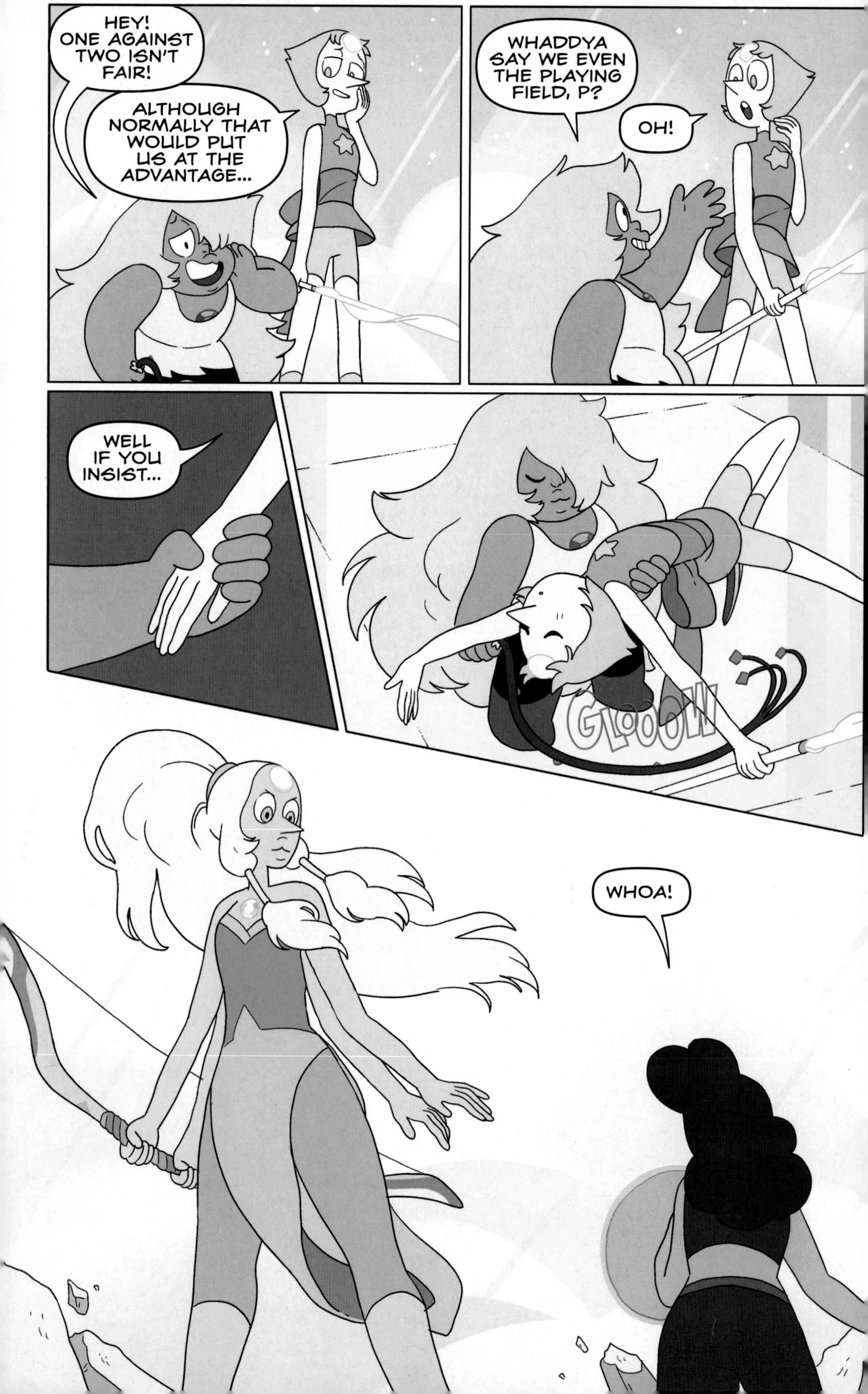
HEY! ONE AGAINST TWO ISN'T FAIR!
ALTHOUGH NORMALLY THAT WOULD PUT US AT THE ADVANTAGE...
WHADDYA SAY WE EVEN THE PLAYING FIELD, P?
OH!
WELL IF YOU INSIST...
GLOOOOW
WHOA!

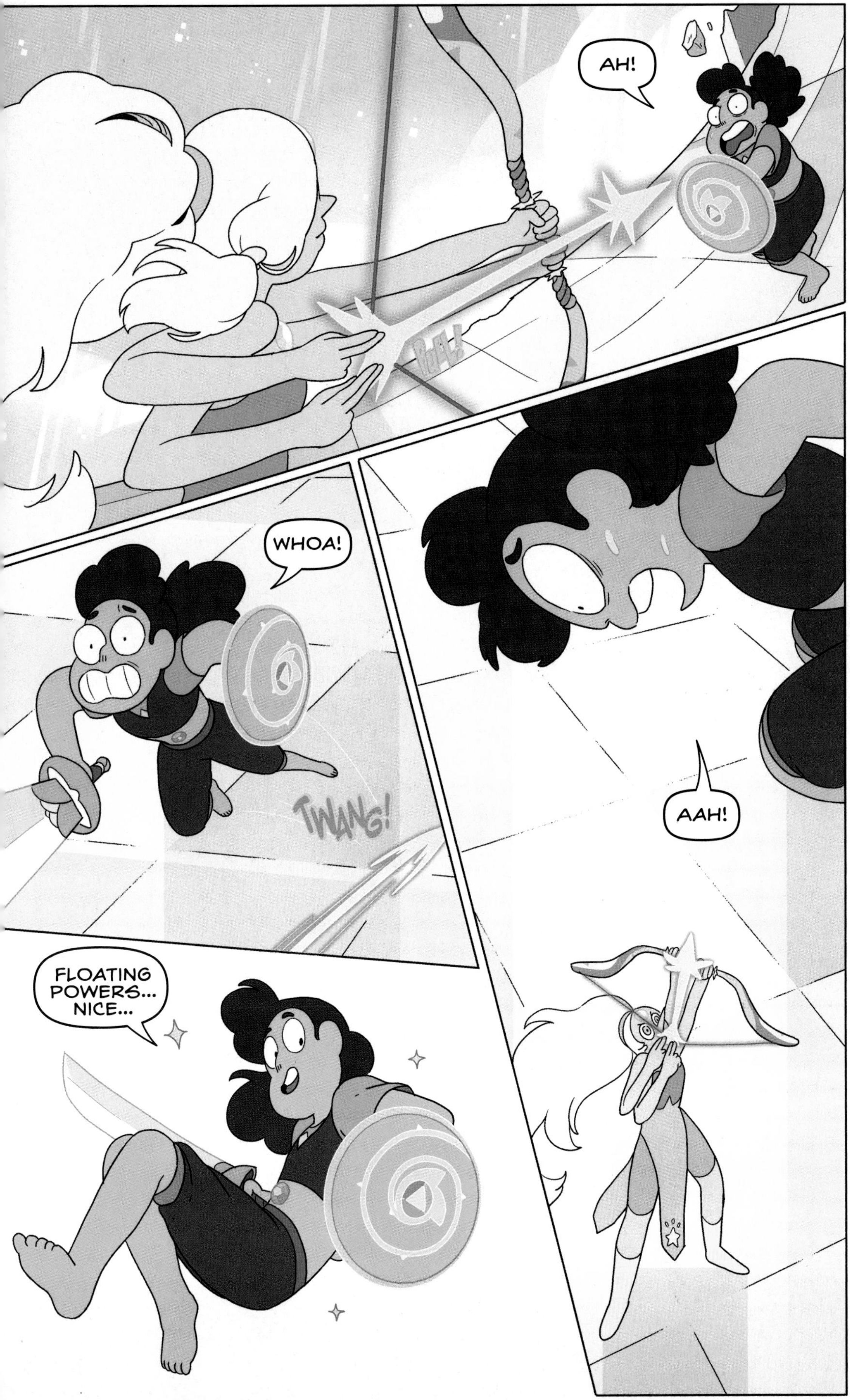
AH!
WHOA!
TWANG!
AAH!
FLOATING POWERS... NICE...

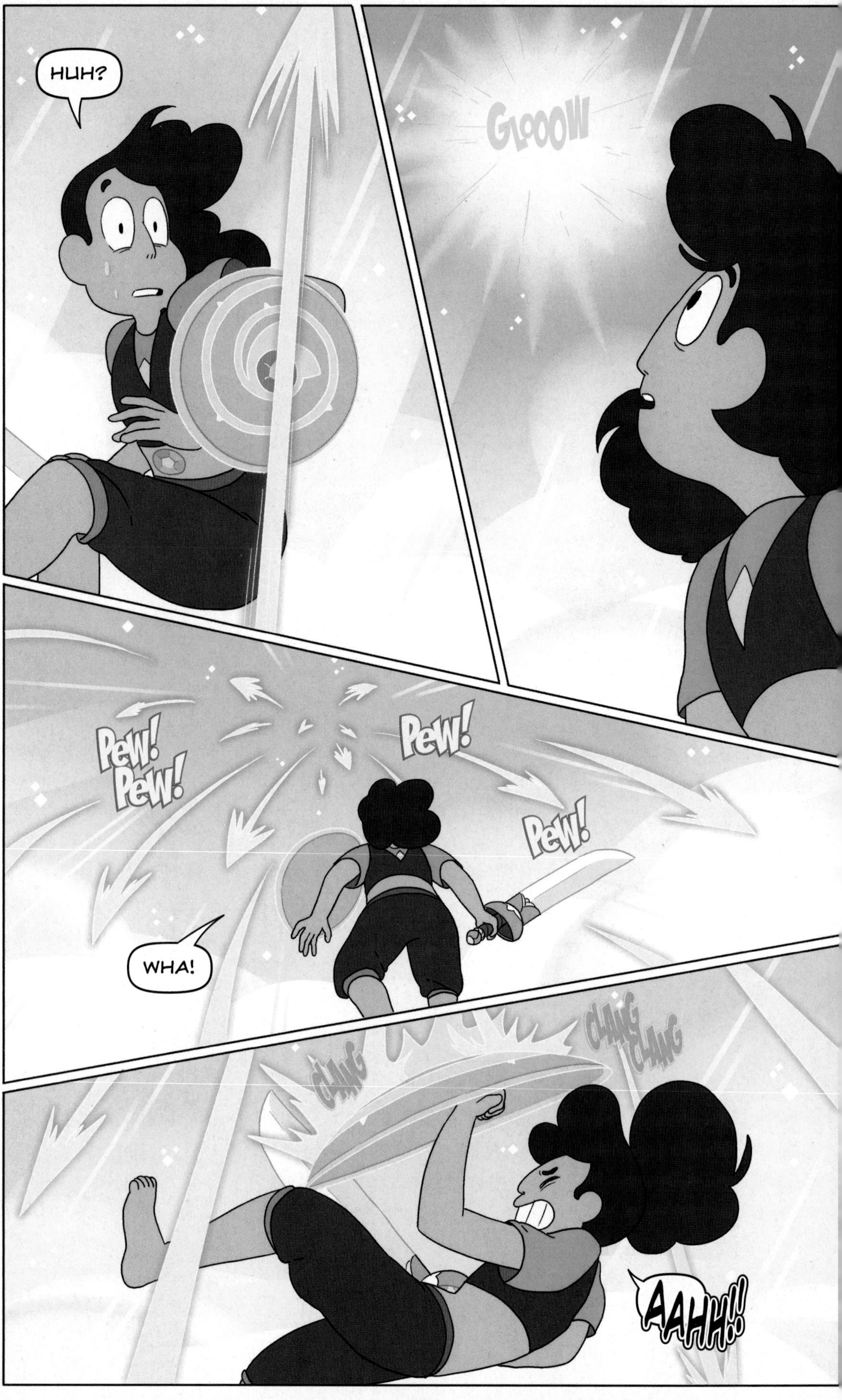
HUH?
GLOOOW
PEW! PEW!
PEW!
PEW!
WHA!
CLANG
CLANG CLANG
AAHH!!

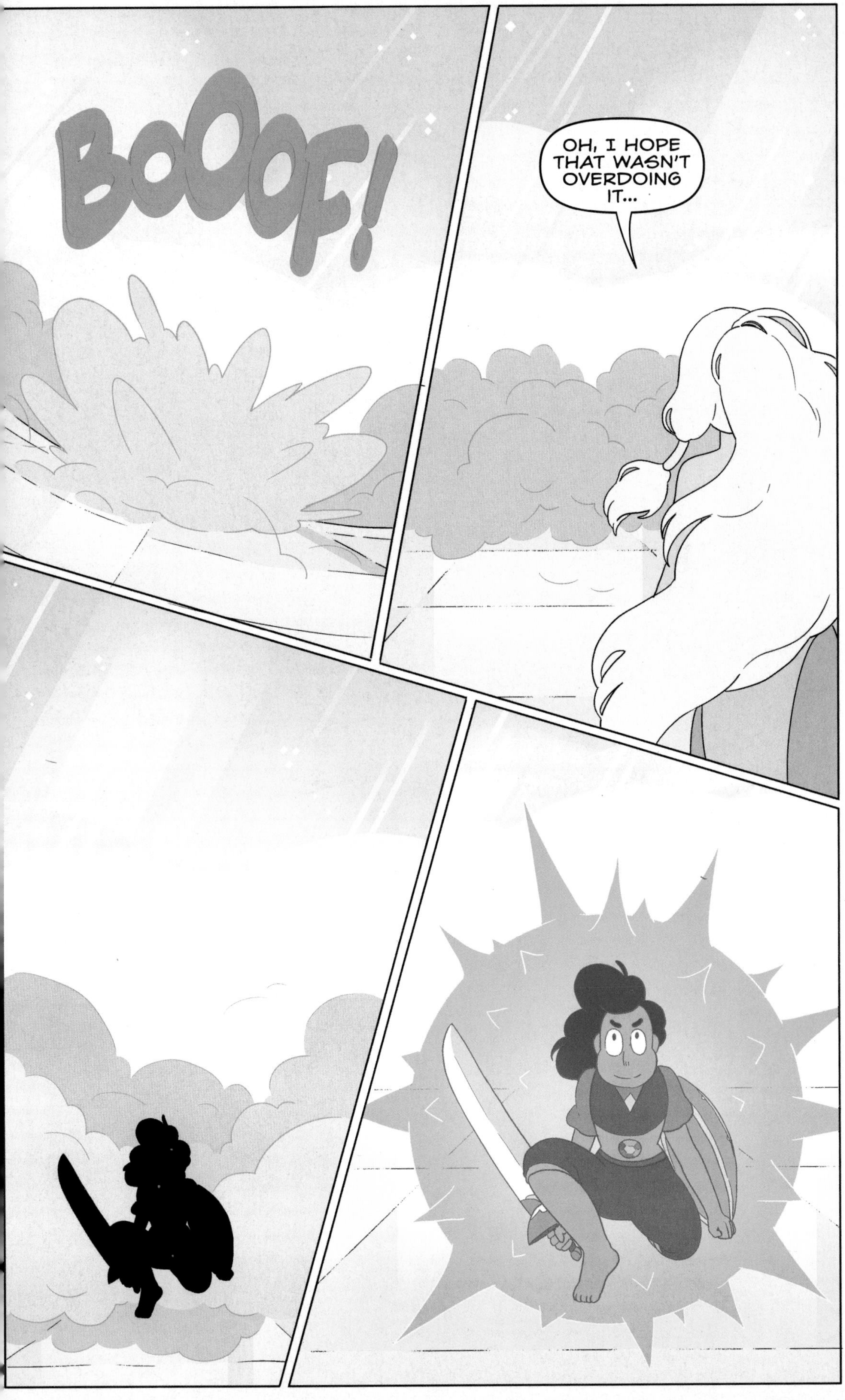
BOOOF!
OH, I HOPE THAT WASN'T OVERDOING IT...

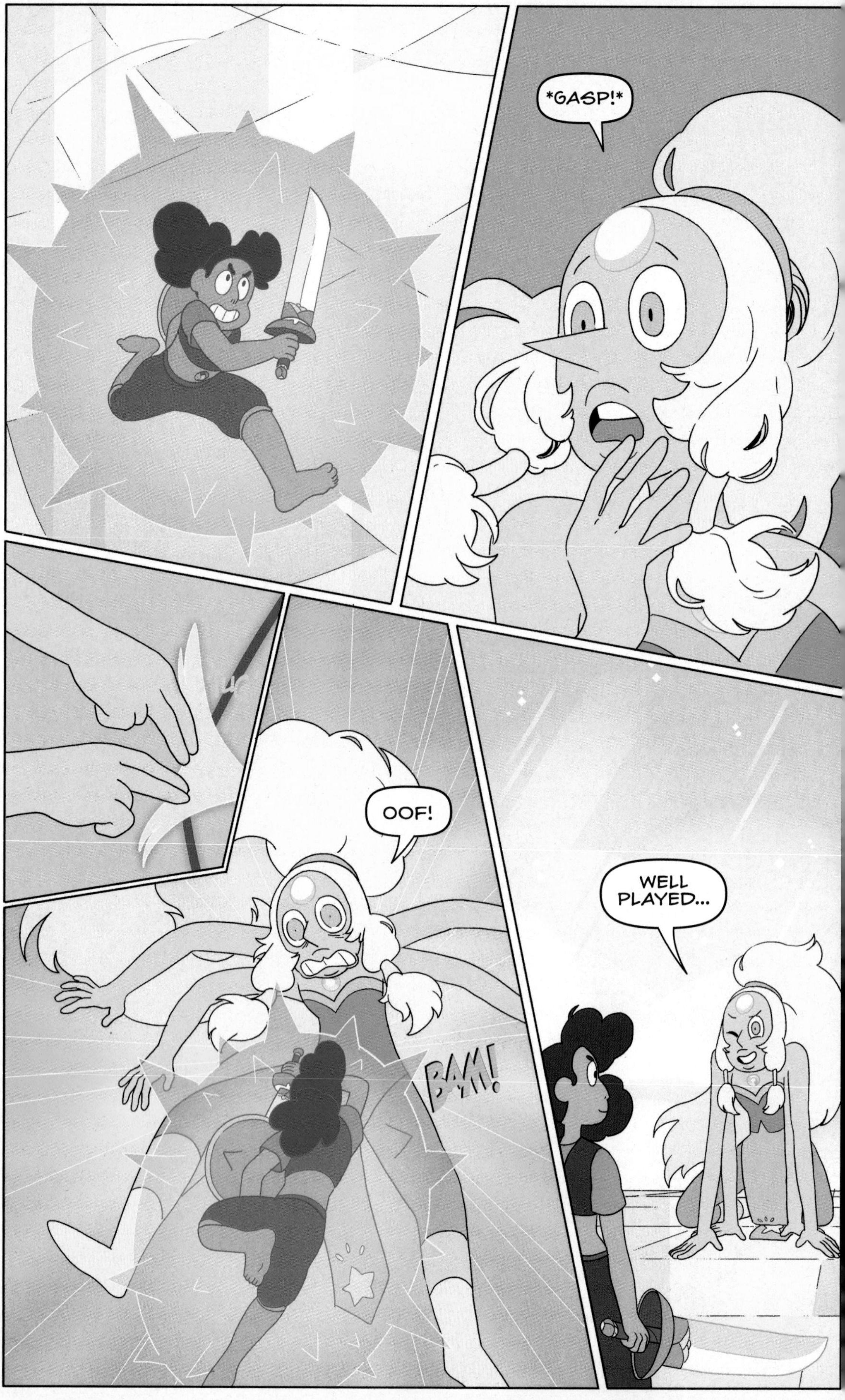
GASP!
OOF!
BAM!
WELL PLAYED...

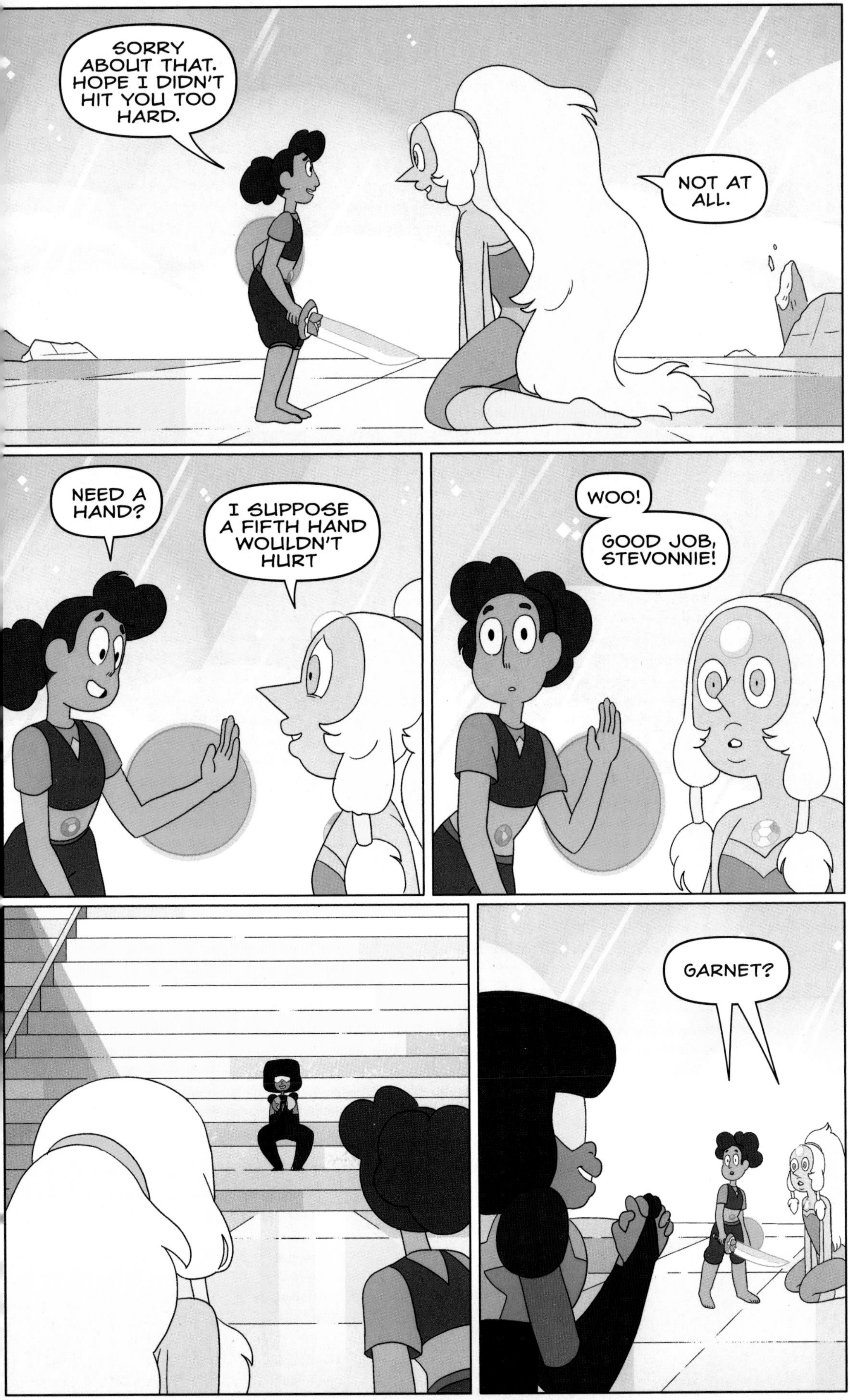
SORRY ABOUT THAT. HOPE I DIDN'T HIT YOU TOO HARD.
NOT AT ALL.
NEED A HAND?
I SUPPOSE A FIFTH HAND WOULDN'T HURT
WOO!
GOOD JOB, STEVONNIE!
GARNET?

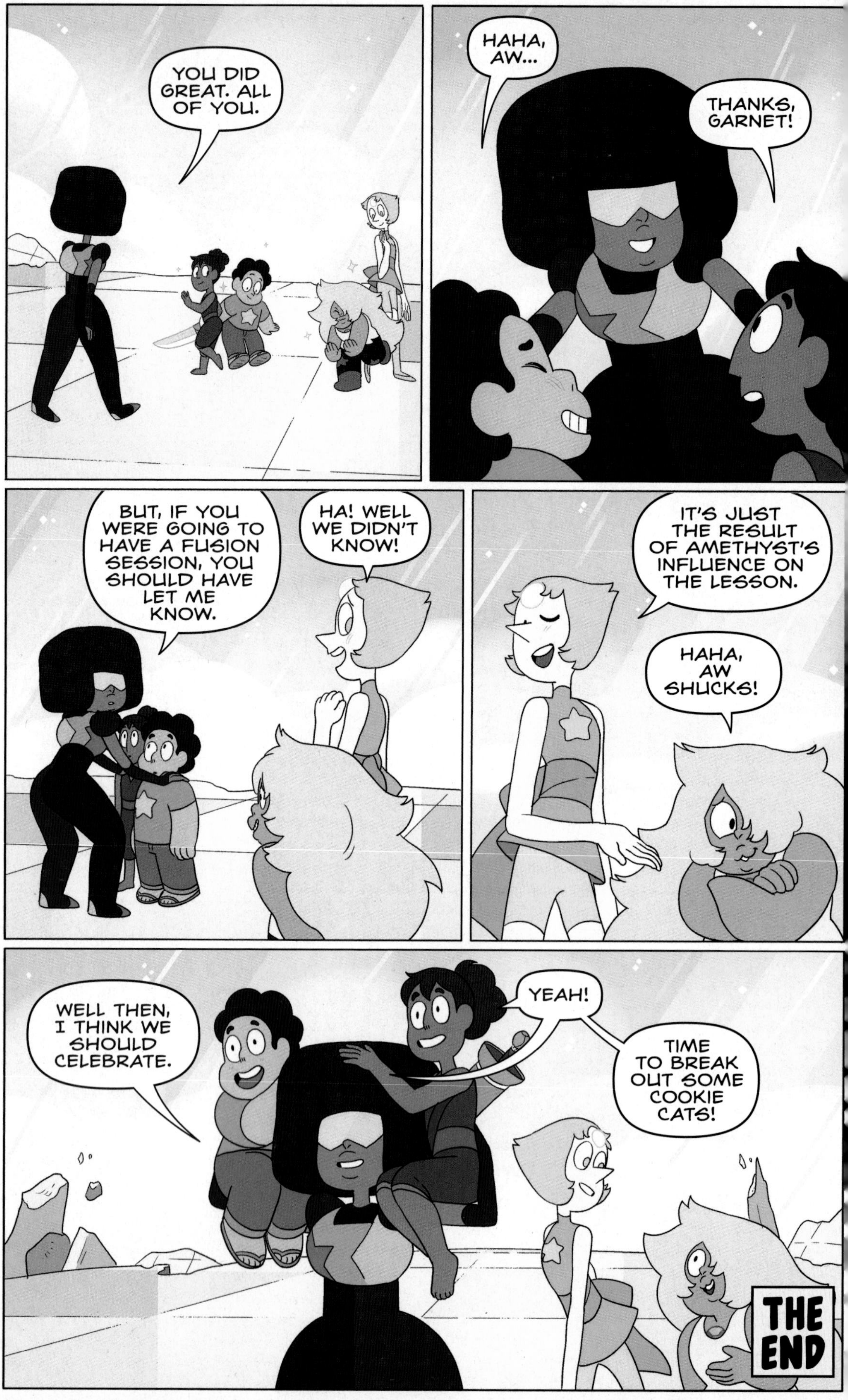
YOU DID GREAT. ALL OF YOU.
HAHA, AW...
THANKS, GARNET!
BUT, IF YOU WERE GOING TO HAVE A FUSION SESSION, YOU SHOULD HAVE LET ME KNOW.
HA! WELL WE DIDN'T KNOW!
IT'S JUST THE RESULT OF AMETHYST'S INFLUENCE ON THE LESSON.
HAHA, AW SHUCKS!
WELL THEN, I THINK WE SHOULD CELEBRATE.
YEAH!
TIME TO BREAK OUT SOME COOKIE CATS!
THE END

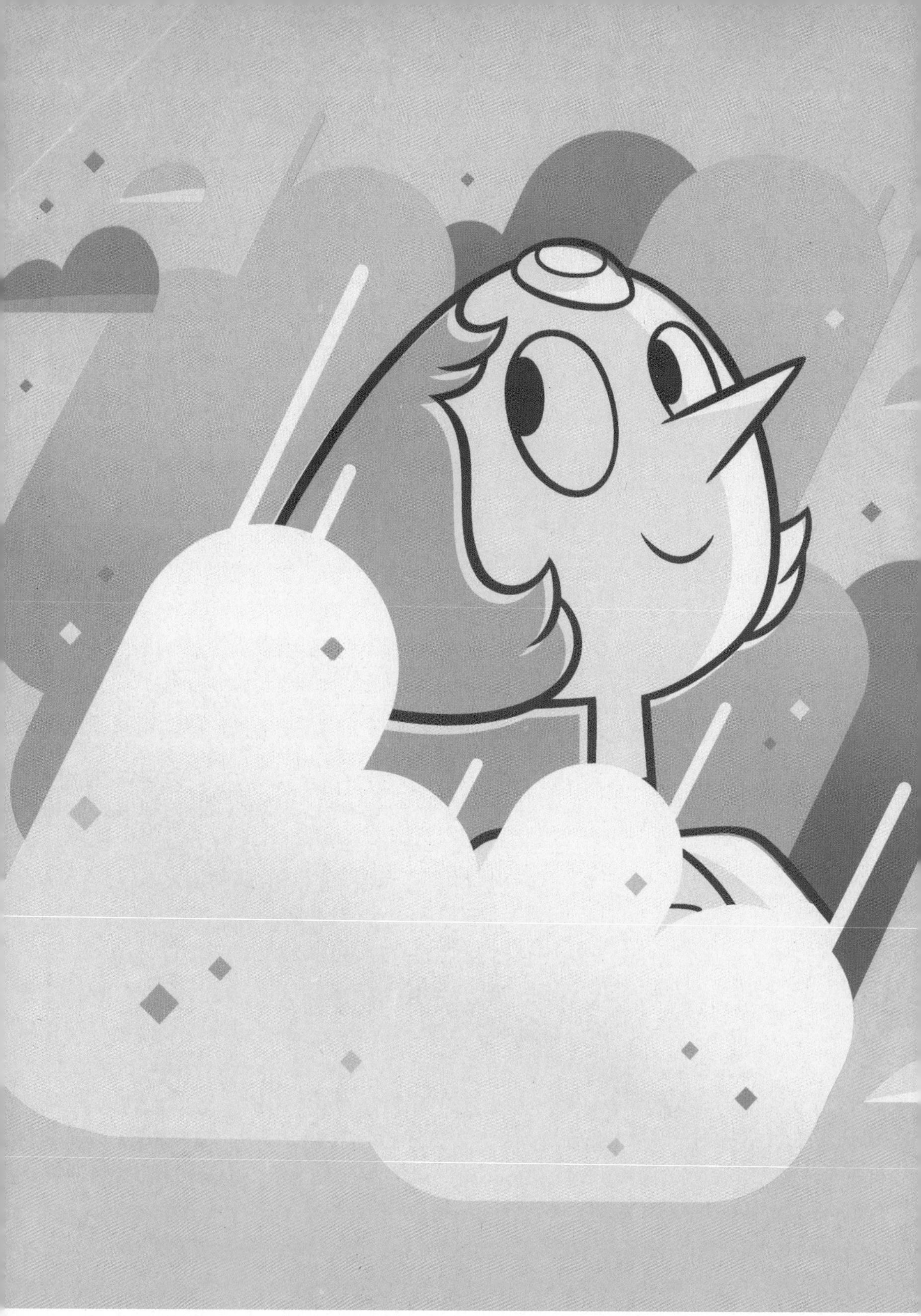

CHAPTER NINETEEN

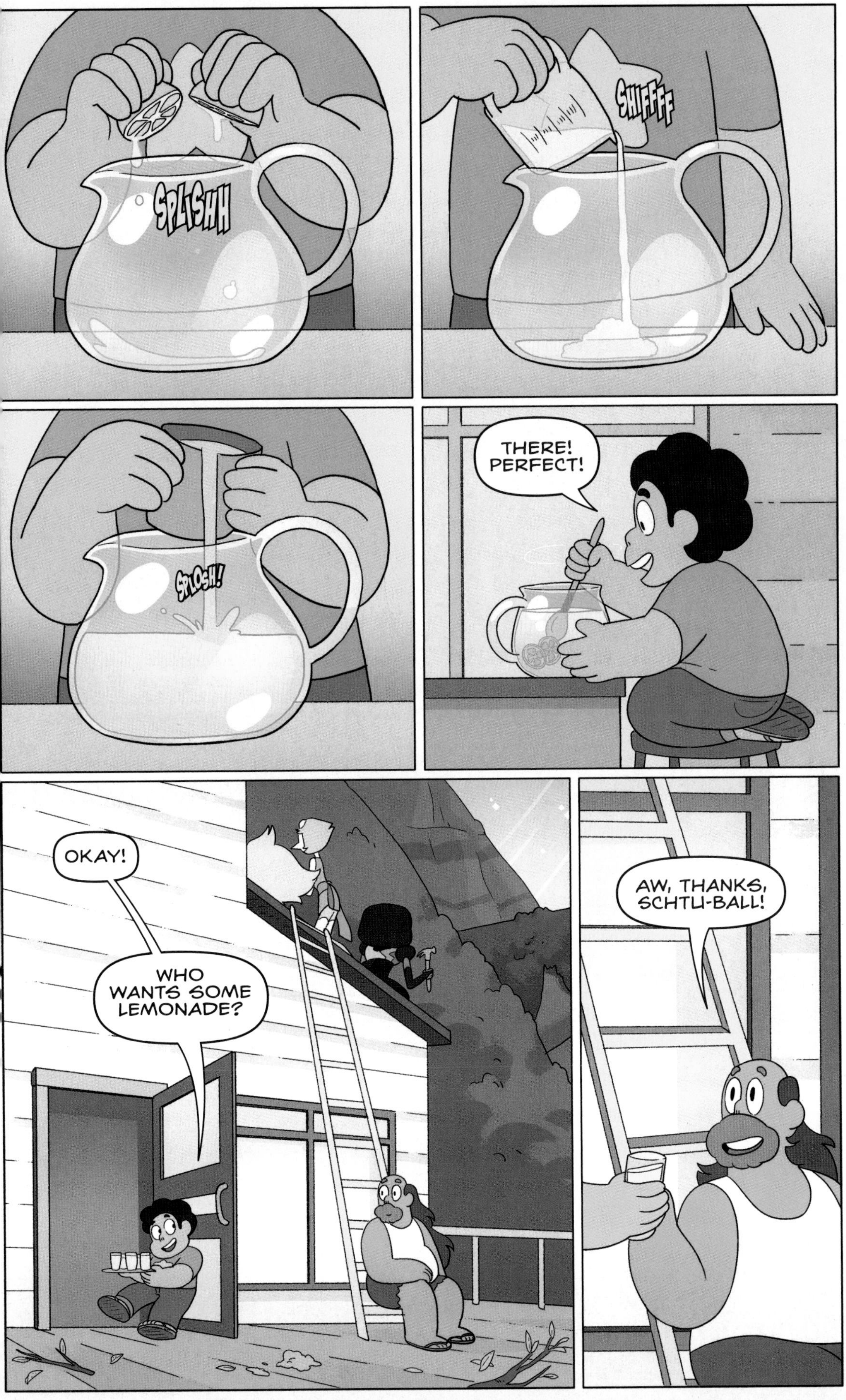
SPLISHH
SHIFFFF
SPLOSH!
THERE! PERFECT!
OKAY!
WHO WANTS SOME LEMONADE?
AW, THANKS, SCHTU-BALL!

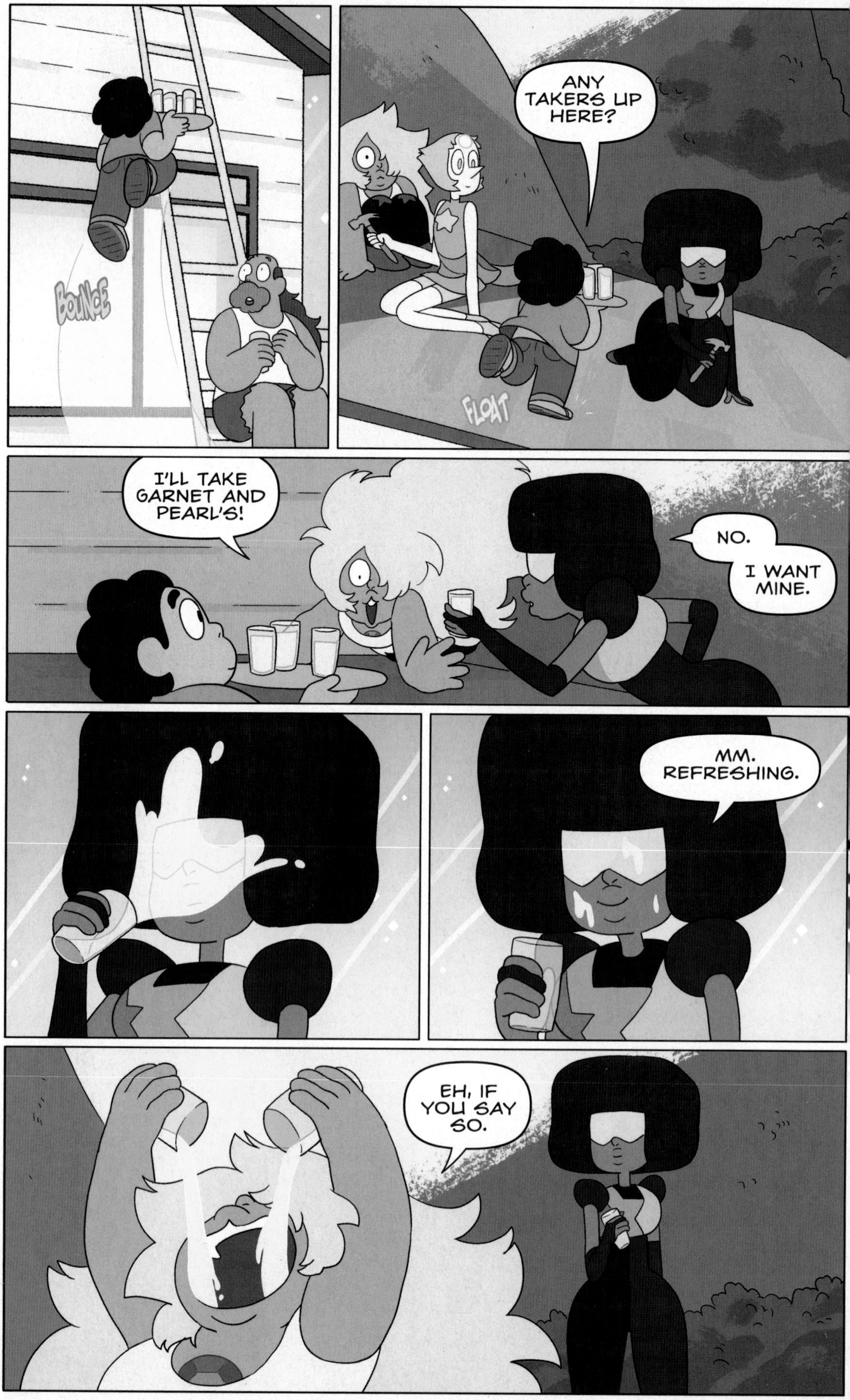
BOUNCE
ANY TAKERS UP HERE?
FLOAT
I'LL TAKE GARNET AND PEARL'S!
NO.
I WANT MINE.
MM. REFRESHING.
EH, IF YOU SAY SO.

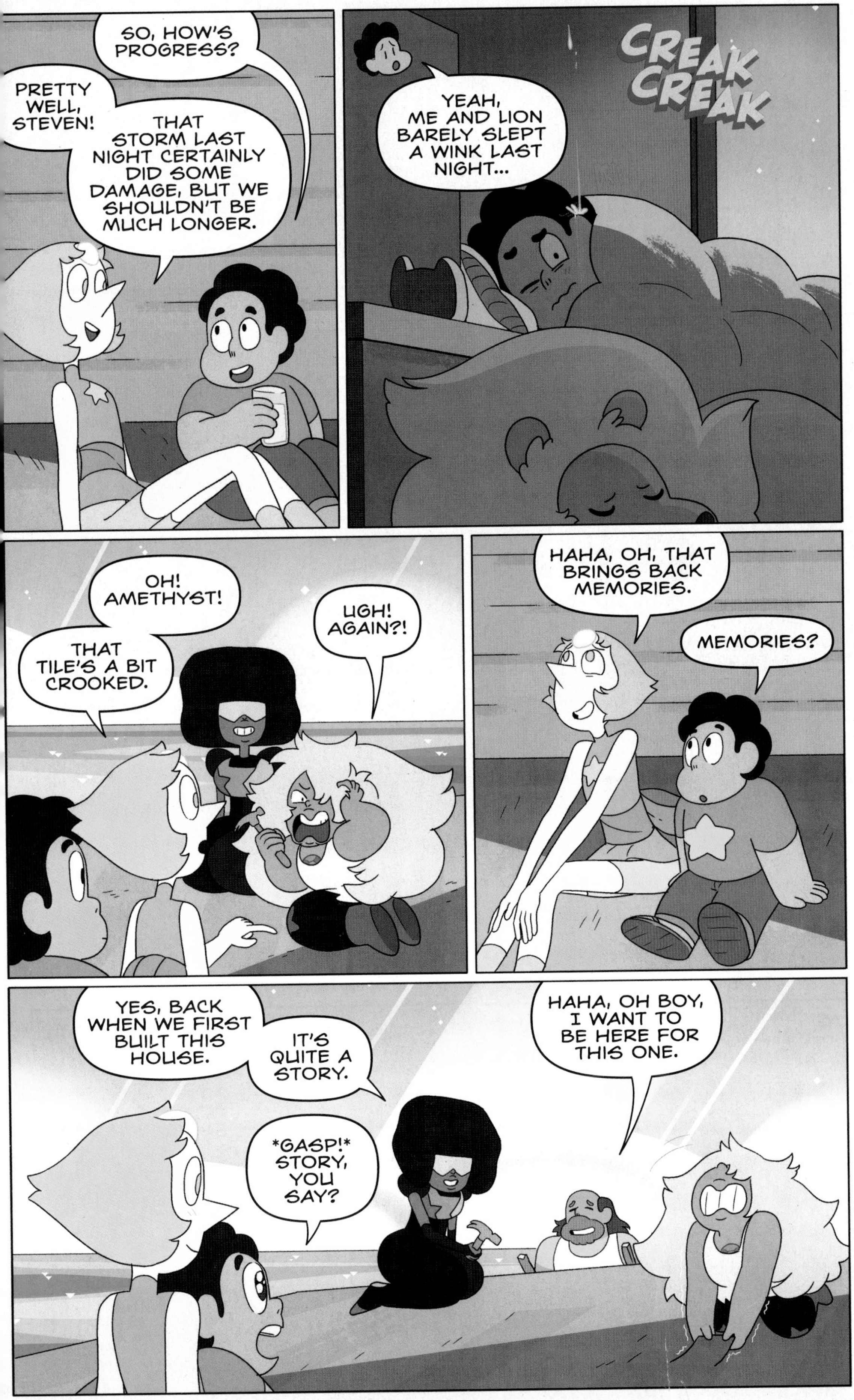
SO, HOW'S PROGRESS?
PRETTY WELL, STEVEN!
THAT STORM LAST NIGHT CERTAINLY DID SOME DAMAGE, BUT WE SHOULDN'T BE MUCH LONGER.
YEAH, ME AND LION BARELY SLEPT A WINK LAST NIGHT...
CREAK CREAK
OH! AMETHYST!
THAT TILE'S A BIT CROOKED.
UGH! AGAIN?!
HAHA, OH, THAT BRINGS BACK MEMORIES.
MEMORIES?
YES, BACK WHEN WE FIRST BUILT THIS HOUSE.
IT'S QUITE A STORY.
GASP! STORY, YOU SAY?
HAHA, OH BOY, I WANT TO BE HERE FOR THIS ONE.

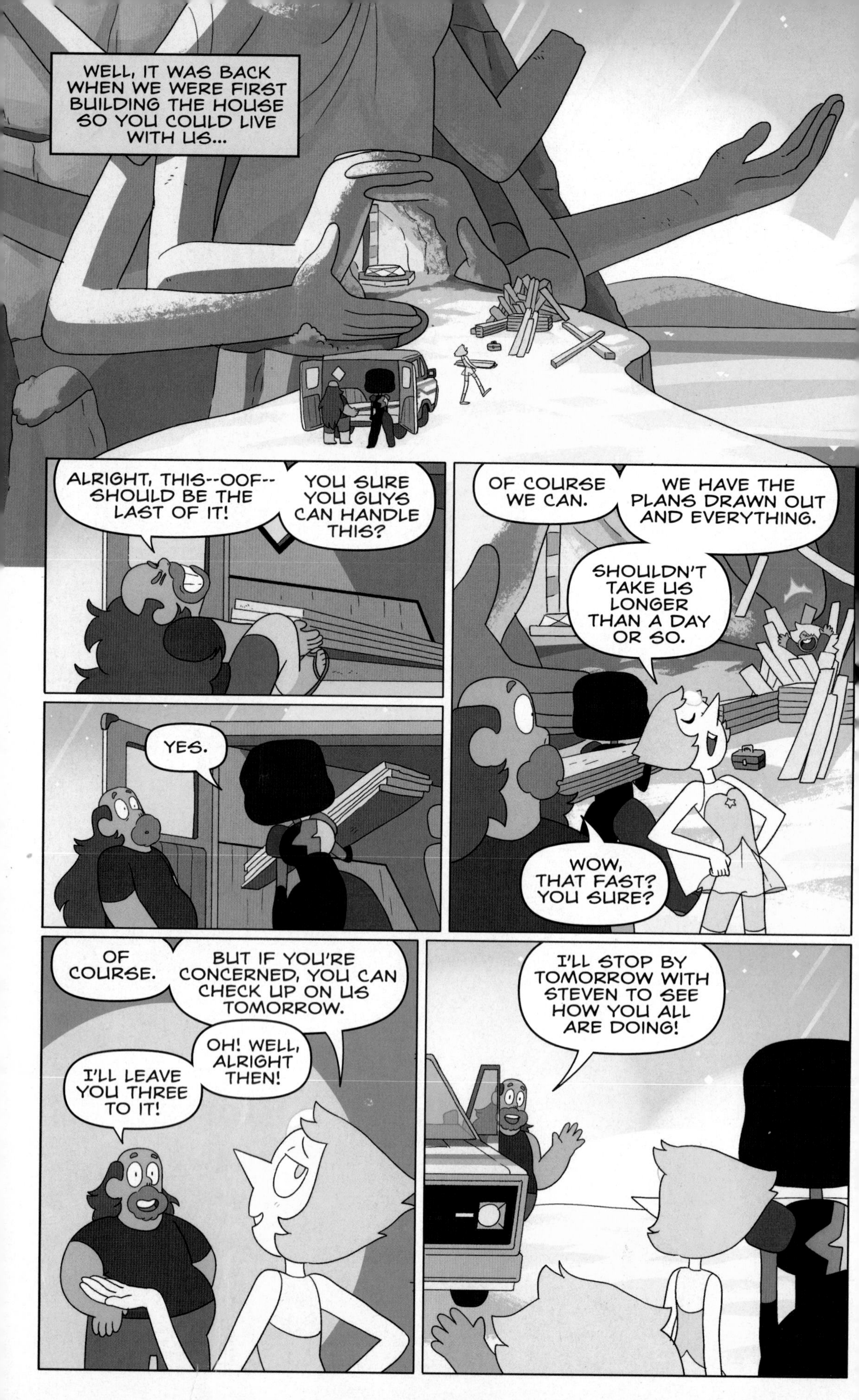
WELL, IT WAS BACK WHEN WE WERE FIRST BUILDING THE HOUSE SO YOU COULD LIVE WITH US...
ALRIGHT, THIS--OOF-- SHOULD BE THE LAST OF IT!
YOU SURE YOU GUYS CAN HANDLE THIS?
YES.
OF COURSE WE CAN.
WE HAVE THE PLANS DRAWN OUT AND EVERYTHING.
SHOULDN'T TAKE US LONGER THAN A DAY OR SO.
WOW, THAT FAST? YOU SURE?
OF COURSE.
BUT IF YOU'RE CONCERNED, YOU CAN CHECK UP ON US TOMORROW.
OH! WELL, ALRIGHT THEN!
I'LL LEAVE YOU THREE TO IT!
I'LL STOP BY TOMORROW WITH STEVEN TO SEE HOW YOU ALL ARE DOING!

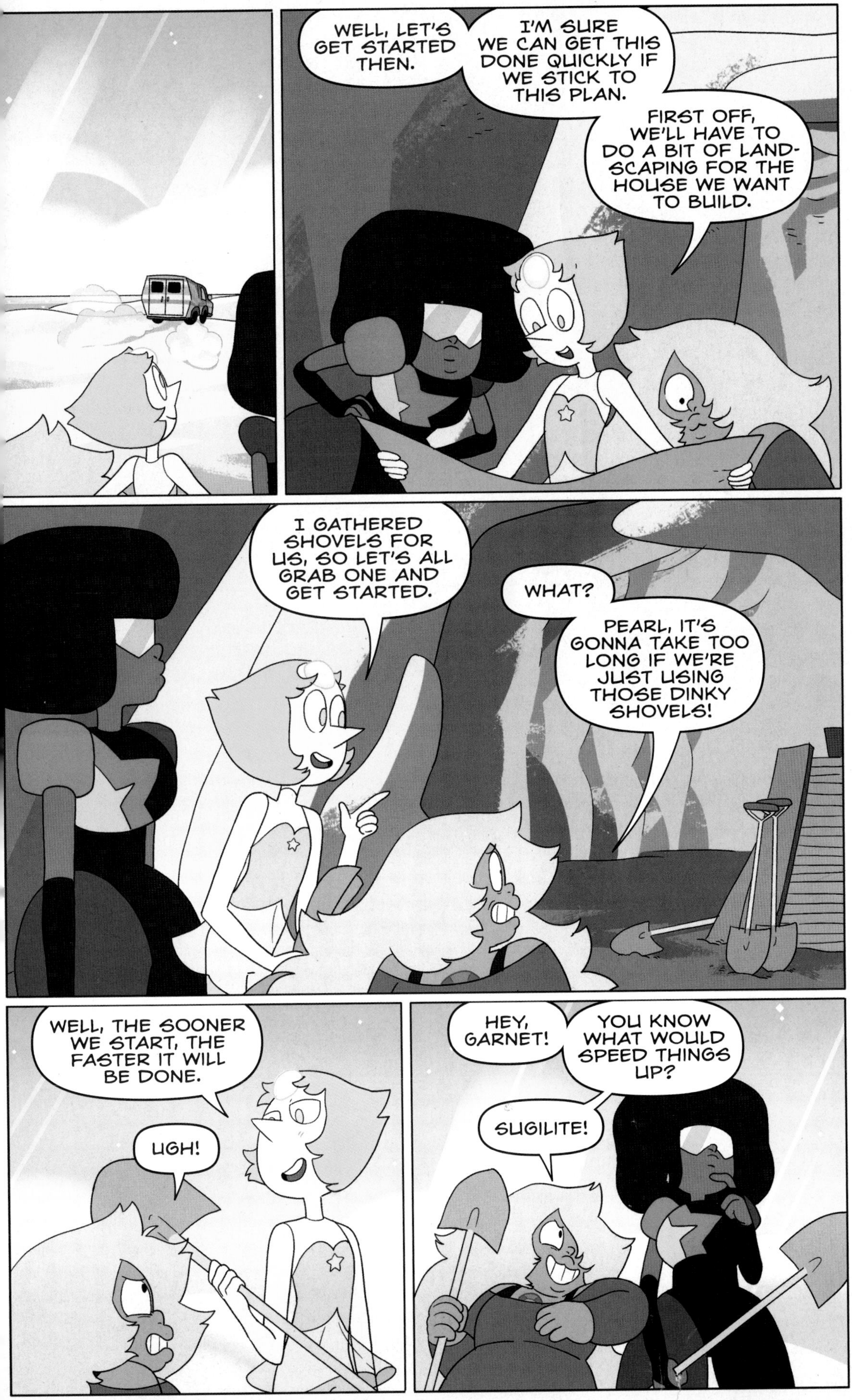
WELL, LET'S GET STARTED THEN.
I'M SURE WE CAN GET THIS DONE QUICKLY IF WE STICK TO THIS PLAN.
FIRST OFF, WE'LL HAVE TO DO A BIT OF LAND-SCAPING FOR THE HOUSE WE WANT TO BUILD.
I GATHERED SHOVELS FOR US, SO LET'S ALL GRAB ONE AND GET STARTED.
WHAT?
PEARL, IT'S GONNA TAKE TOO LONG IF WE'RE JUST USING THOSE DINKY SHOVELS!
WELL, THE SOONER WE START, THE FASTER IT WILL BE DONE.
UGH!
HEY, GARNET!
YOU KNOW WHAT WOULD SPEED THINGS UP?
SUGILITE!

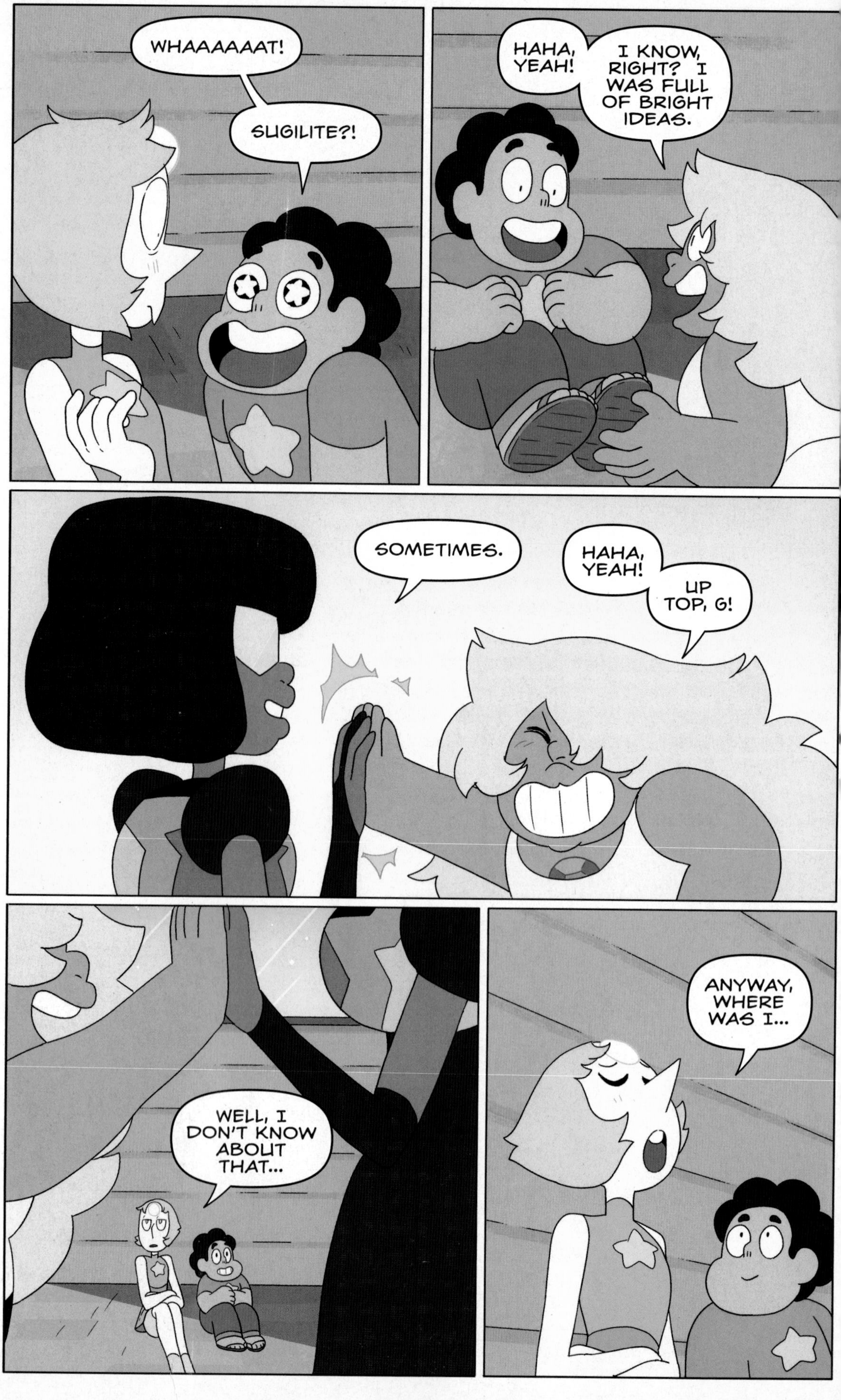
WHAAAAAAT!
SUGILITE?!
HAHA, YEAH!
I KNOW, RIGHT? I WAS FULL OF BRIGHT IDEAS.
SOMETIMES.
HAHA, YEAH!
UP TOP, G!
WELL, I DON'T KNOW ABOUT THAT...
ANYWAY, WHERE WAS I...

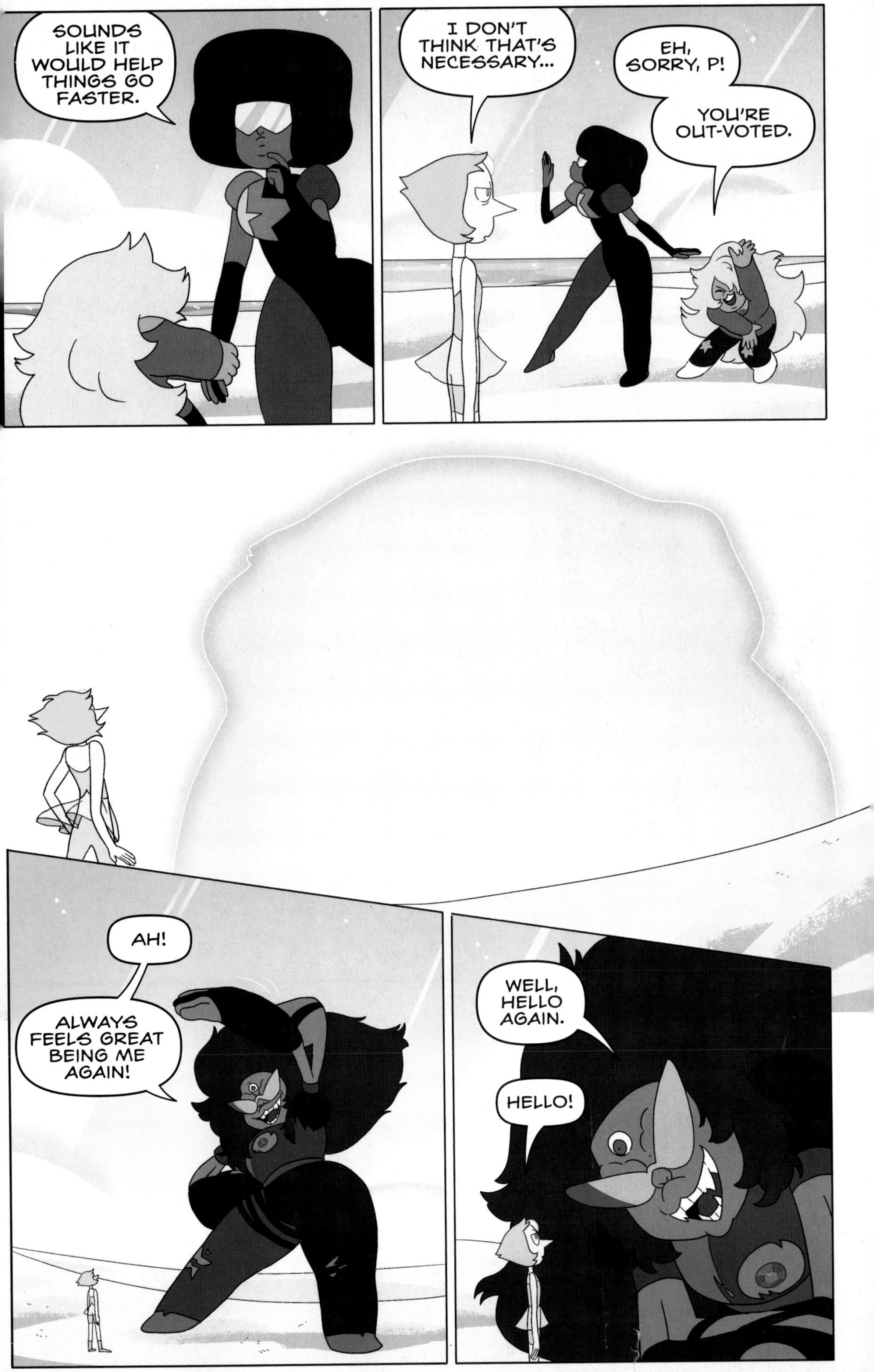
SOUNDS LIKE IT WOULD HELP THINGS GO FASTER.
I DON'T THINK THAT'S NECESSARY...
EH, SORRY, P!
YOU'RE OUT-VOTED.
AH!
ALWAYS FEELS GREAT BEING ME AGAIN!
WELL, HELLO AGAIN.
HELLO!

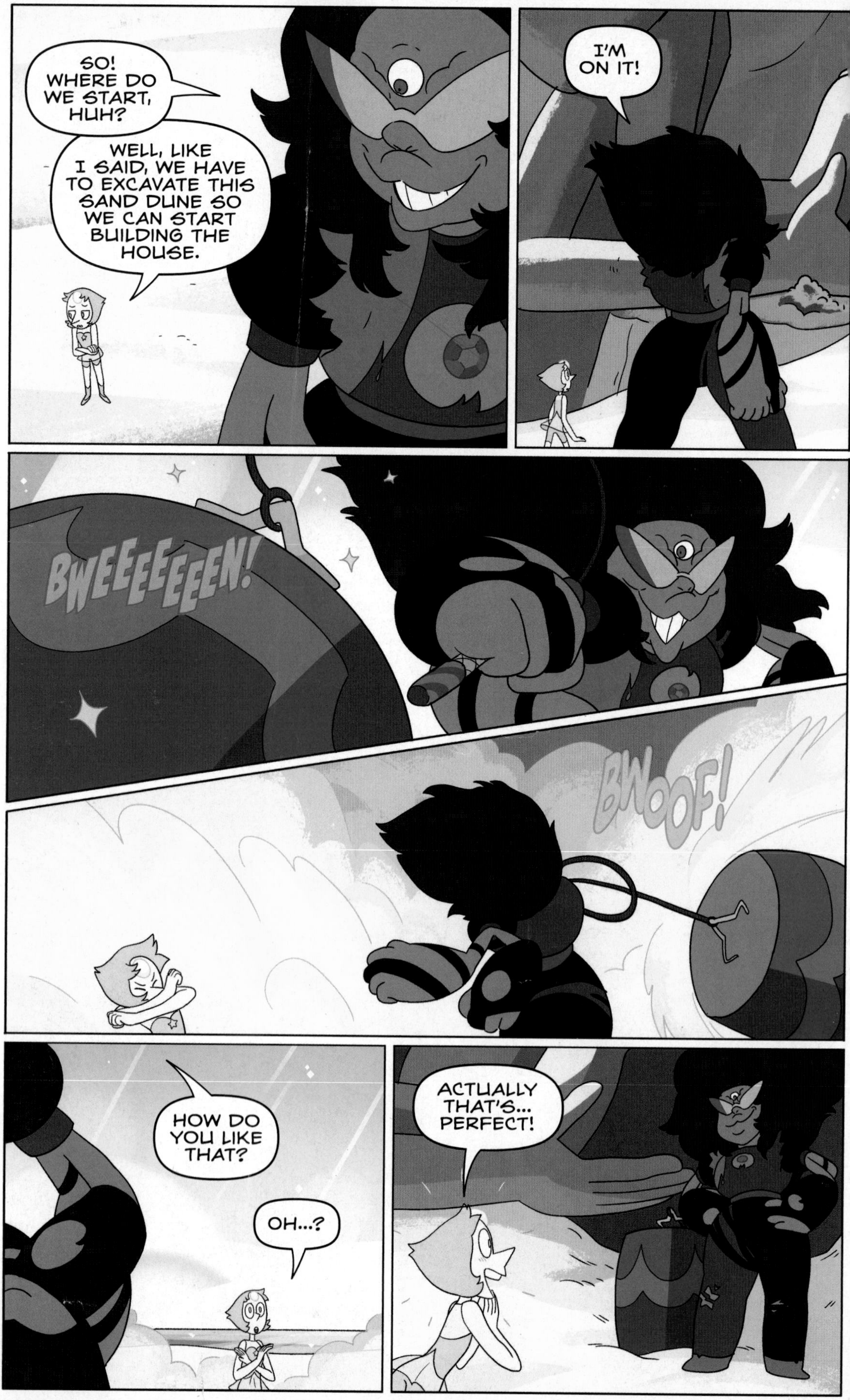
SO! WHERE DO WE START, HUH?
WELL, LIKE I SAID, WE HAVE TO EXCAVATE THIS SAND DUNE SO WE CAN START BUILDING THE HOUSE.
I'M ON IT!
BWEEEEEEEN!
BWOOF!
HOW DO YOU LIKE THAT?
OH...?
ACTUALLY THAT'S... PERFECT!

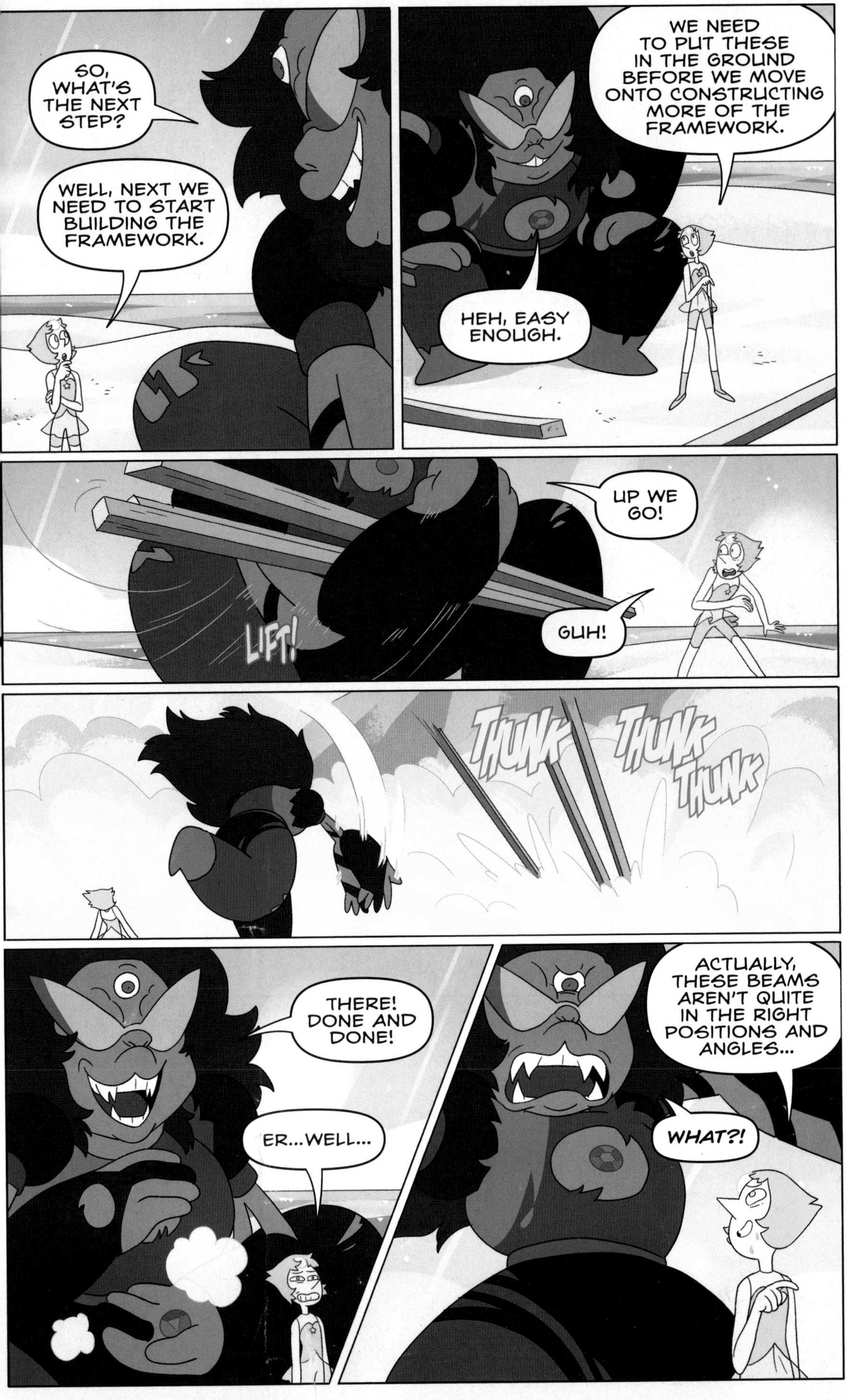
SO, WHAT'S THE NEXT STEP?
WELL, NEXT WE NEED TO START BUILDING THE FRAMEWORK.
WE NEED TO PUT THESE IN THE GROUND BEFORE WE MOVE ONTO CONSTRUCTING MORE OF THE FRAMEWORK.
HEH, EASY ENOUGH.
UP WE GO!
LIFT!
GUH!
THUNK
THUNK
THUNK
THERE! DONE AND DONE!
ER...WELL...
ACTUALLY, THESE BEAMS AREN'T QUITE IN THE RIGHT POSITIONS AND ANGLES...
WHAT?!

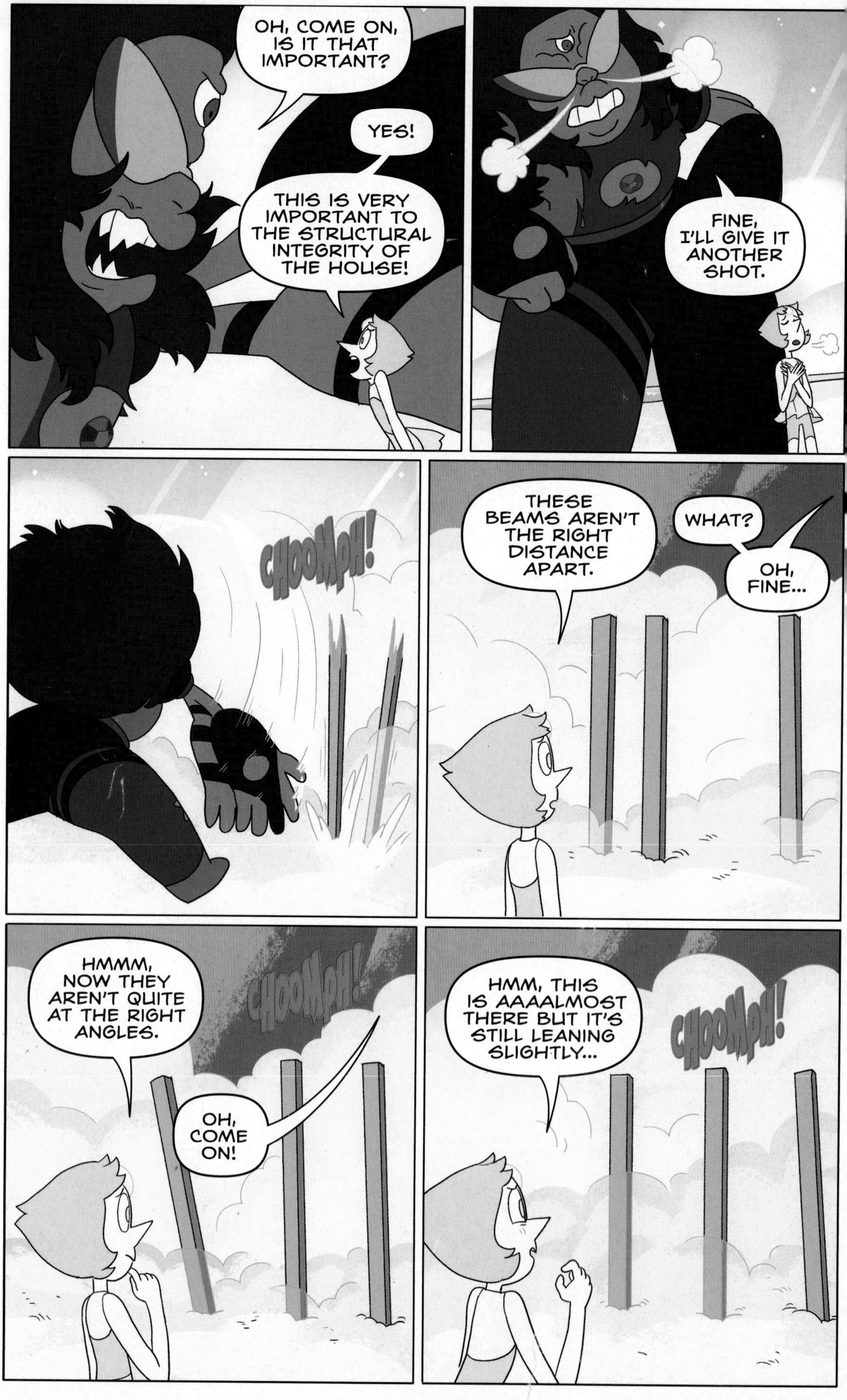
OH, COME ON, IS IT THAT IMPORTANT?
YES!
THIS IS VERY IMPORTANT TO THE STRUCTURAL INTEGRITY OF THE HOUSE!
FINE, I'LL GIVE IT ANOTHER SHOT.
CHOOMPH!
THESE BEAMS AREN'T THE RIGHT DISTANCE APART.
WHAT?
OH, FINE...
HMMM, NOW THEY AREN'T QUITE AT THE RIGHT ANGLES.
CHOOMPH!
OH, COME ON!
HMM, THIS IS AAAALMOST THERE BUT IT'S STILL LEANING SLIGHTLY...
CHOOMPH!

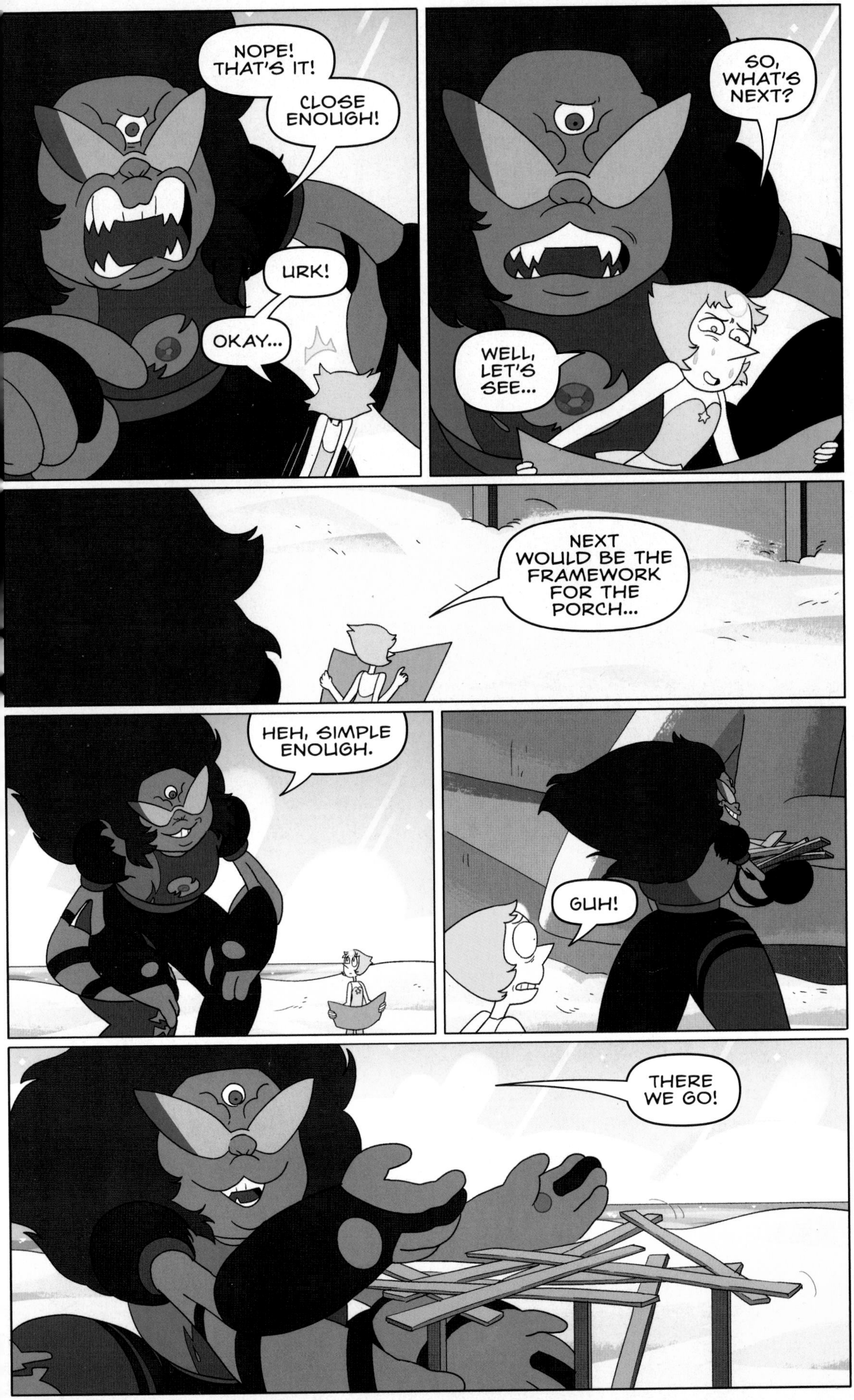
NOPE! THAT'S IT!
CLOSE ENOUGH!
URK!
OKAY...
SO, WHAT'S NEXT?
WELL, LET'S SEE...
NEXT WOULD BE THE FRAMEWORK FOR THE PORCH...
HEH, SIMPLE ENOUGH.
GUH!
THERE WE GO!

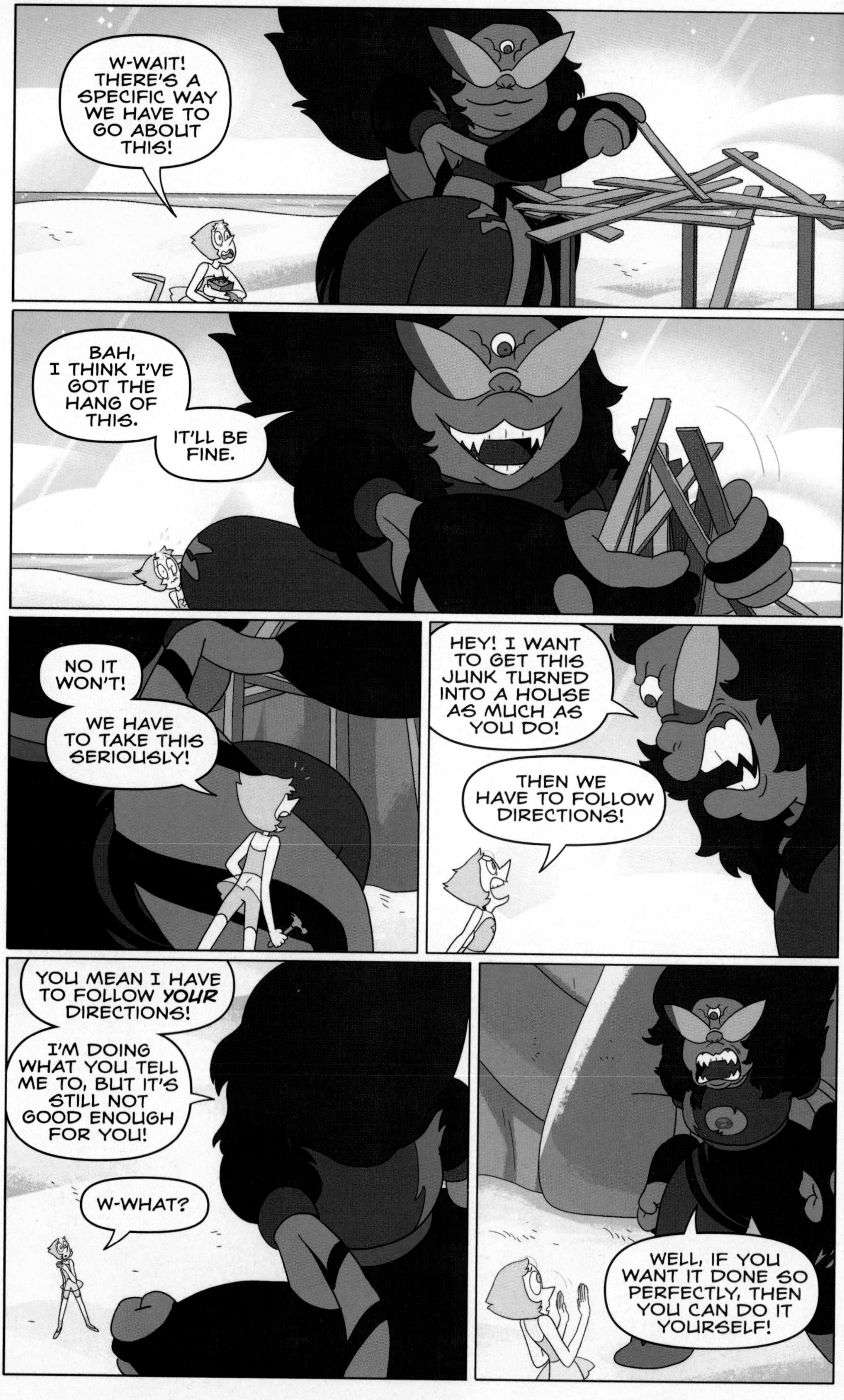
W-WAIT! THERE'S A SPECIFIC WAY WE HAVE TO GO ABOUT THIS!
BAH, I THINK I'VE GOT THE HANG OF THIS.
IT'LL BE FINE.
NO IT WON'T!
WE HAVE TO TAKE THIS SERIOUSLY!
HEY! I WANT TO GET THIS JUNK TURNED INTO A HOUSE AS MUCH AS YOU DO!
THEN WE HAVE TO FOLLOW DIRECTIONS!
YOU MEAN I HAVE TO FOLLOW *YOUR* DIRECTIONS!
I'M DOING WHAT YOU TELL ME TO, BUT IT'S STILL NOT GOOD ENOUGH FOR YOU!
W-WHAT?
WELL, IF YOU WANT IT DONE SO PERFECTLY, THEN YOU CAN DO IT YOURSELF!

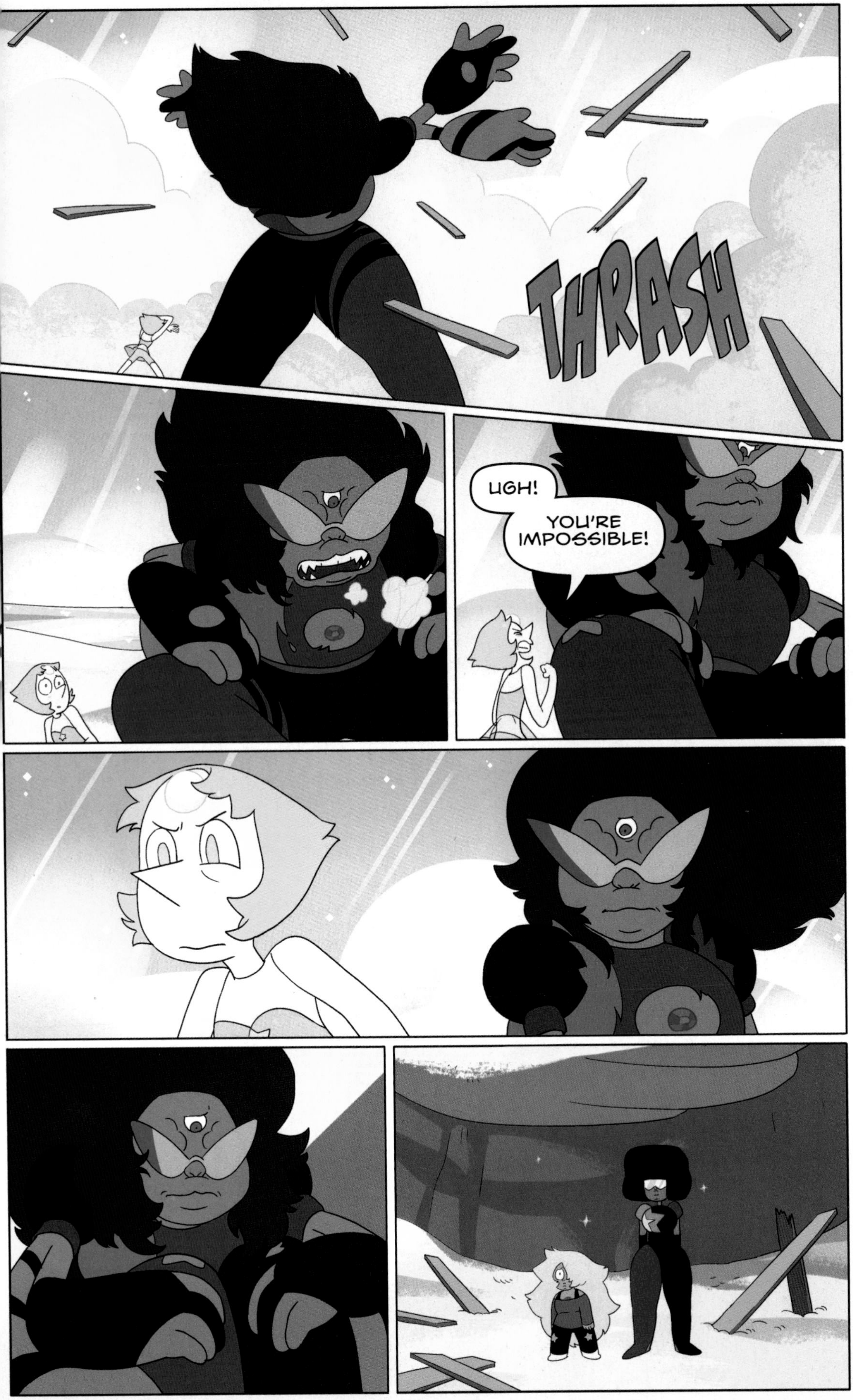
THRASH
UGH!
YOU'RE IMPOSSIBLE!

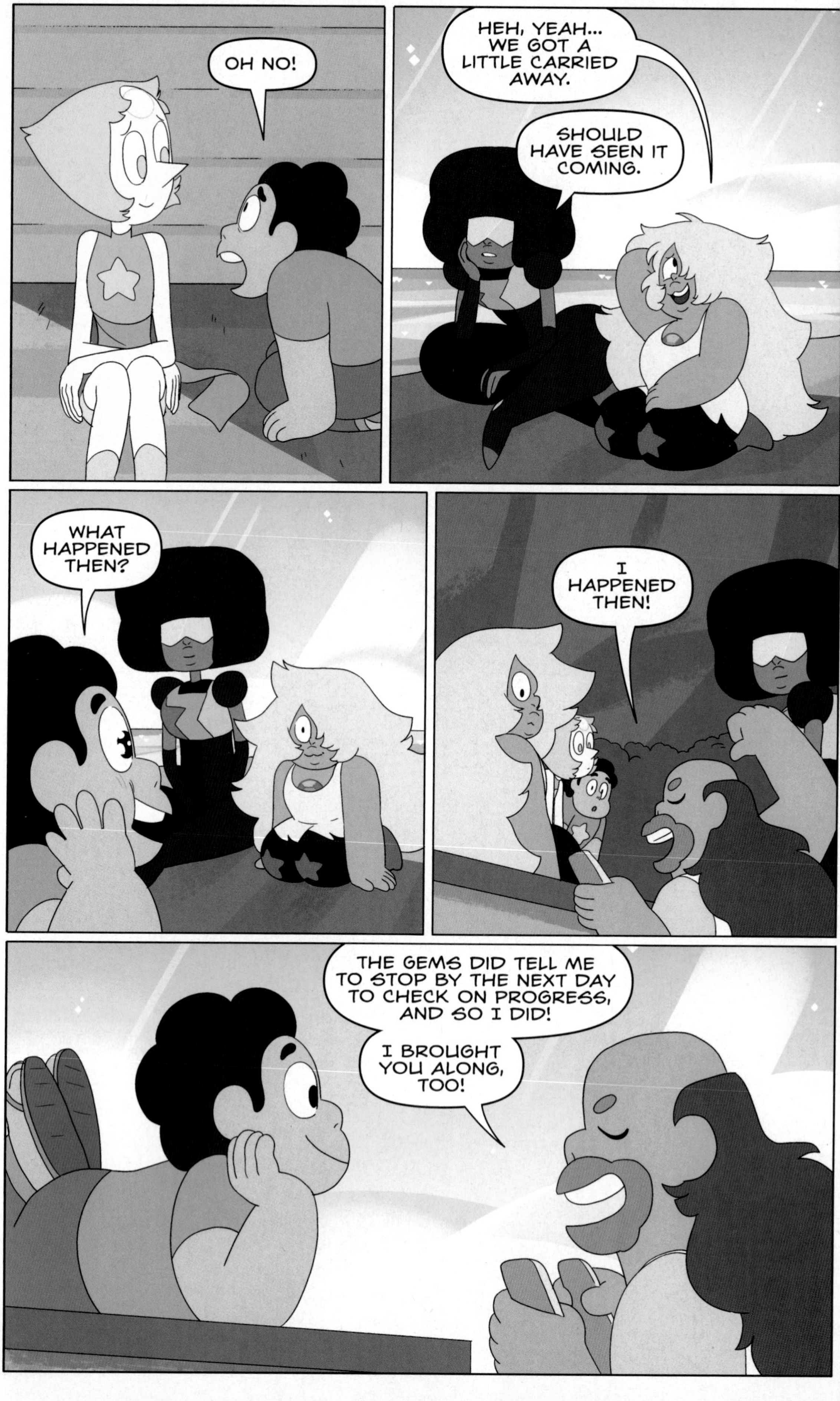
OH NO!
HEH, YEAH... WE GOT A LITTLE CARRIED AWAY.
SHOULD HAVE SEEN IT COMING.
WHAT HAPPENED THEN?
I HAPPENED THEN!
THE GEMS DID TELL ME TO STOP BY THE NEXT DAY TO CHECK ON PROGRESS, AND SO I DID!
I BROUGHT YOU ALONG, TOO!

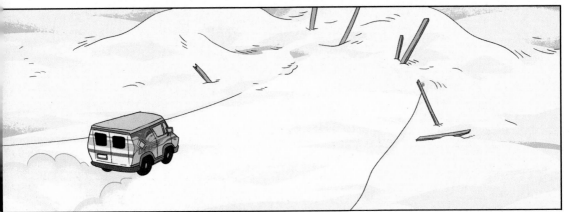

SEE, BUDDY? EVERYTHING'S COMING ALONG...

...SMOOTHLY?

WAIT HERE, SCHTU-BALL. I'LL BE RIGHT BACK.

WHAT HAPPENED?

WE MAY HAVE GOTTEN A BIT AHEAD OF OURSELVES.

YEAH... WE BLEW IT.

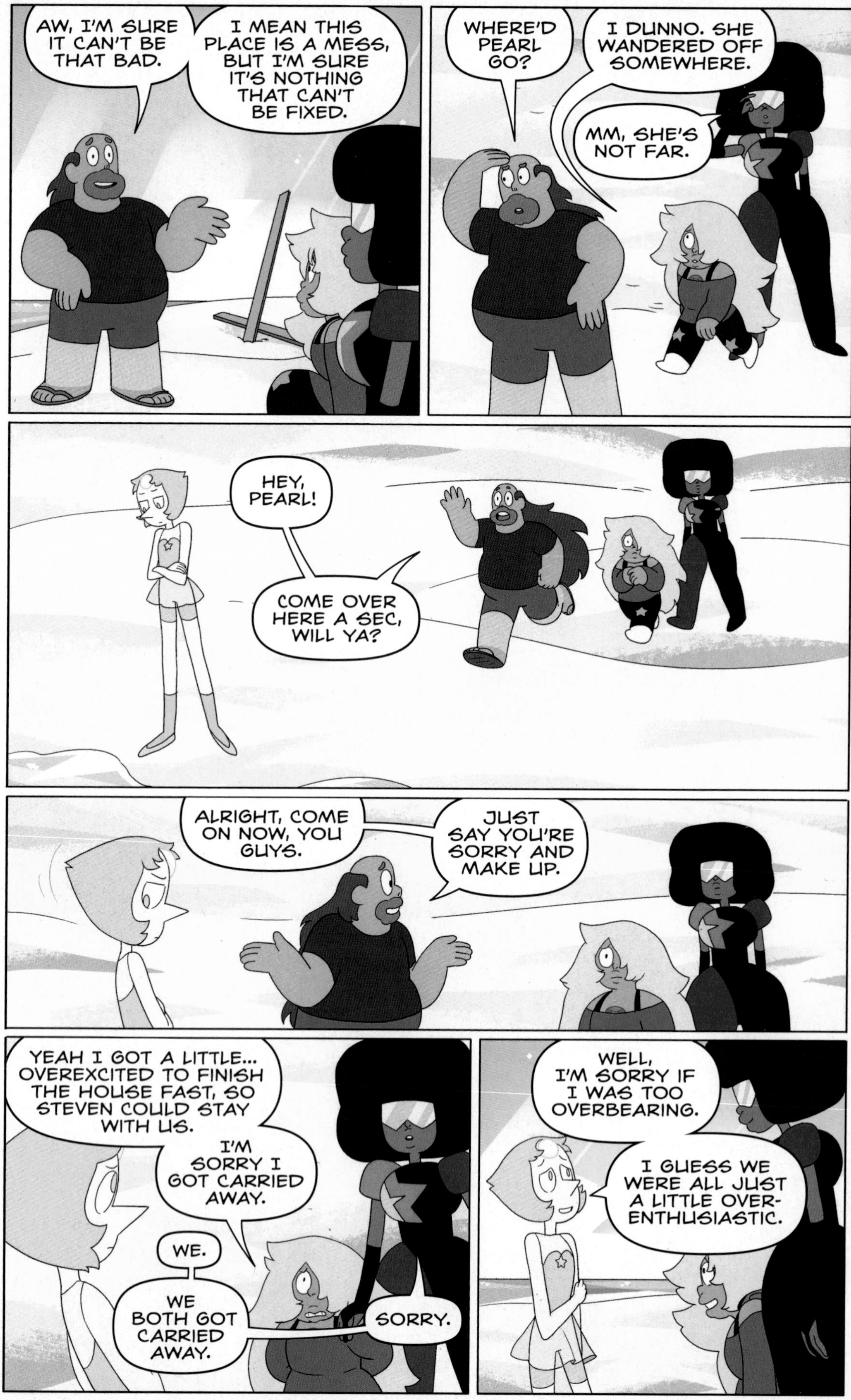
AW, I'M SURE IT CAN'T BE THAT BAD.
I MEAN THIS PLACE IS A MESS, BUT I'M SURE IT'S NOTHING THAT CAN'T BE FIXED.
WHERE'D PEARL GO?
I DUNNO. SHE WANDERED OFF SOMEWHERE.
MM, SHE'S NOT FAR.
HEY, PEARL!
COME OVER HERE A SEC, WILL YA?
ALRIGHT, COME ON NOW, YOU GUYS.
JUST SAY YOU'RE SORRY AND MAKE UP.
YEAH I GOT A LITTLE... OVEREXCITED TO FINISH THE HOUSE FAST, SO STEVEN COULD STAY WITH US.
I'M SORRY I GOT CARRIED AWAY.
WE.
WE BOTH GOT CARRIED AWAY.
SORRY.
WELL, I'M SORRY IF I WAS TOO OVERBEARING.
I GUESS WE WERE ALL JUST A LITTLE OVER-ENTHUSIASTIC.

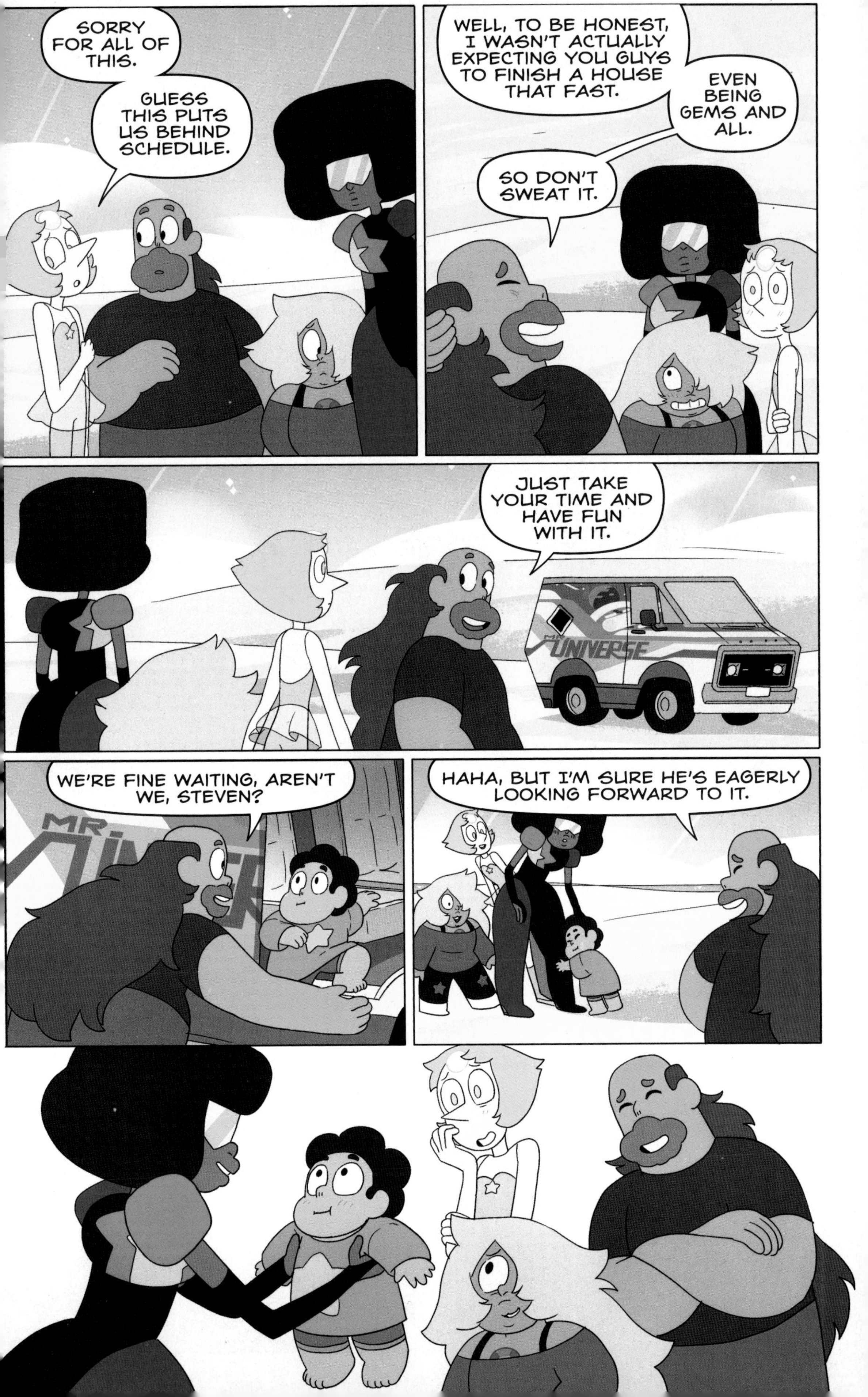
SORRY FOR ALL OF THIS.
GUESS THIS PUTS US BEHIND SCHEDULE.
WELL, TO BE HONEST, I WASN'T ACTUALLY EXPECTING YOU GUYS TO FINISH A HOUSE THAT FAST.
EVEN BEING GEMS AND ALL.
SO DON'T SWEAT IT.
JUST TAKE YOUR TIME AND HAVE FUN WITH IT.
MR. UNIVERSE
WE'RE FINE WAITING, AREN'T WE, STEVEN?
HAHA, BUT I'M SURE HE'S EAGERLY LOOKING FORWARD TO IT.

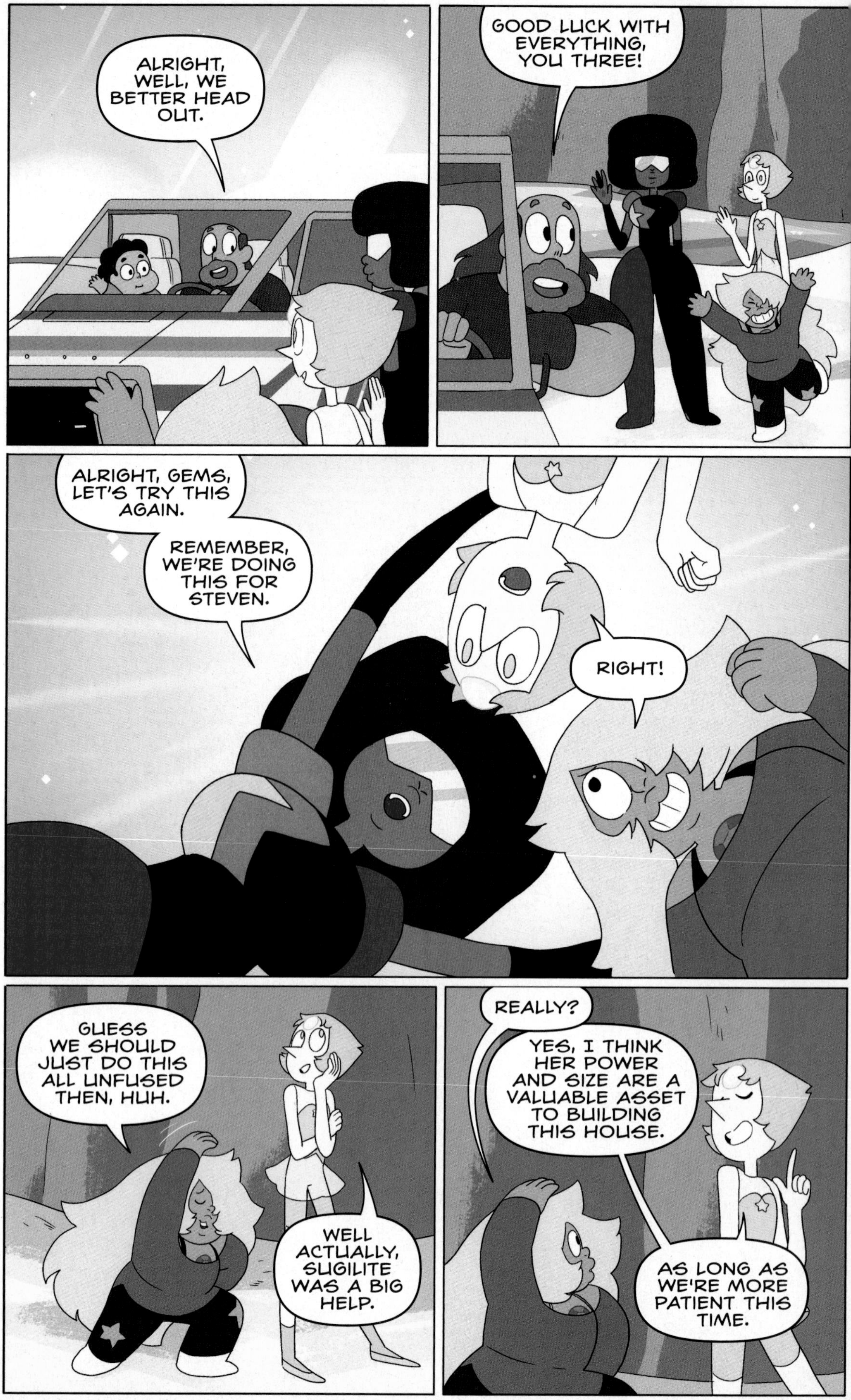
ALRIGHT, WELL, WE BETTER HEAD OUT.
GOOD LUCK WITH EVERYTHING, YOU THREE!
ALRIGHT, GEMS, LET'S TRY THIS AGAIN.
REMEMBER, WE'RE DOING THIS FOR STEVEN.
RIGHT!
GUESS WE SHOULD JUST DO THIS ALL UNFUSED THEN, HUH.
WELL ACTUALLY, SUGILITE WAS A BIG HELP.
REALLY?
YES, I THINK HER POWER AND SIZE ARE A VALUABLE ASSET TO BUILDING THIS HOUSE.
AS LONG AS WE'RE MORE PATIENT THIS TIME.

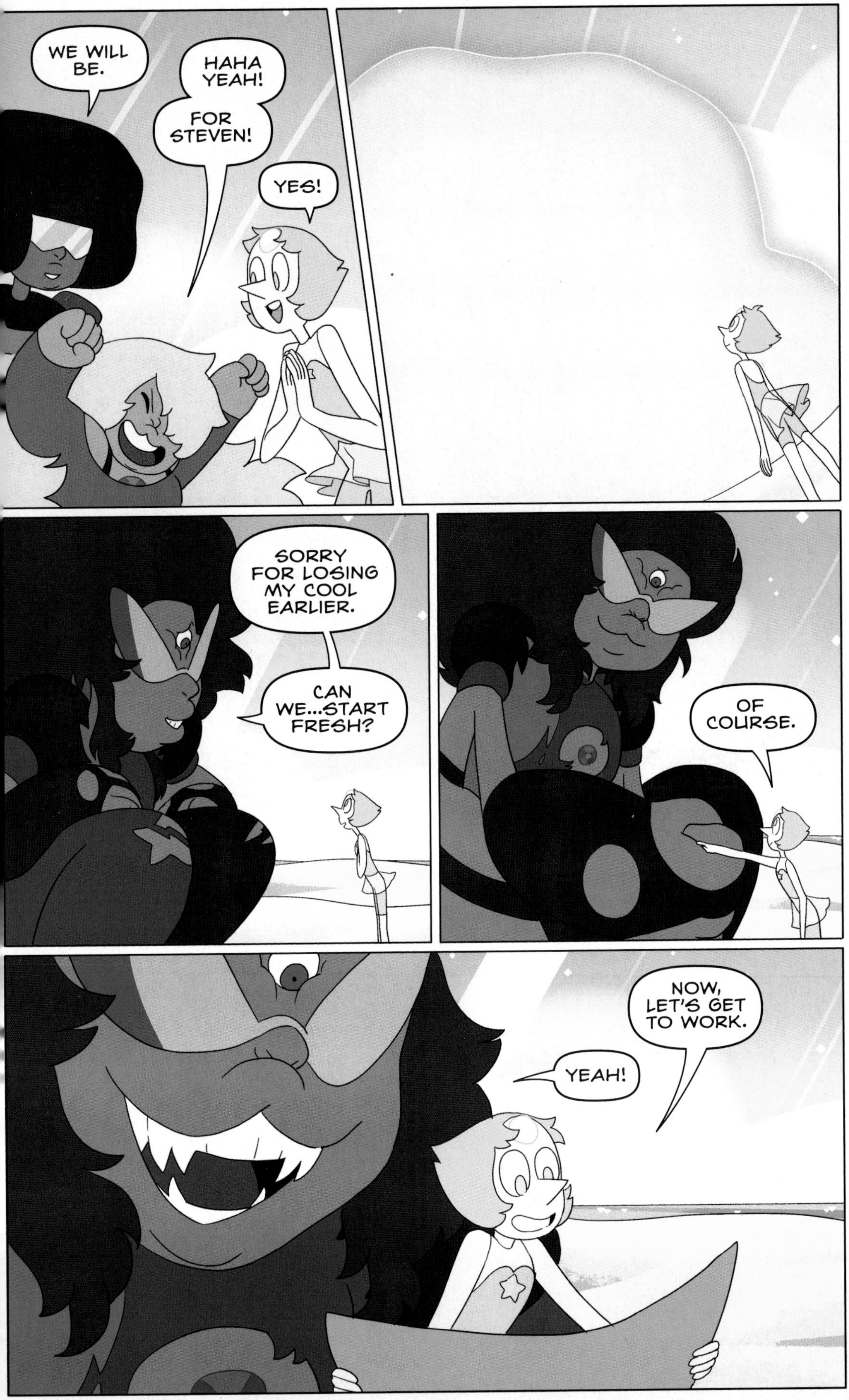
WE WILL BE.
HAHA YEAH!
FOR STEVEN!
YES!
SORRY FOR LOSING MY COOL EARLIER.
CAN WE...START FRESH?
OF COURSE.
NOW, LET'S GET TO WORK.
YEAH!

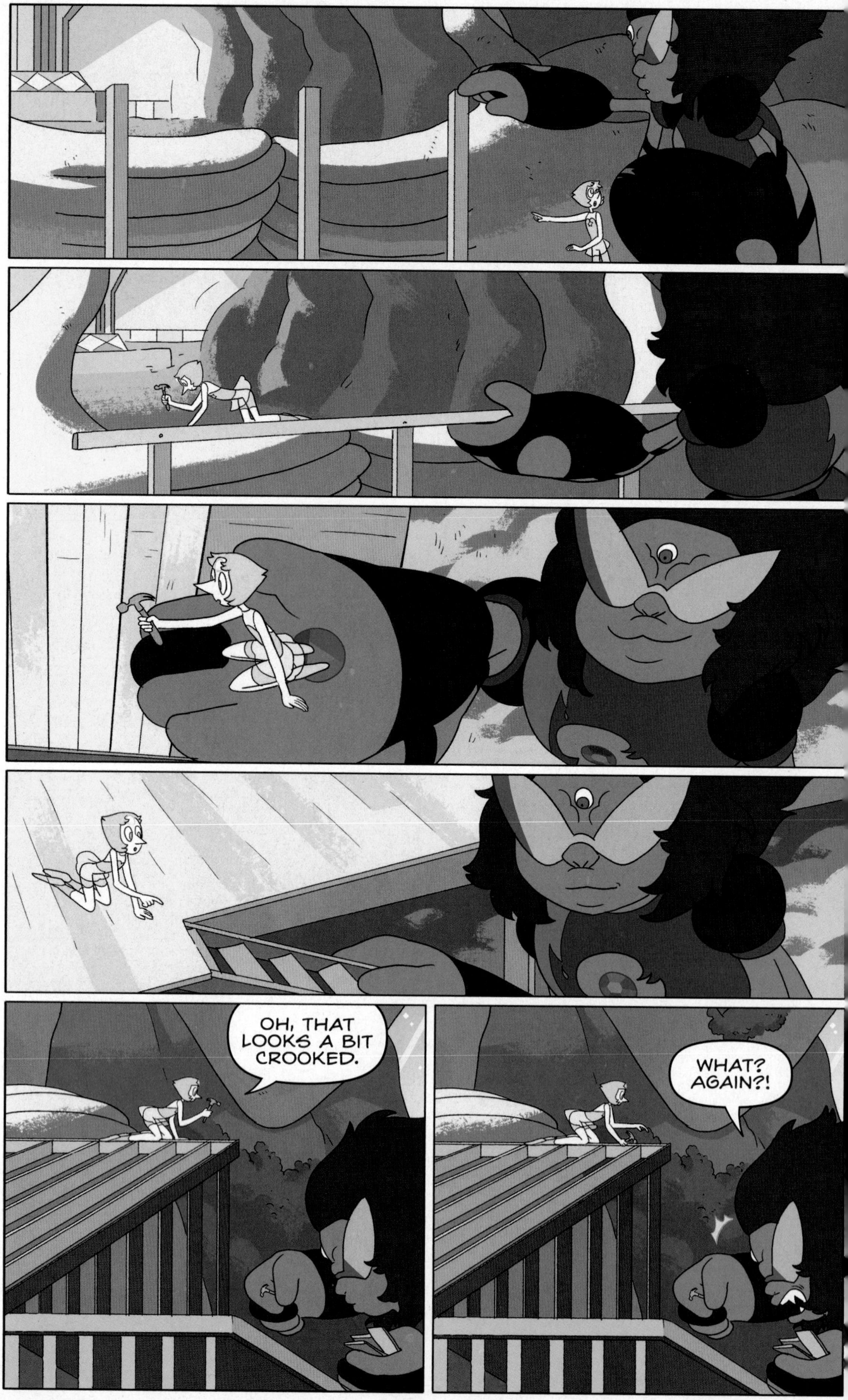
OH, THAT LOOKS A BIT CROOKED.
WHAT? AGAIN?!

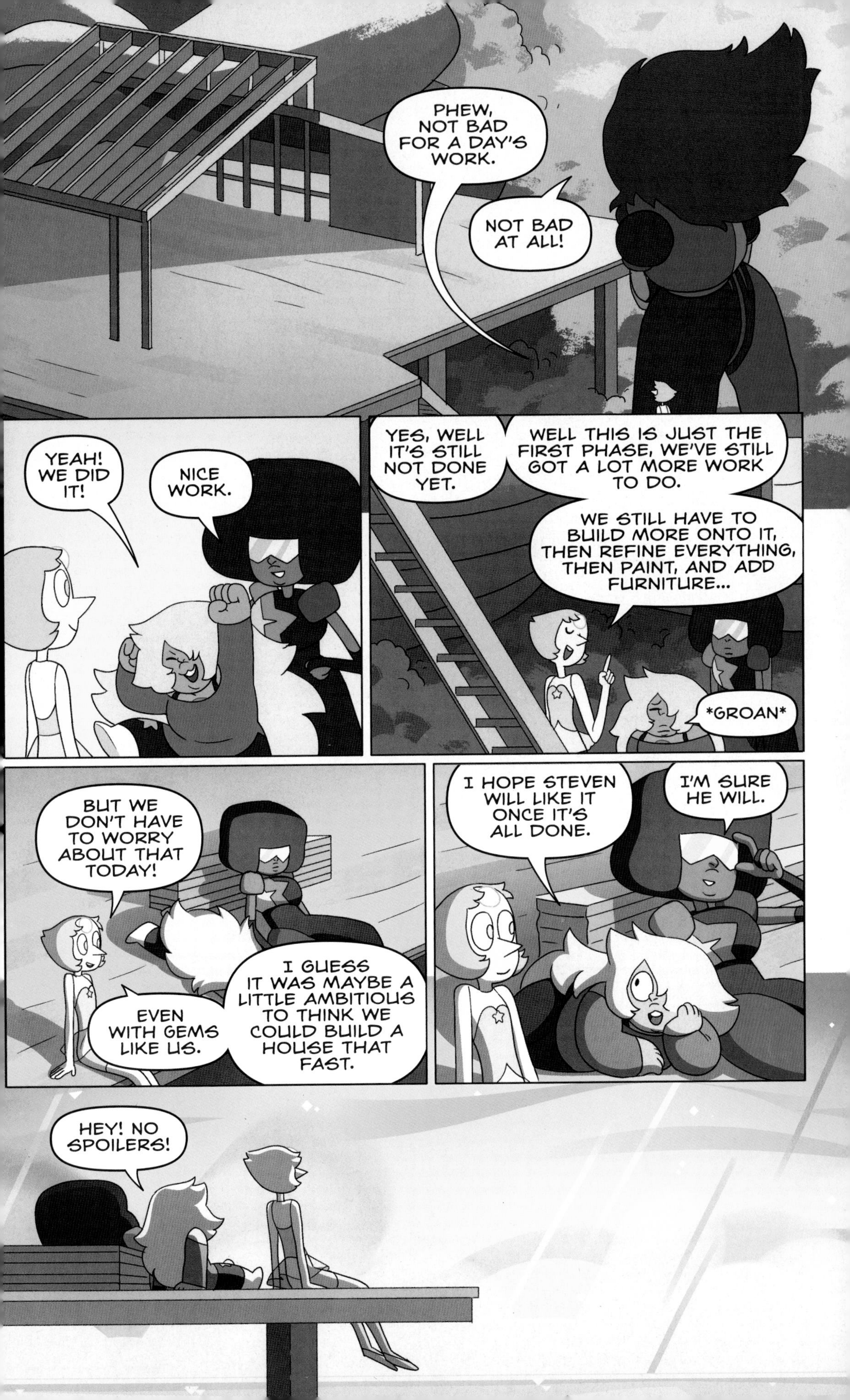
PHEW, NOT BAD FOR A DAY'S WORK.
NOT BAD AT ALL!
YEAH! WE DID IT!
NICE WORK.
YES, WELL IT'S STILL NOT DONE YET.
WELL THIS IS JUST THE FIRST PHASE, WE'VE STILL GOT A LOT MORE WORK TO DO.
WE STILL HAVE TO BUILD MORE ONTO IT, THEN REFINE EVERYTHING, THEN PAINT, AND ADD FURNITURE...
GROAN
BUT WE DON'T HAVE TO WORRY ABOUT THAT TODAY!
EVEN WITH GEMS LIKE US.
I GUESS IT WAS MAYBE A LITTLE AMBITIOUS TO THINK WE COULD BUILD A HOUSE THAT FAST.
I HOPE STEVEN WILL LIKE IT ONCE IT'S ALL DONE.
I'M SURE HE WILL.
HEY! NO SPOILERS!

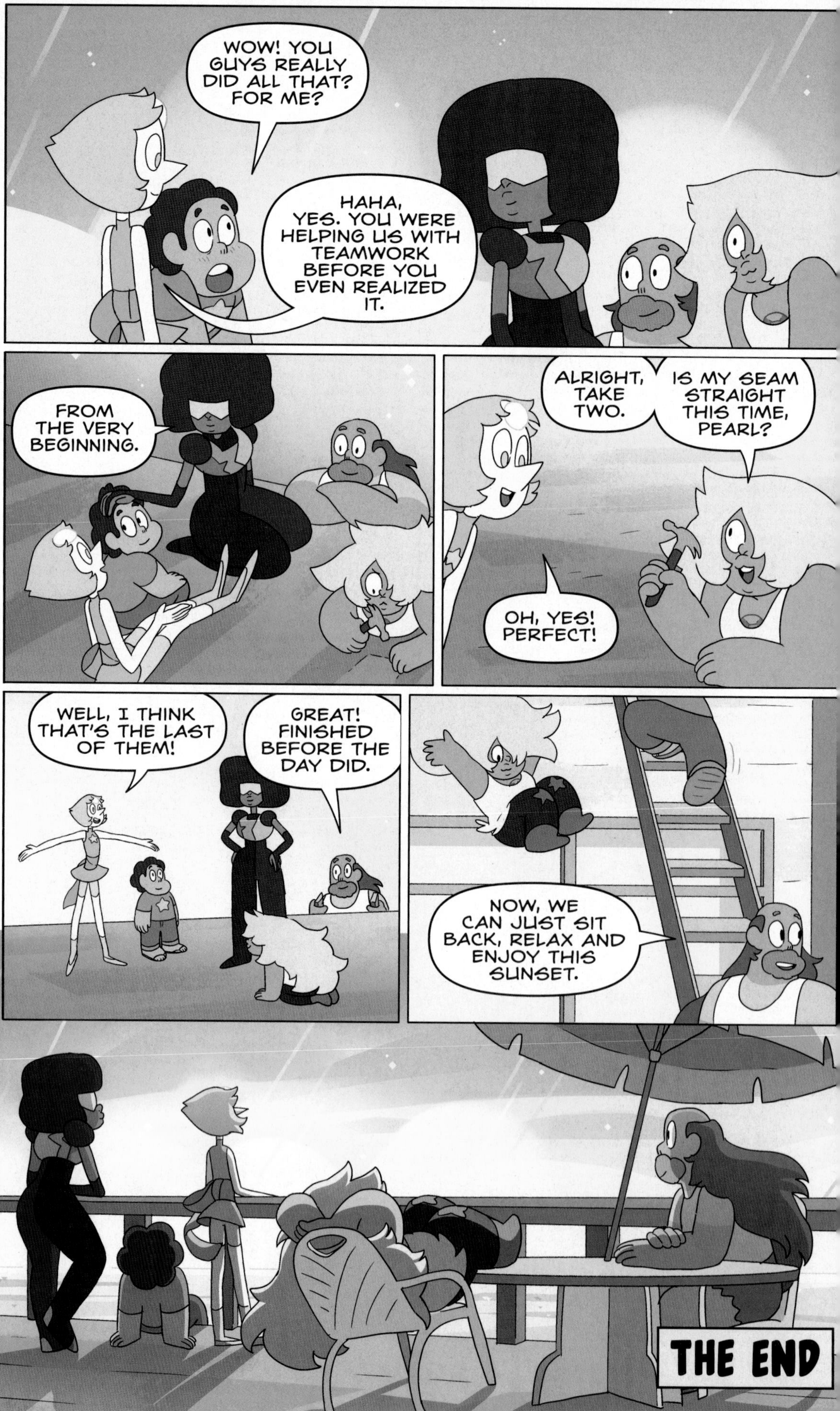
WOW! YOU GUYS REALLY DID ALL THAT? FOR ME?
HAHA, YES. YOU WERE HELPING US WITH TEAMWORK BEFORE YOU EVEN REALIZED IT.
FROM THE VERY BEGINNING.
ALRIGHT, TAKE TWO.
IS MY SEAM STRAIGHT THIS TIME, PEARL?
OH, YES! PERFECT!
WELL, I THINK THAT'S THE LAST OF THEM!
GREAT! FINISHED BEFORE THE DAY DID.
NOW, WE CAN JUST SIT BACK, RELAX AND ENJOY THIS SUNSET.
THE END

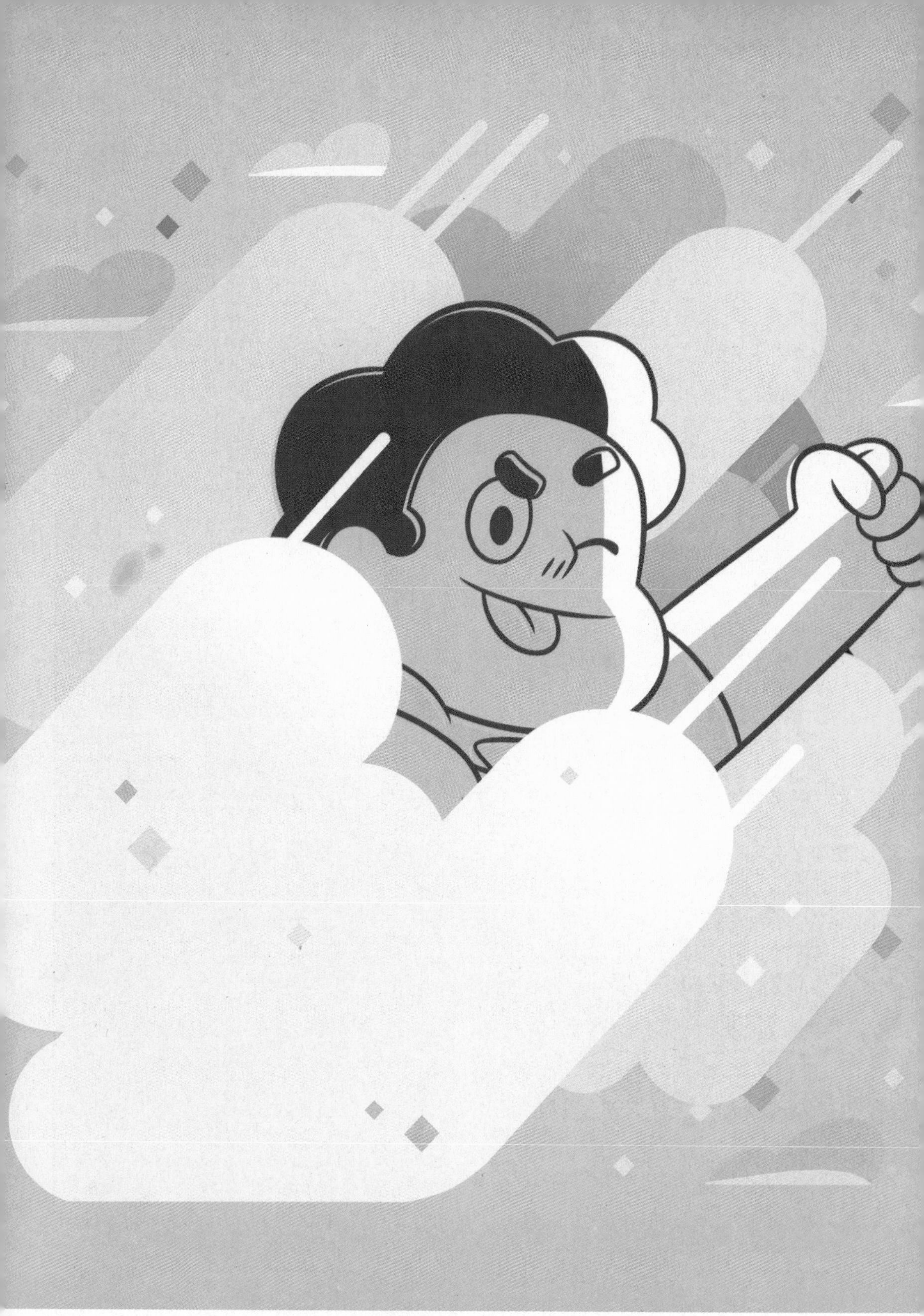

CHAPTER TWENTY

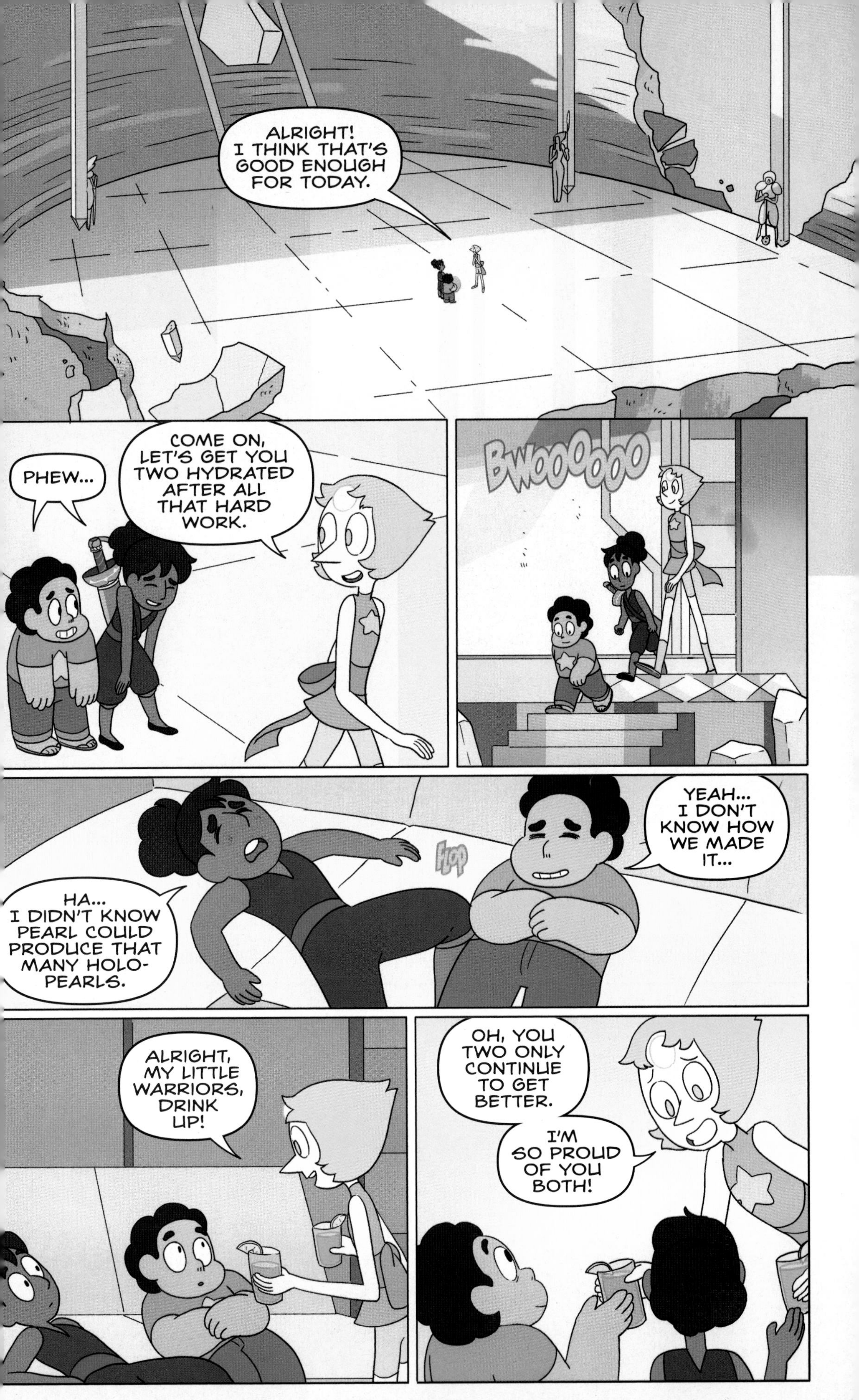
ALRIGHT! I THINK THAT'S GOOD ENOUGH FOR TODAY.
PHEW...
COME ON, LET'S GET YOU TWO HYDRATED AFTER ALL THAT HARD WORK.
BWOOOOOO
HA... I DIDN'T KNOW PEARL COULD PRODUCE THAT MANY HOLO-PEARLS.
FLOP
YEAH... I DON'T KNOW HOW WE MADE IT...
ALRIGHT, MY LITTLE WARRIORS, DRINK UP!
OH, YOU TWO ONLY CONTINUE TO GET BETTER.
I'M SO PROUD OF YOU BOTH!

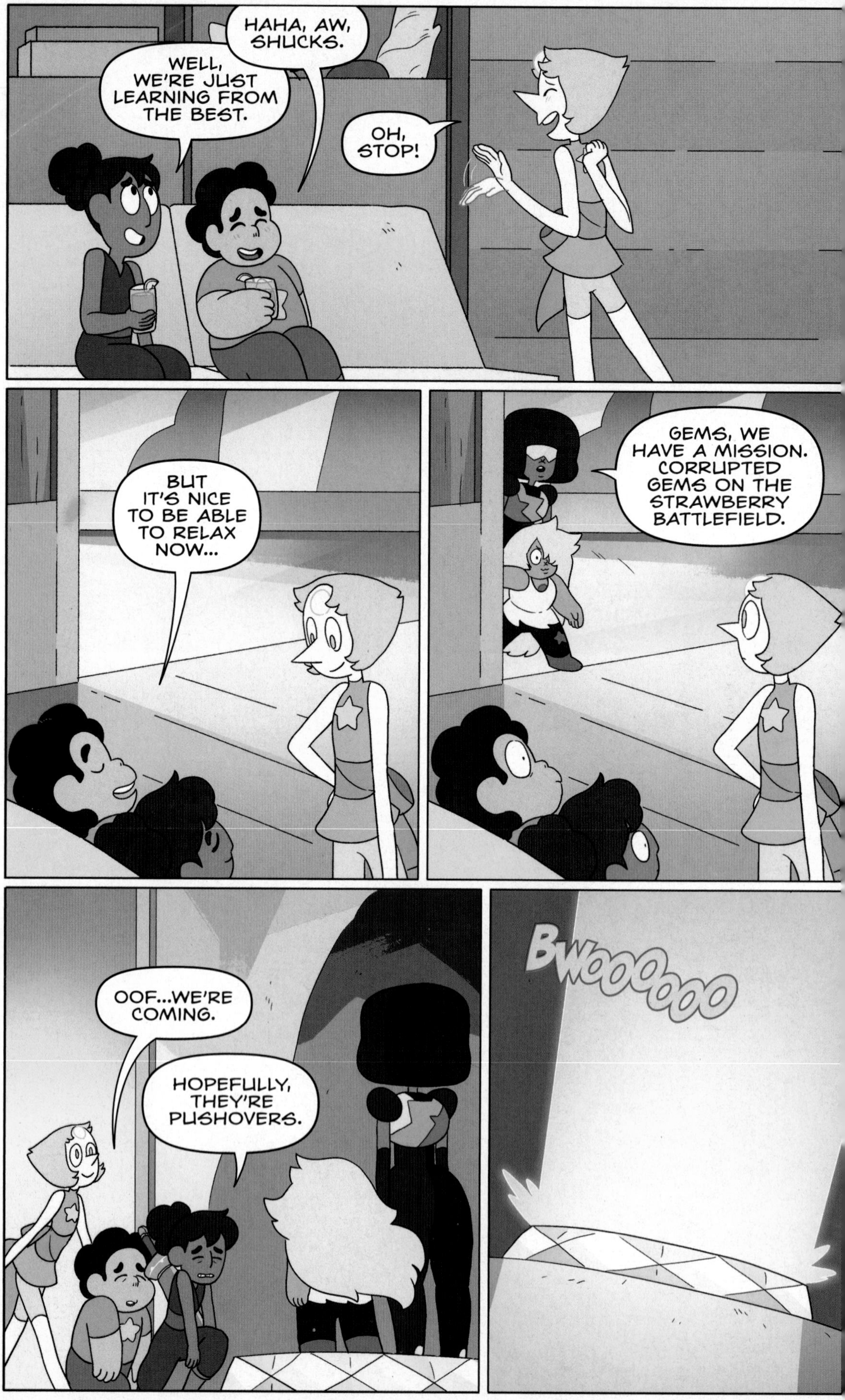
WELL, WE'RE JUST LEARNING FROM THE BEST.
HAHA, AW, SHUCKS.
OH, STOP!
BUT IT'S NICE TO BE ABLE TO RELAX NOW...
GEMS, WE HAVE A MISSION. CORRUPTED GEMS ON THE STRAWBERRY BATTLEFIELD.
OOF...WE'RE COMING.
HOPEFULLY, THEY'RE PUSHOVERS.
BWOOOOOO

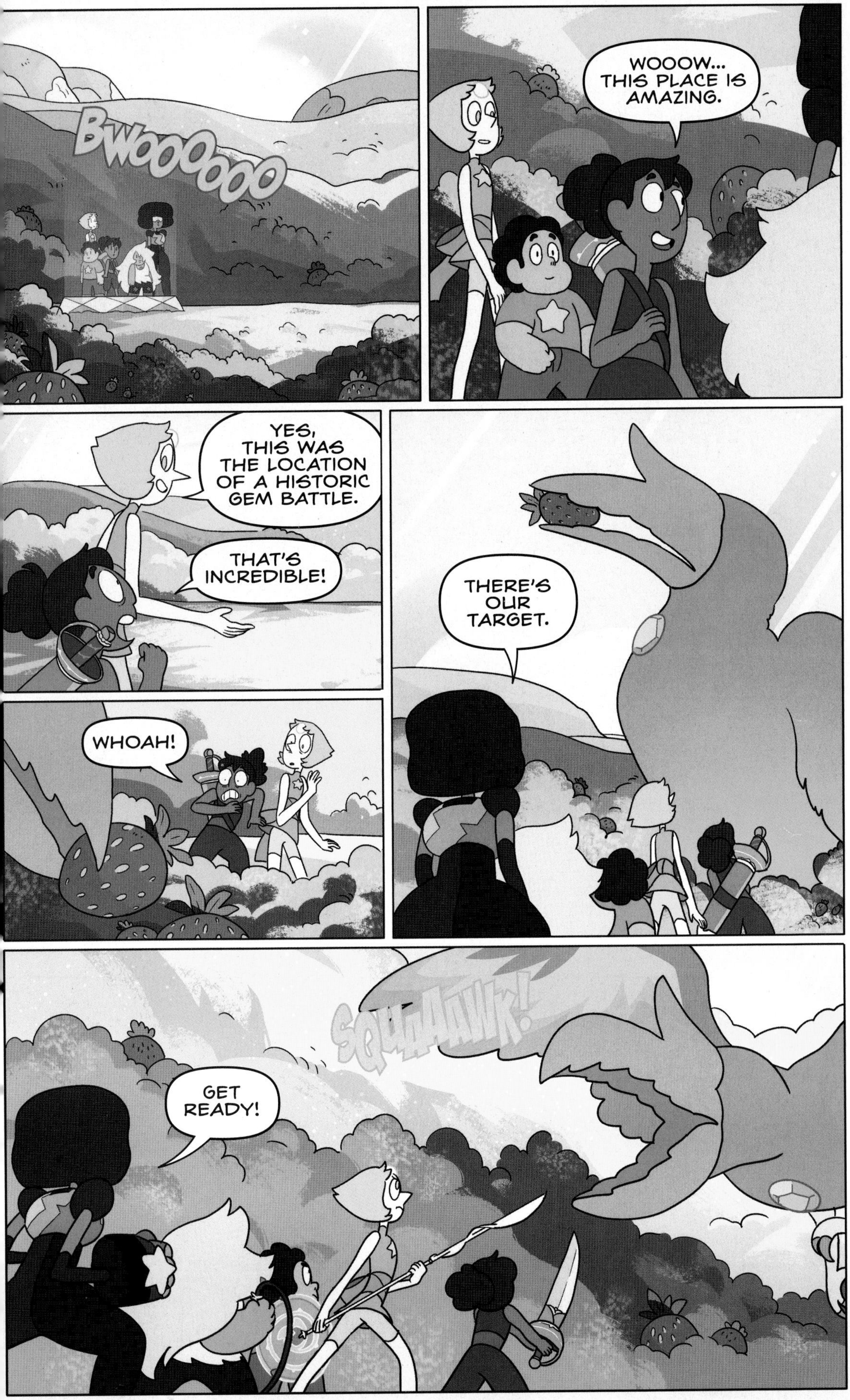
BWOOOOOO
WOOOW... THIS PLACE IS AMAZING.
YES, THIS WAS THE LOCATION OF A HISTORIC GEM BATTLE.
THAT'S INCREDIBLE!
WHOAH!
THERE'S OUR TARGET.
SQUAAAWK!
GET READY!

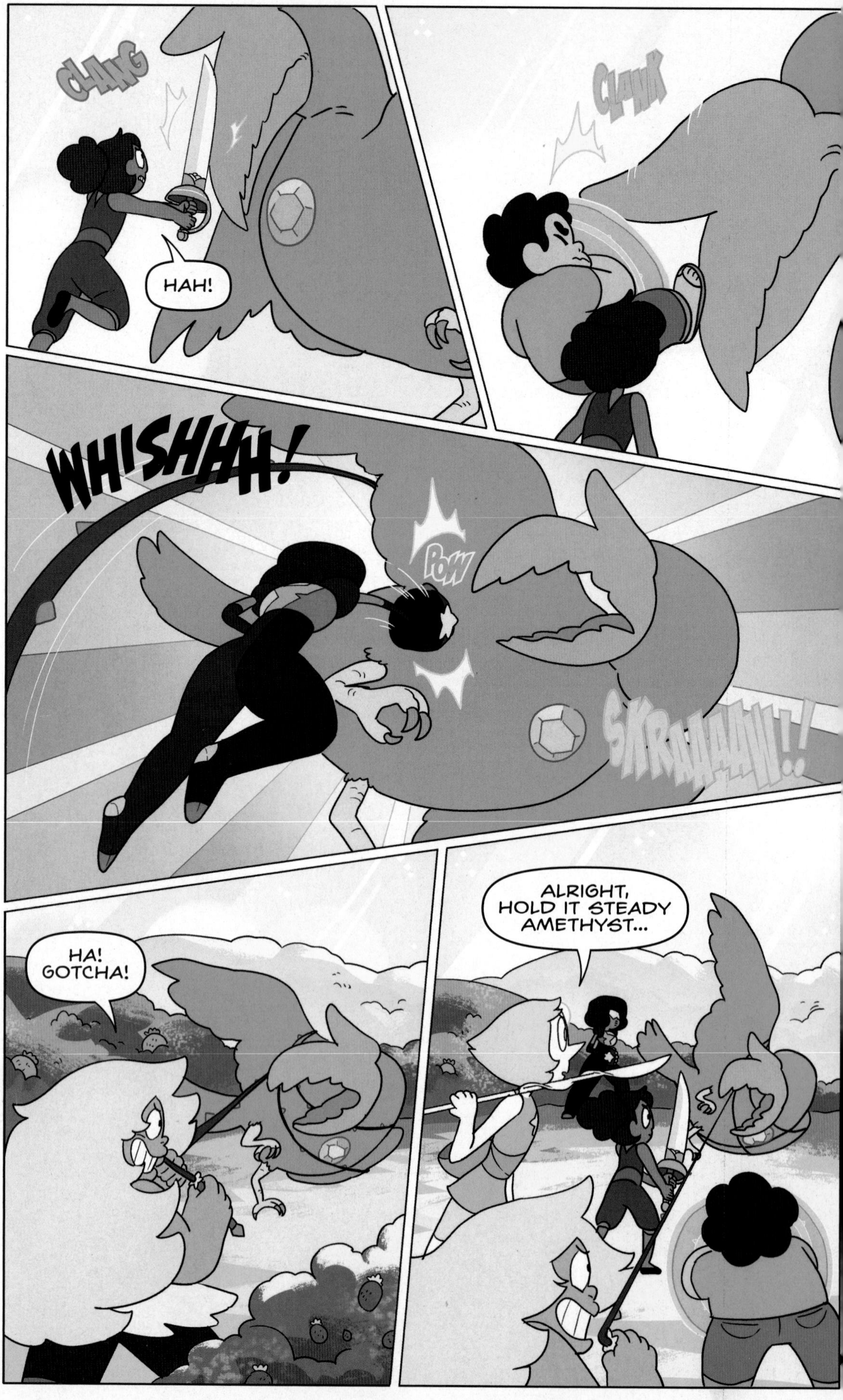
CLANG
HAH!
CLANK
WHISHHH!
POW
SKRAAAAW!!
HA! GOTCHA!
ALRIGHT, HOLD IT STEADY AMETHYST...

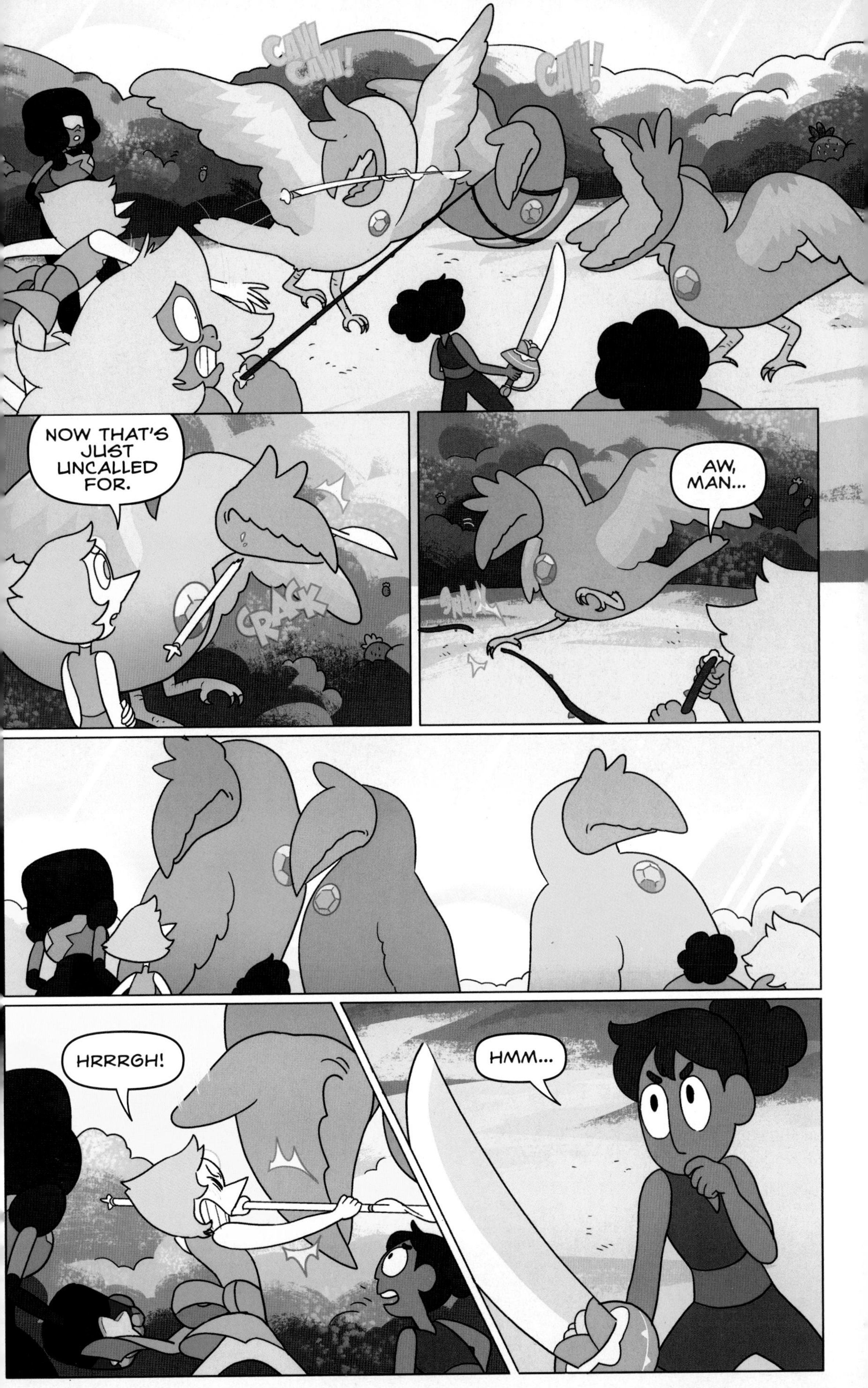
CAW CAW!
CAW!
NOW THAT'S JUST UNCALLED FOR.
CRACK
AW, MAN...
SNAP
HRRRGH!
HMM...

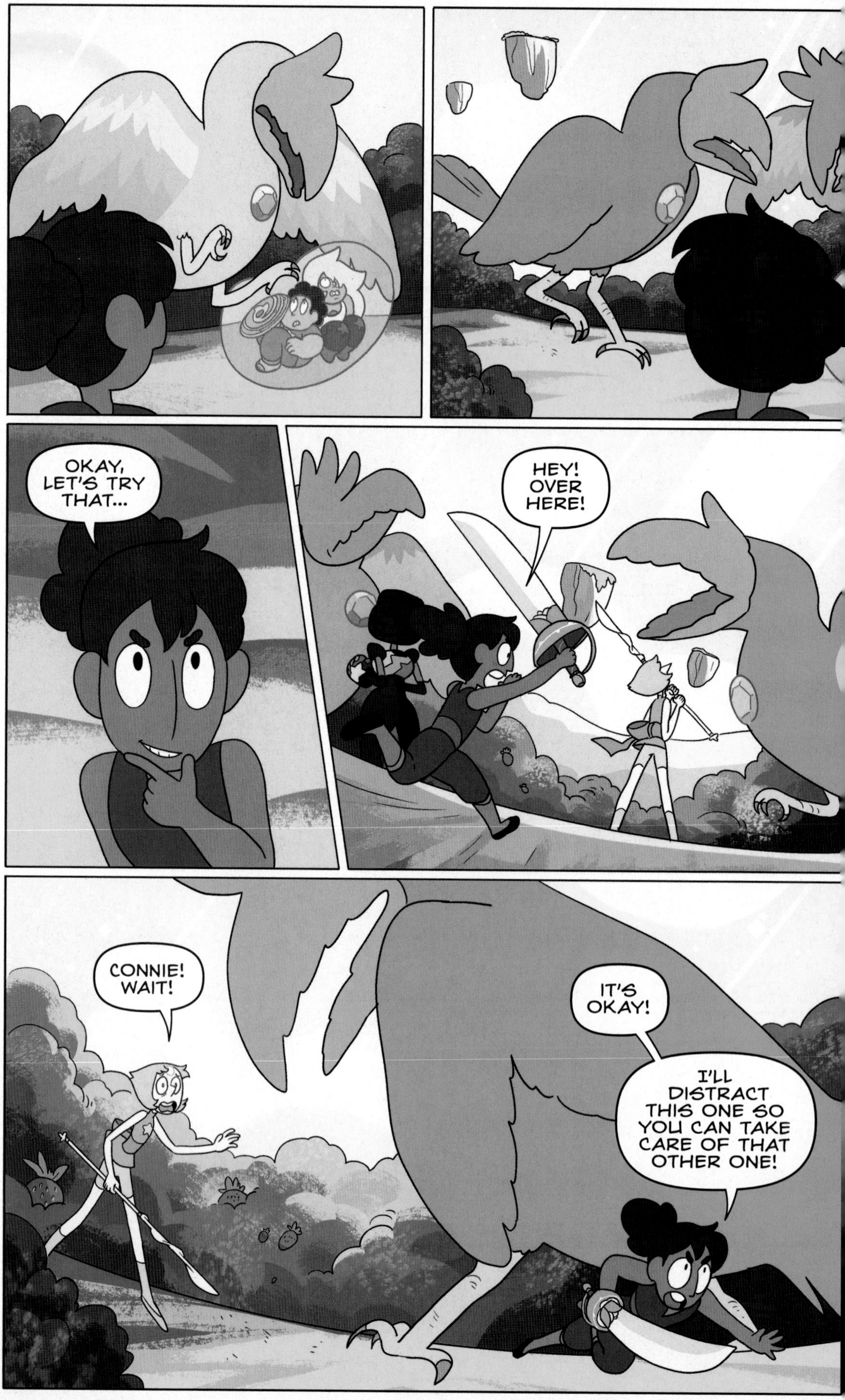
OKAY, LET'S TRY THAT...
HEY! OVER HERE!
CONNIE! WAIT!
IT'S OKAY!
I'LL DISTRACT THIS ONE SO YOU CAN TAKE CARE OF THAT OTHER ONE!

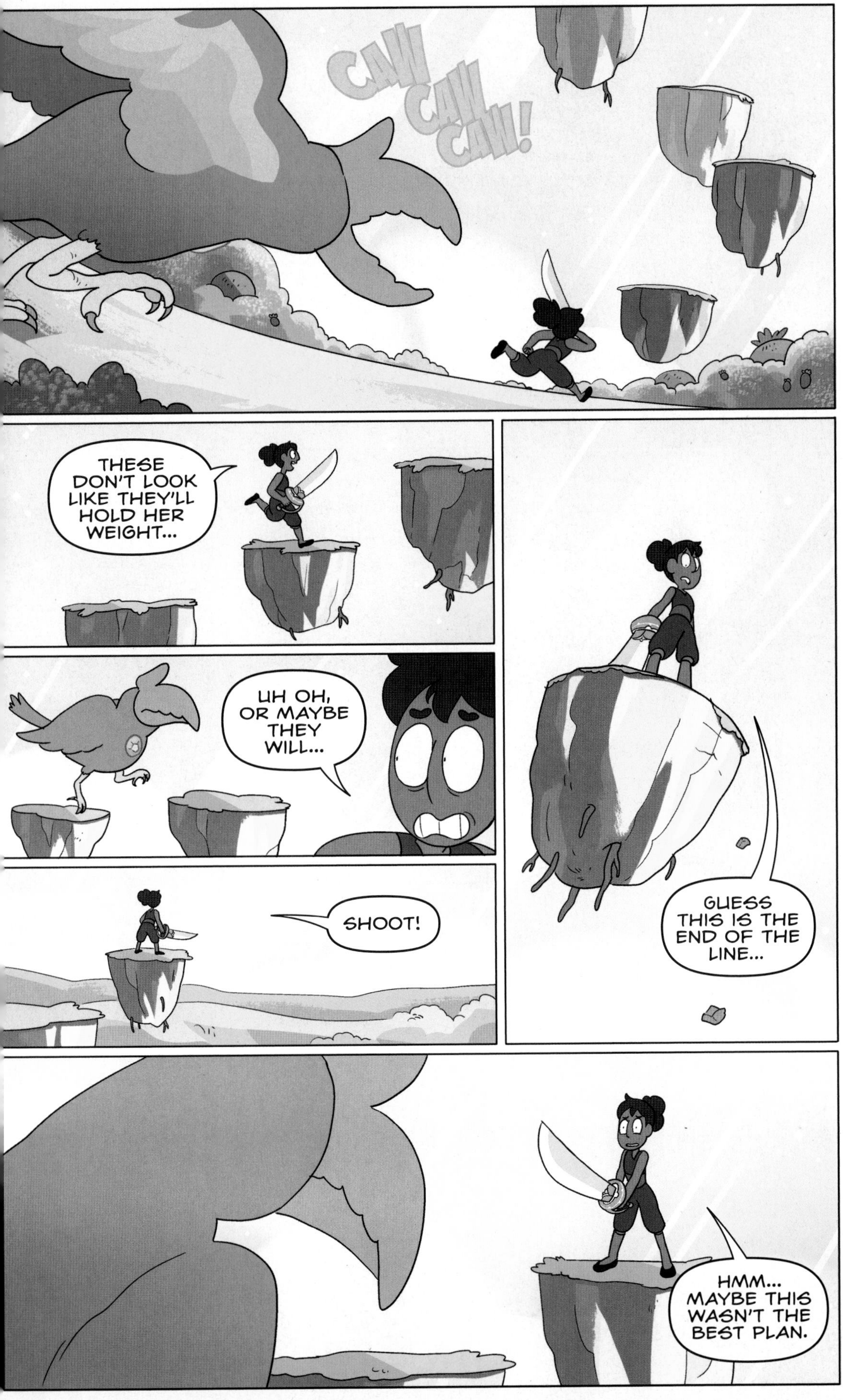
CAW CAW CAW!
THESE DON'T LOOK LIKE THEY'LL HOLD HER WEIGHT...
UH OH, OR MAYBE THEY WILL...
SHOOT!
GUESS THIS IS THE END OF THE LINE...
HMM... MAYBE THIS WASN'T THE BEST PLAN.

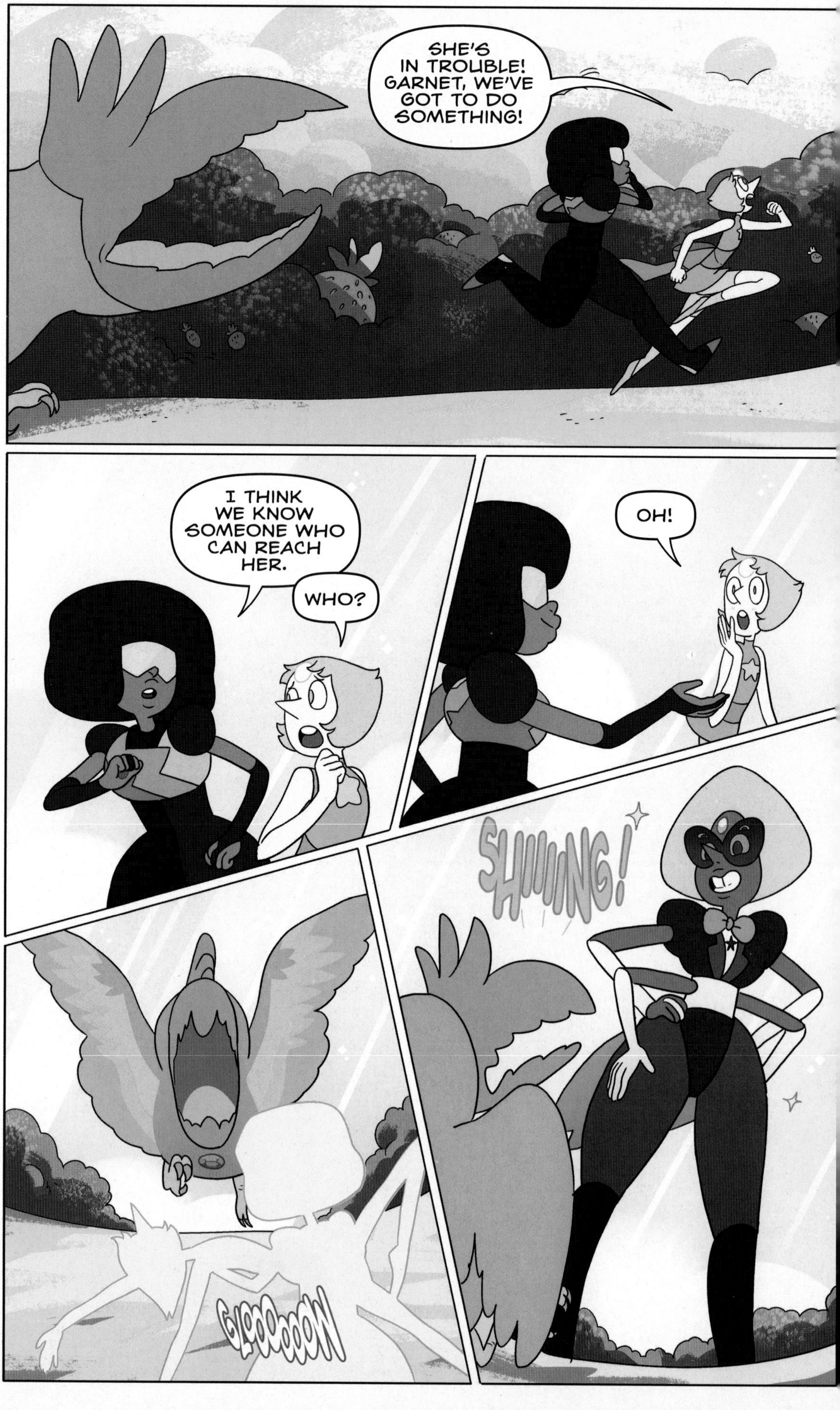
SHE'S IN TROUBLE! GARNET, WE'VE GOT TO DO SOMETHING!
I THINK WE KNOW SOMEONE WHO CAN REACH HER.
WHO?
OH!
SHIIIING!
GLOOOOOOON

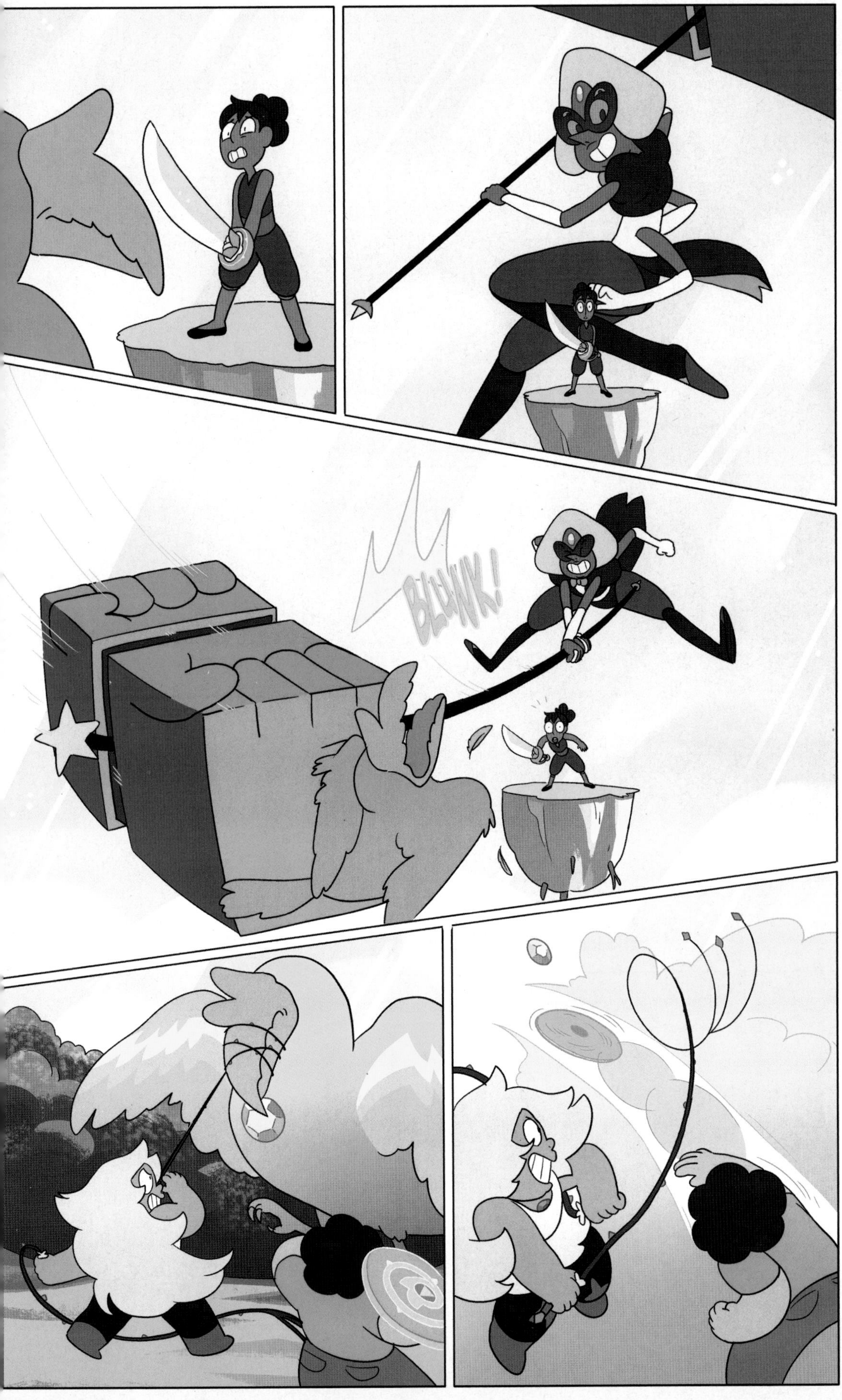
BLUNK!

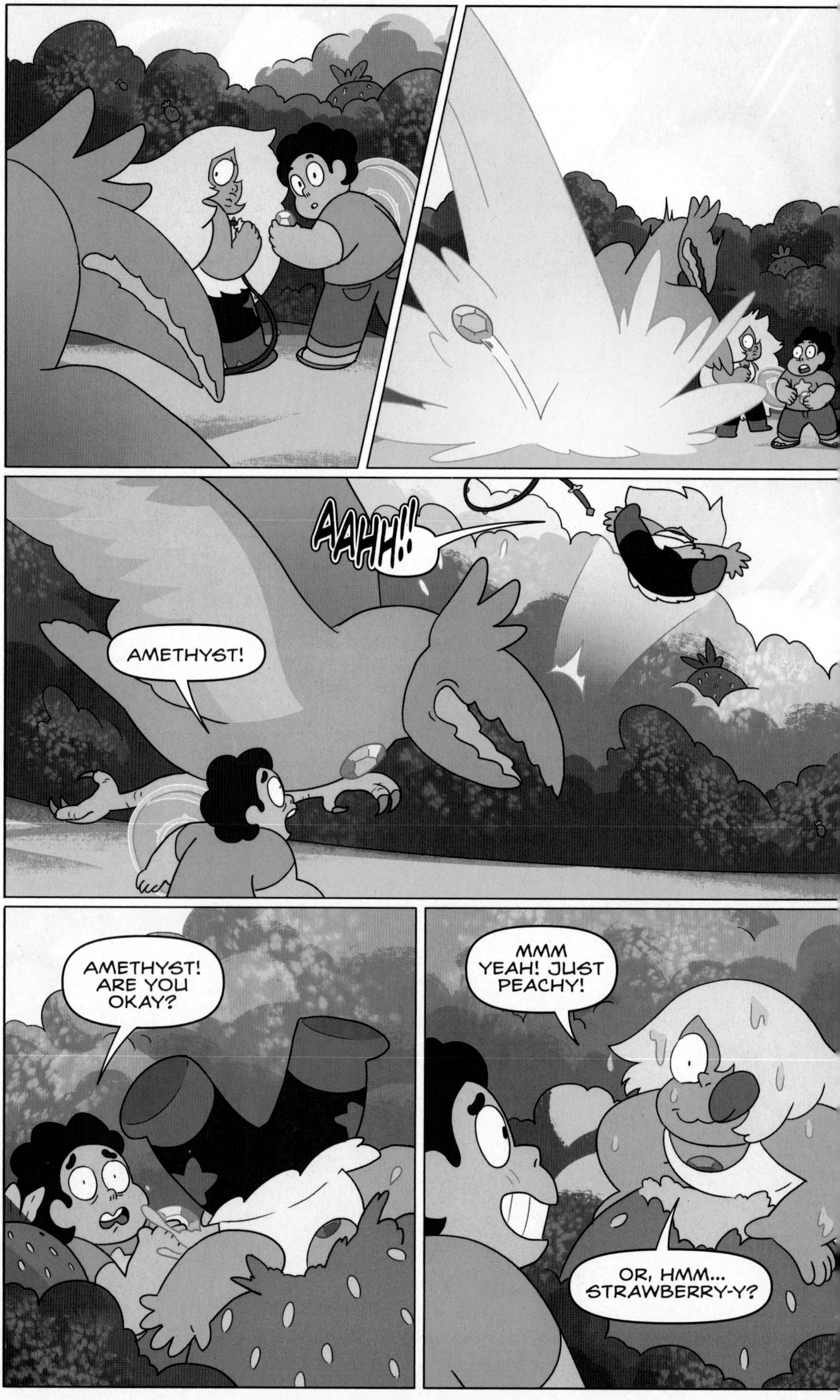
AAHH!!
AMETHYST!
AMETHYST! ARE YOU OKAY?
MMM YEAH! JUST PEACHY!
OR, HMM... STRAWBERRY-Y?

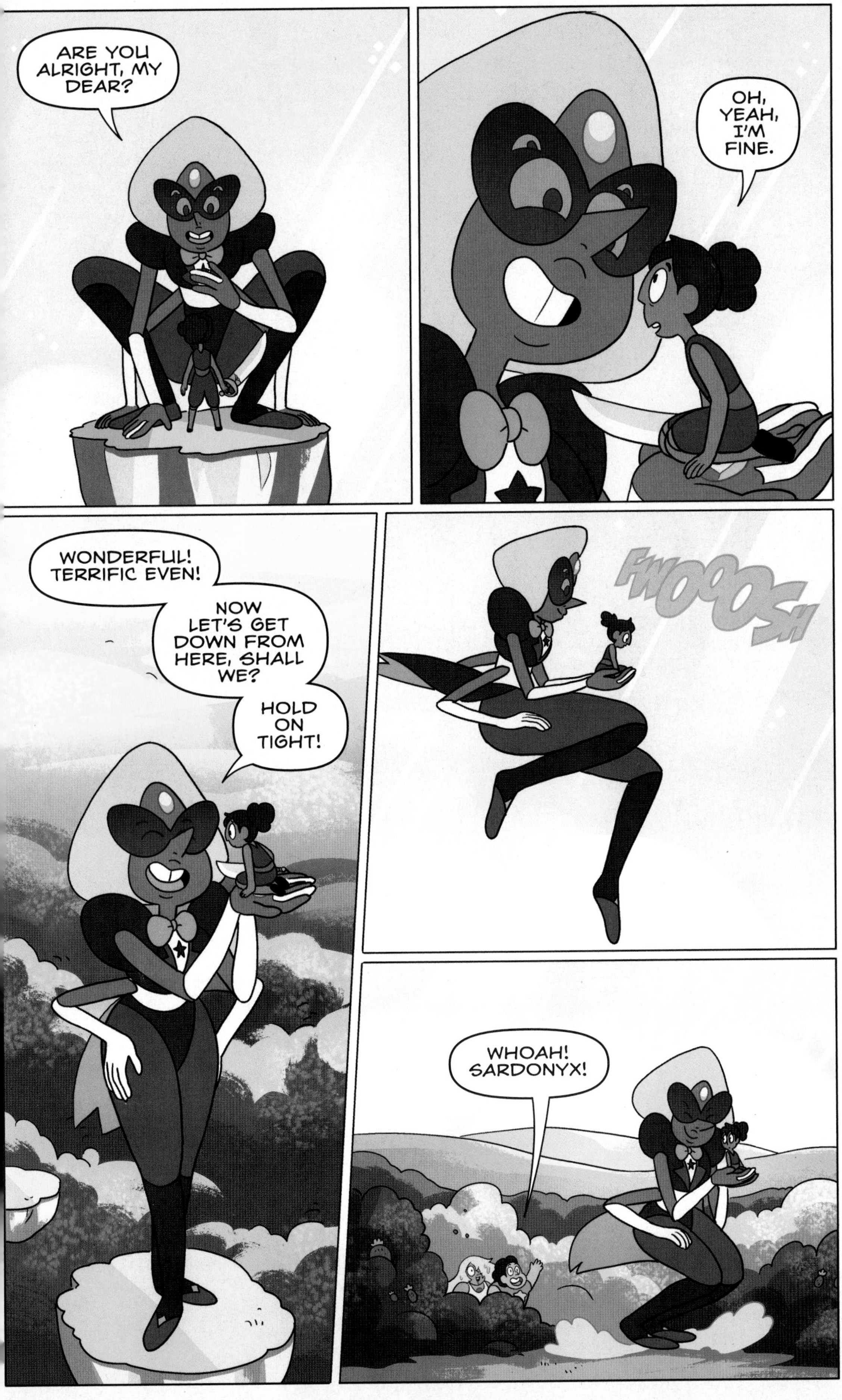
ARE YOU ALRIGHT, MY DEAR?
OH, YEAH, I'M FINE.
WONDERFUL! TERRIFIC EVEN!
NOW LET'S GET DOWN FROM HERE, SHALL WE?
HOLD ON TIGHT!
FWOOOSH
WHOAH! SARDONYX!

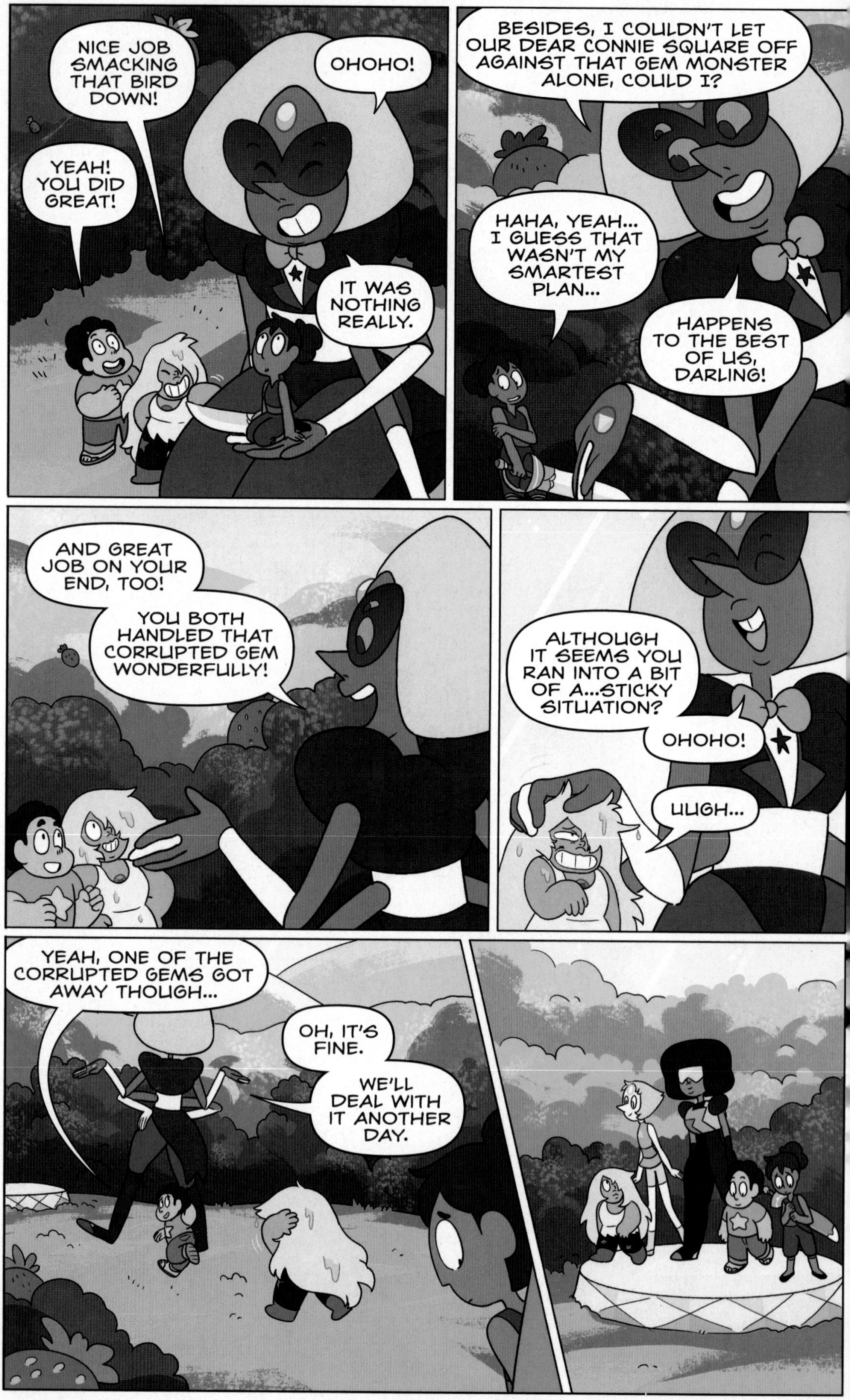
NICE JOB SMACKING THAT BIRD DOWN!
YEAH! YOU DID GREAT!
OHOHO!
IT WAS NOTHING REALLY.
BESIDES, I COULDN'T LET OUR DEAR CONNIE SQUARE OFF AGAINST THAT GEM MONSTER ALONE, COULD I?
HAHA, YEAH... I GUESS THAT WASN'T MY SMARTEST PLAN...
HAPPENS TO THE BEST OF US, DARLING!
AND GREAT JOB ON YOUR END, TOO!
YOU BOTH HANDLED THAT CORRUPTED GEM WONDERFULLY!
ALTHOUGH IT SEEMS YOU RAN INTO A BIT OF A...STICKY SITUATION?
OHOHO!
UUGH...
YEAH, ONE OF THE CORRUPTED GEMS GOT AWAY THOUGH...
OH, IT'S FINE.
WE'LL DEAL WITH IT ANOTHER DAY.

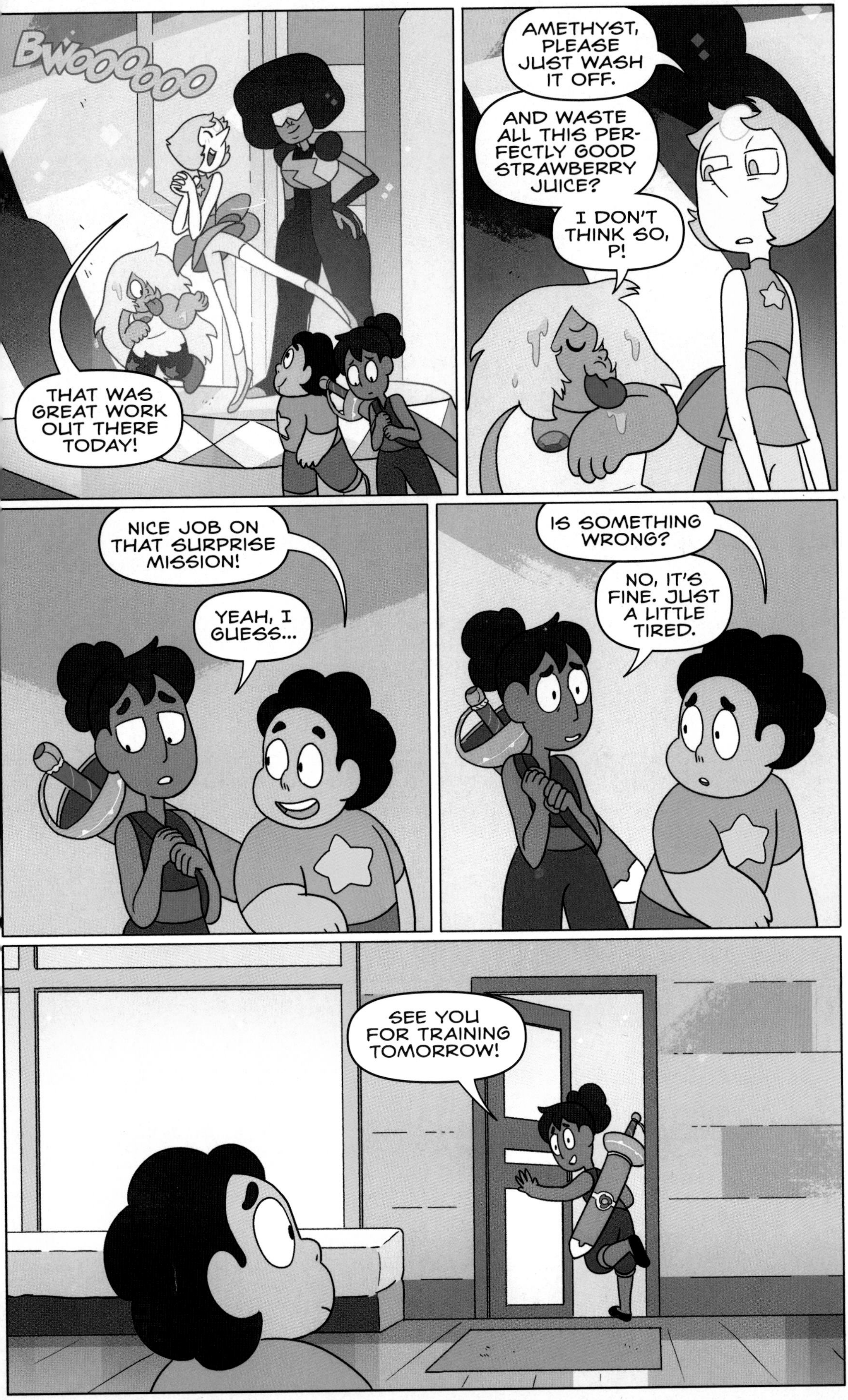
BWOOOOOO
THAT WAS GREAT WORK OUT THERE TODAY!
AMETHYST, PLEASE JUST WASH IT OFF.
AND WASTE ALL THIS PERFECTLY GOOD STRAWBERRY JUICE?
I DON'T THINK SO, P!
NICE JOB ON THAT SURPRISE MISSION!
YEAH, I GUESS...
IS SOMETHING WRONG?
NO, IT'S FINE. JUST A LITTLE TIRED.
SEE YOU FOR TRAINING TOMORROW!

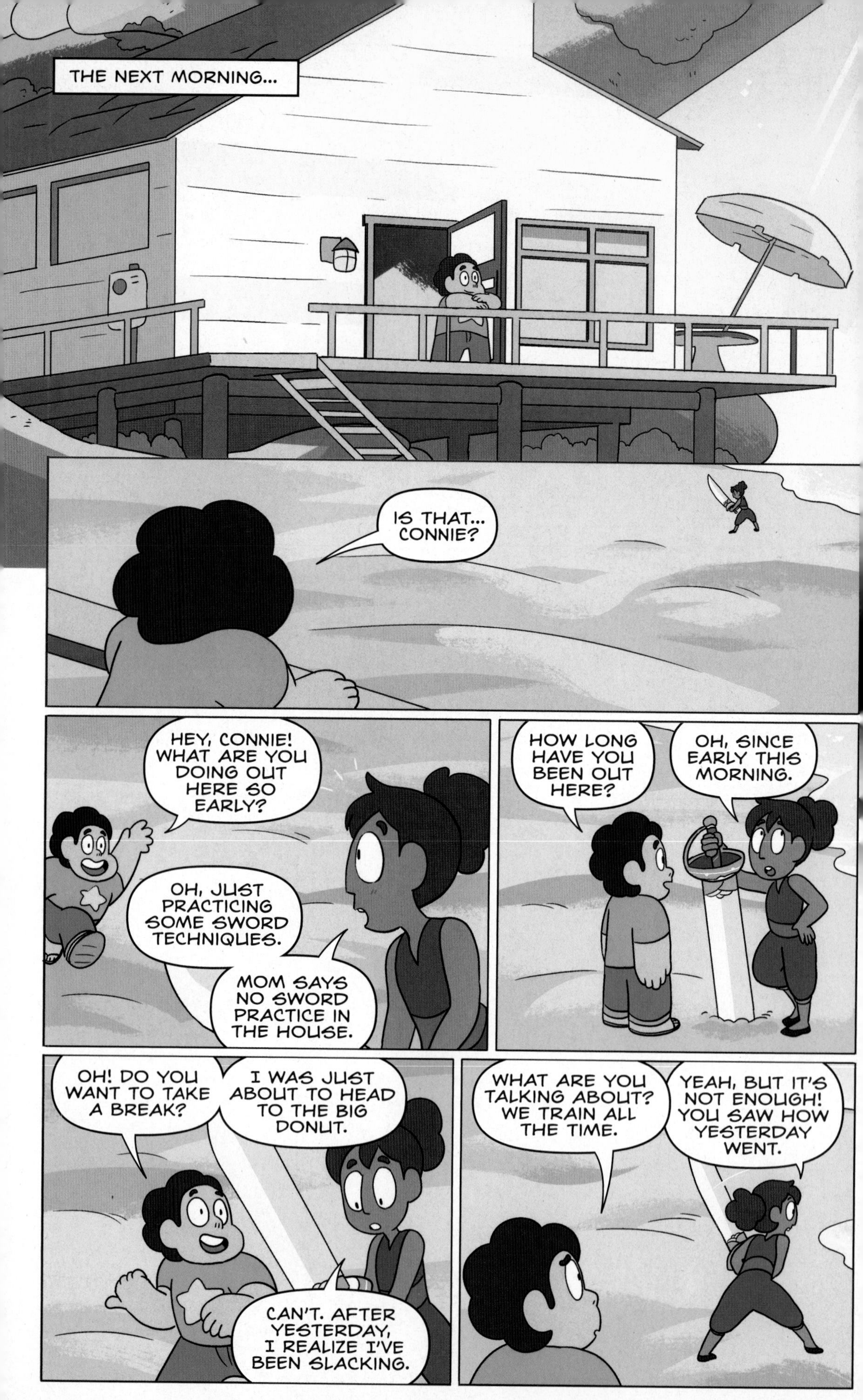
THE NEXT MORNING...
IS THAT... CONNIE?
HEY, CONNIE! WHAT ARE YOU DOING OUT HERE SO EARLY?
OH, JUST PRACTICING SOME SWORD TECHNIQUES.
MOM SAYS NO SWORD PRACTICE IN THE HOUSE.
HOW LONG HAVE YOU BEEN OUT HERE?
OH, SINCE EARLY THIS MORNING.
OH! DO YOU WANT TO TAKE A BREAK?
I WAS JUST ABOUT TO HEAD TO THE BIG DONUT.
CAN'T. AFTER YESTERDAY, I REALIZE I'VE BEEN SLACKING.
WHAT ARE YOU TALKING ABOUT? WE TRAIN ALL THE TIME.
YEAH, BUT IT'S NOT ENOUGH! YOU SAW HOW YESTERDAY WENT.

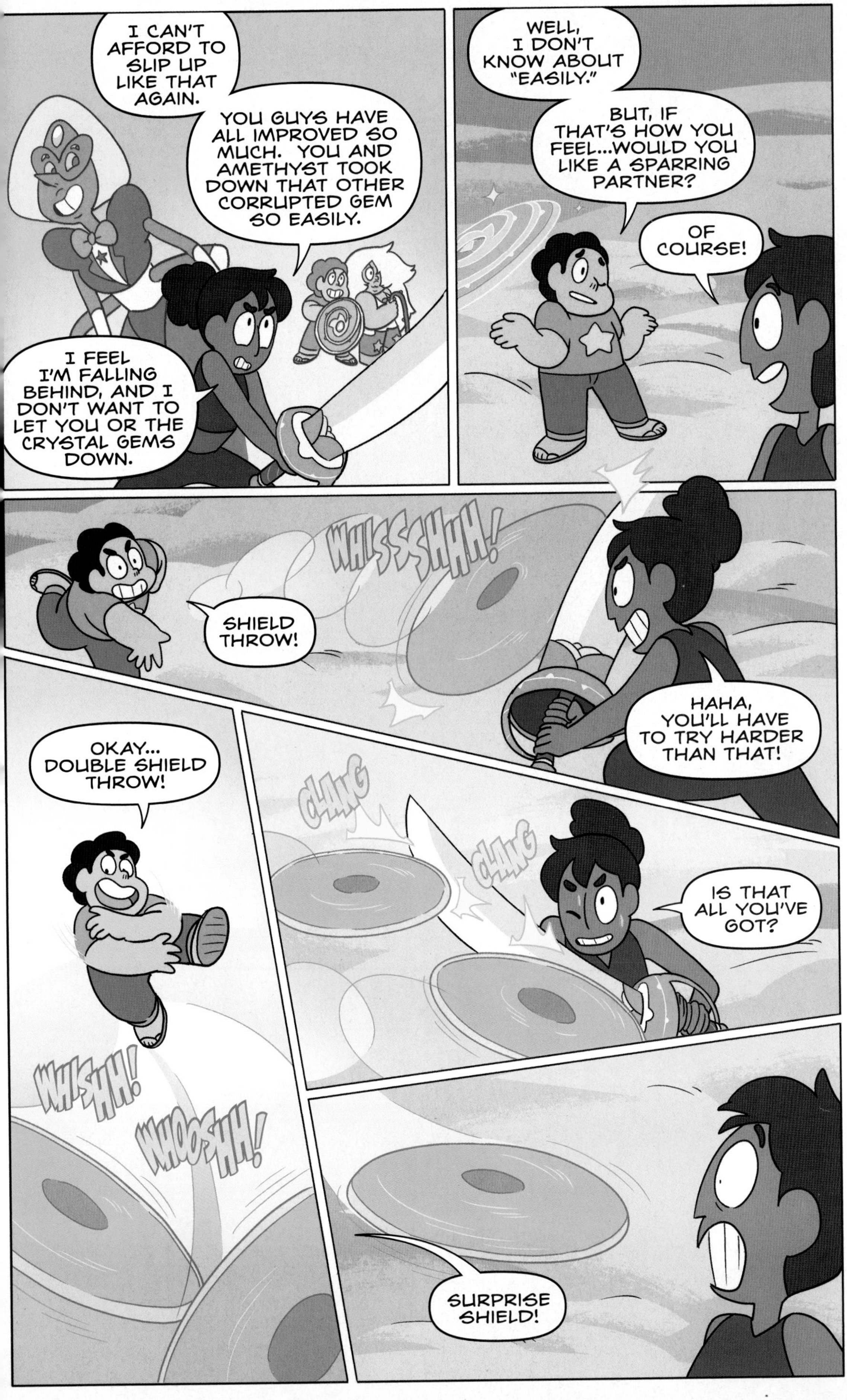
I CAN'T AFFORD TO SLIP UP LIKE THAT AGAIN.
YOU GUYS HAVE ALL IMPROVED SO MUCH. YOU AND AMETHYST TOOK DOWN THAT OTHER CORRUPTED GEM SO EASILY.
I FEEL I'M FALLING BEHIND, AND I DON'T WANT TO LET YOU OR THE CRYSTAL GEMS DOWN.
WELL, I DON'T KNOW ABOUT "EASILY."
BUT, IF THAT'S HOW YOU FEEL...WOULD YOU LIKE A SPARRING PARTNER?
OF COURSE!
WHISSSHHH!
SHIELD THROW!
HAHA, YOU'LL HAVE TO TRY HARDER THAN THAT!
OKAY... DOUBLE SHIELD THROW!
WHISHH!
WHOOSHH!
CLANG
CLANG
IS THAT ALL YOU'VE GOT?
SURPRISE SHIELD!

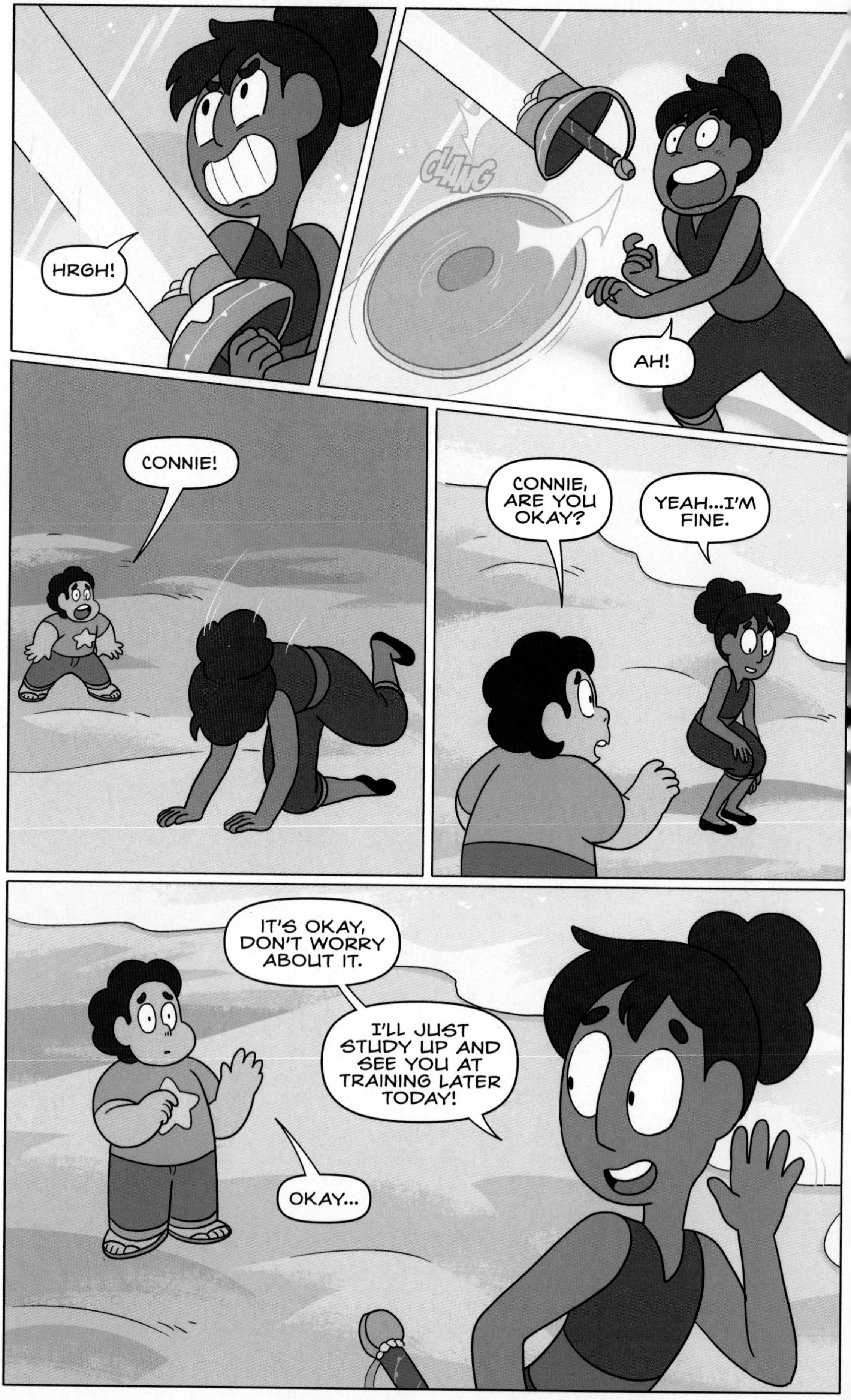
HRGH!
CLANG
AH!
CONNIE!
CONNIE, ARE YOU OKAY?
YEAH...I'M FINE.
IT'S OKAY, DON'T WORRY ABOUT IT.
I'LL JUST STUDY UP AND SEE YOU AT TRAINING LATER TODAY!
OKAY...

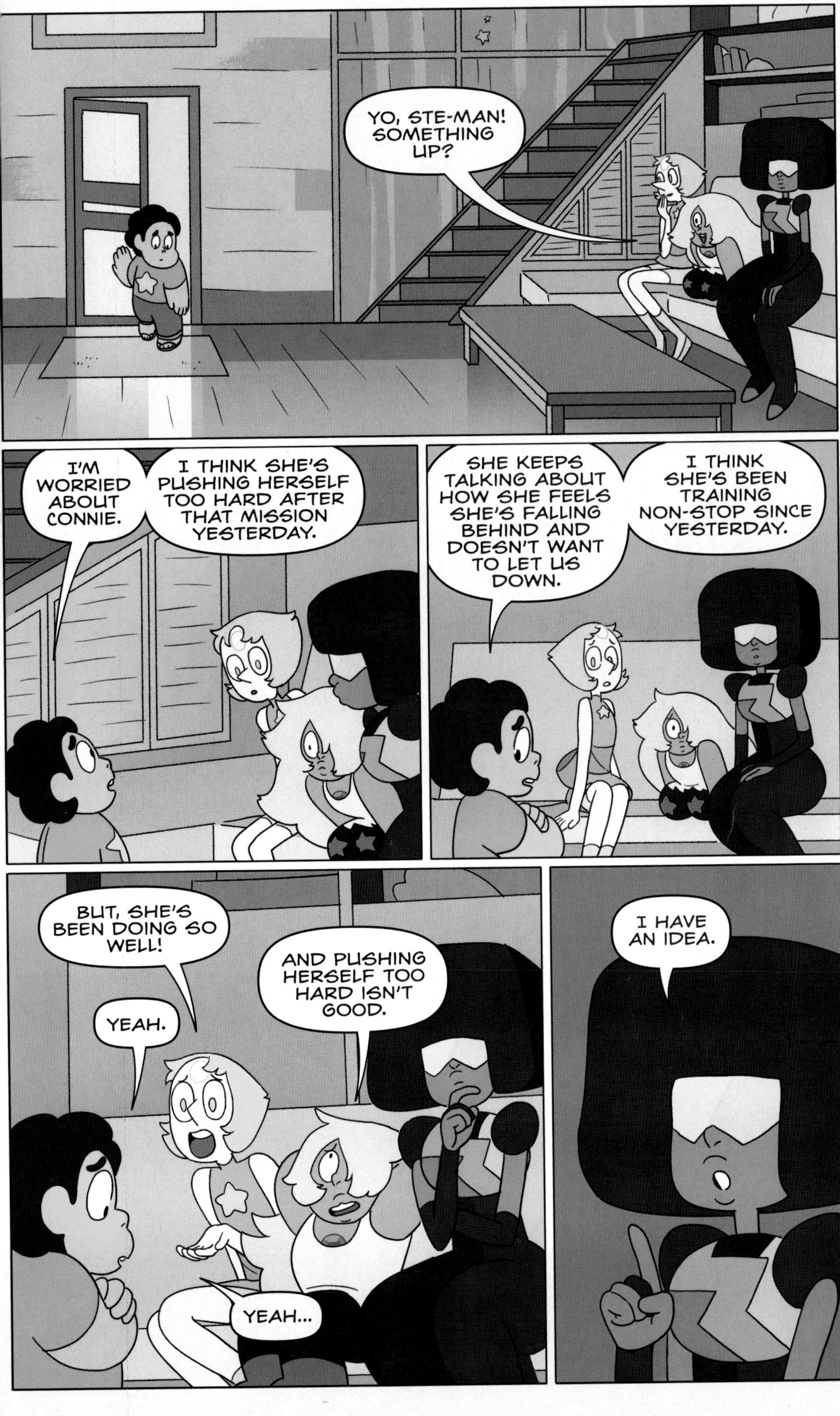
YO, STE-MAN! SOMETHING UP?
I'M WORRIED ABOUT CONNIE.
I THINK SHE'S PUSHING HERSELF TOO HARD AFTER THAT MISSION YESTERDAY.
SHE KEEPS TALKING ABOUT HOW SHE FEELS SHE'S FALLING BEHIND AND DOESN'T WANT TO LET US DOWN.
I THINK SHE'S BEEN TRAINING NON-STOP SINCE YESTERDAY.
BUT, SHE'S BEEN DOING SO WELL!
YEAH.
AND PUSHING HERSELF TOO HARD ISN'T GOOD.
YEAH...
I HAVE AN IDEA.

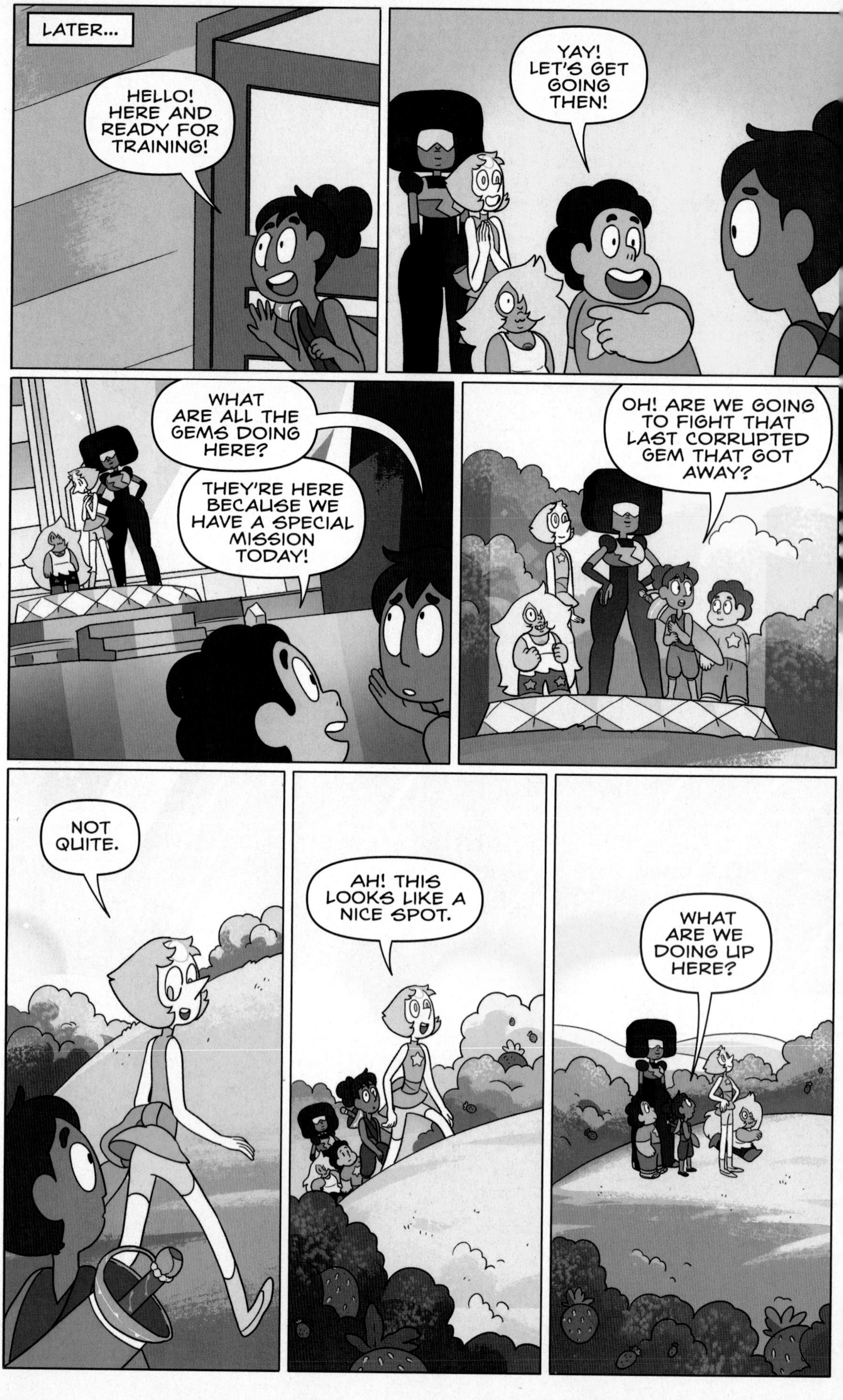
LATER...
HELLO! HERE AND READY FOR TRAINING!
YAY! LET'S GET GOING THEN!
WHAT ARE ALL THE GEMS DOING HERE?
THEY'RE HERE BECAUSE WE HAVE A SPECIAL MISSION TODAY!
OH! ARE WE GOING TO FIGHT THAT LAST CORRUPTED GEM THAT GOT AWAY?
NOT QUITE.
AH! THIS LOOKS LIKE A NICE SPOT.
WHAT ARE WE DOING UP HERE?

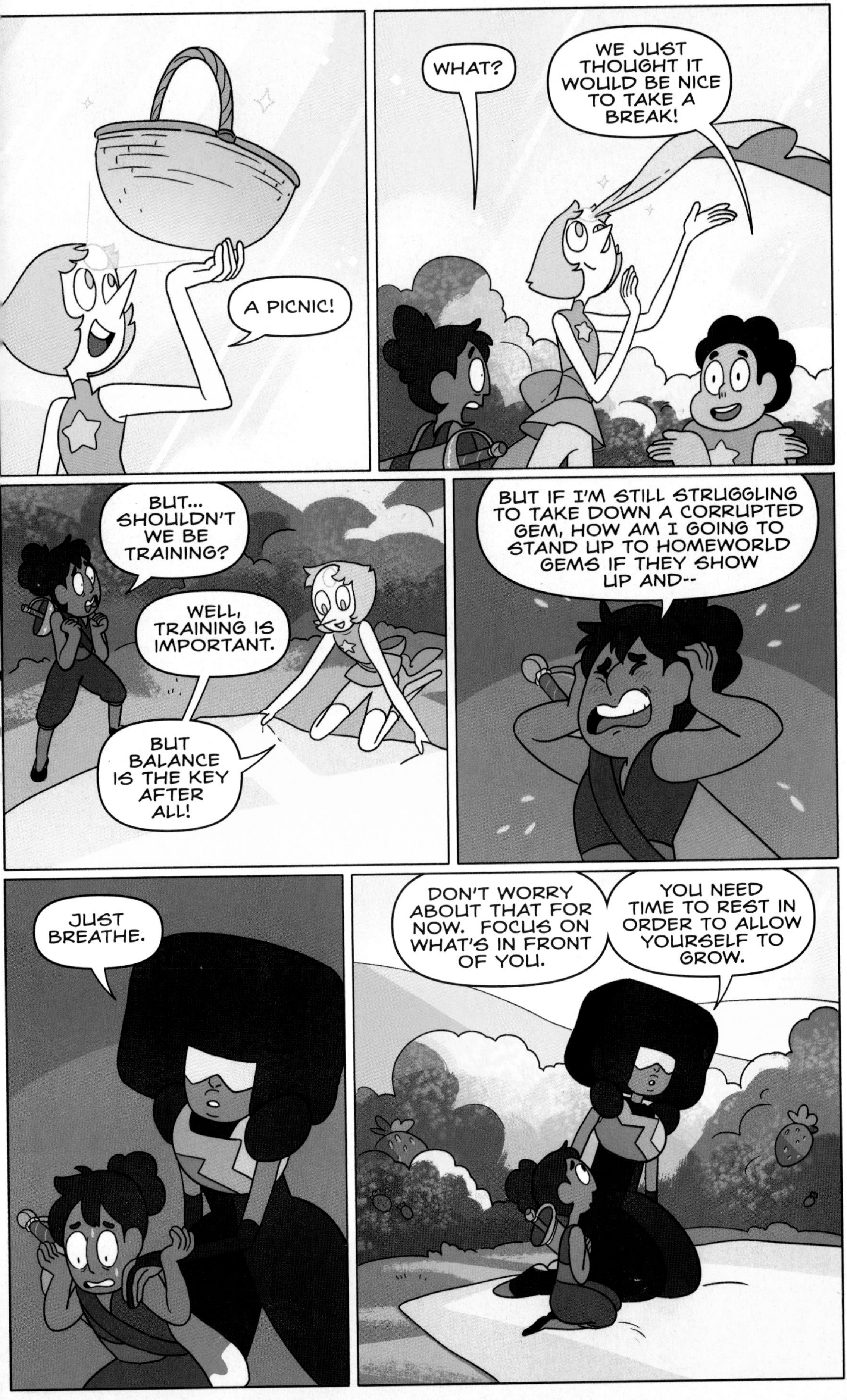
A PICNIC!
WHAT?
WE JUST THOUGHT IT WOULD BE NICE TO TAKE A BREAK!
BUT... SHOULDN'T WE BE TRAINING?
WELL, TRAINING IS IMPORTANT.
BUT BALANCE IS THE KEY AFTER ALL!
BUT IF I'M STILL STRUGGLING TO TAKE DOWN A CORRUPTED GEM, HOW AM I GOING TO STAND UP TO HOMEWORLD GEMS IF THEY SHOW UP AND--
JUST BREATHE.
DON'T WORRY ABOUT THAT FOR NOW. FOCUS ON WHAT'S IN FRONT OF YOU.
YOU NEED TIME TO REST IN ORDER TO ALLOW YOURSELF TO GROW.

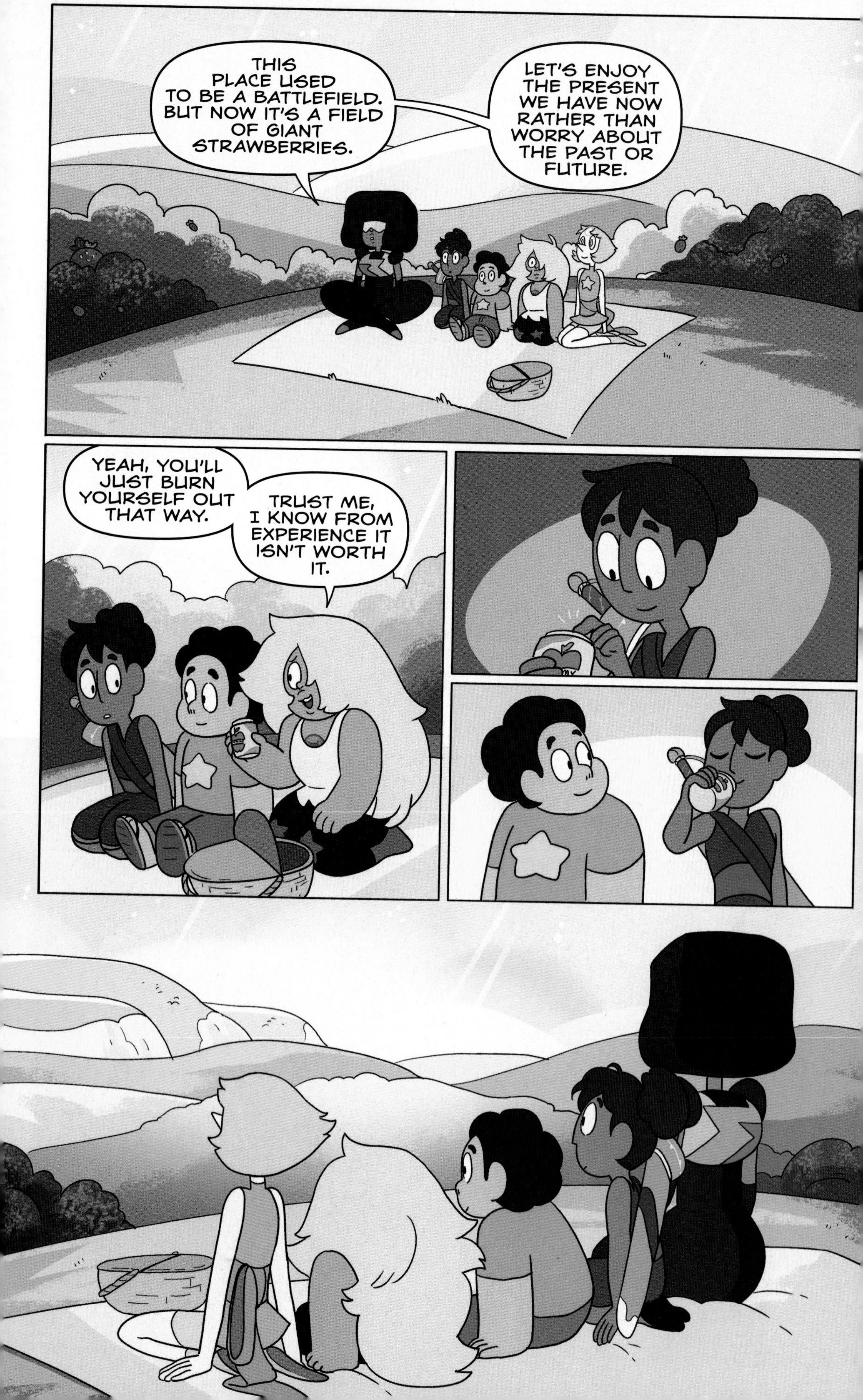
THIS PLACE USED TO BE A BATTLEFIELD. BUT NOW IT'S A FIELD OF GIANT STRAWBERRIES.
LET'S ENJOY THE PRESENT WE HAVE NOW RATHER THAN WORRY ABOUT THE PAST OR FUTURE.
YEAH, YOU'LL JUST BURN YOURSELF OUT THAT WAY.
TRUST ME, I KNOW FROM EXPERIENCE IT ISN'T WORTH IT.

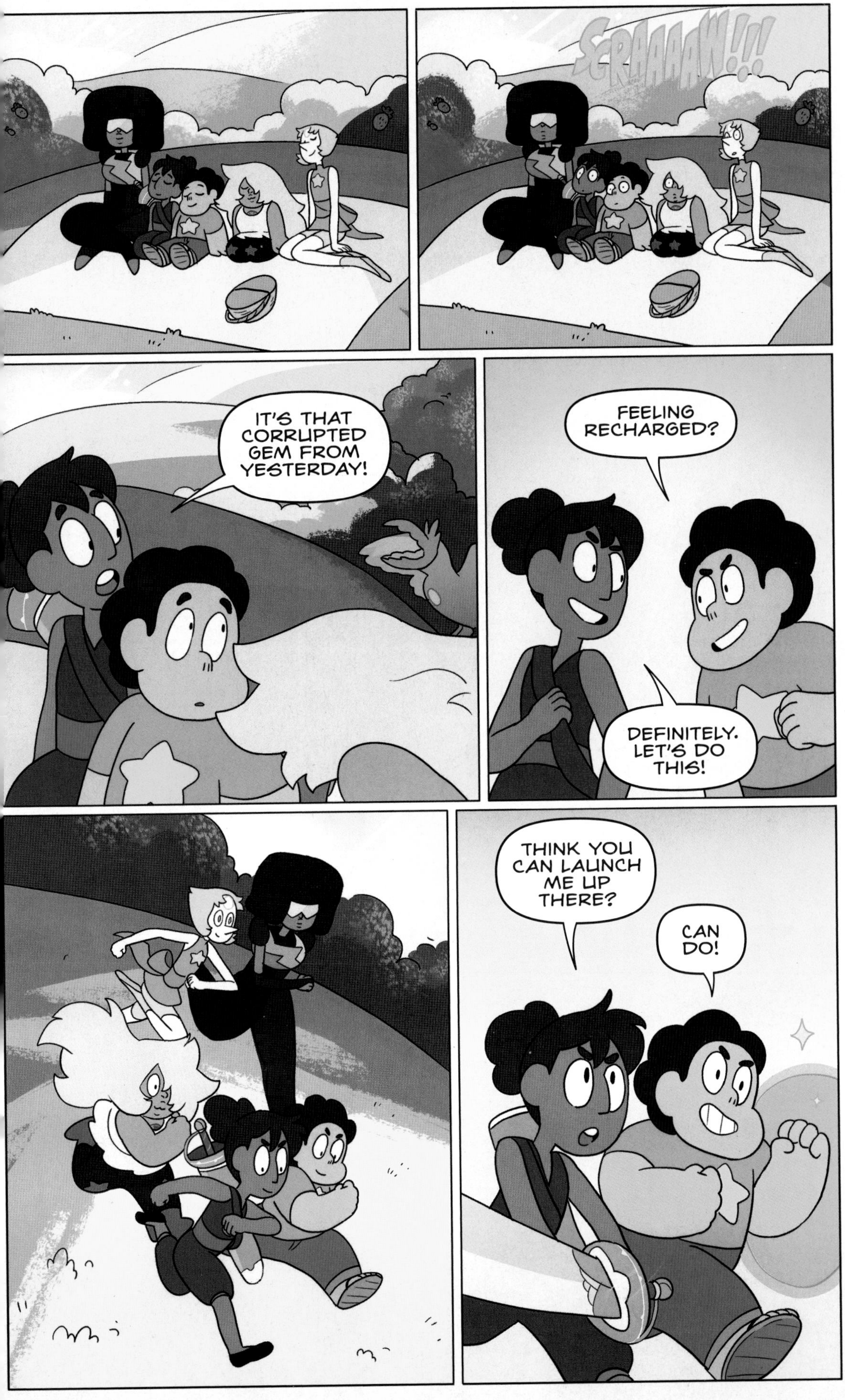
SCRAAAAW!!!
IT'S THAT CORRUPTED GEM FROM YESTERDAY!
FEELING RECHARGED?
DEFINITELY. LET'S DO THIS!
THINK YOU CAN LAUNCH ME UP THERE?
CAN DO!

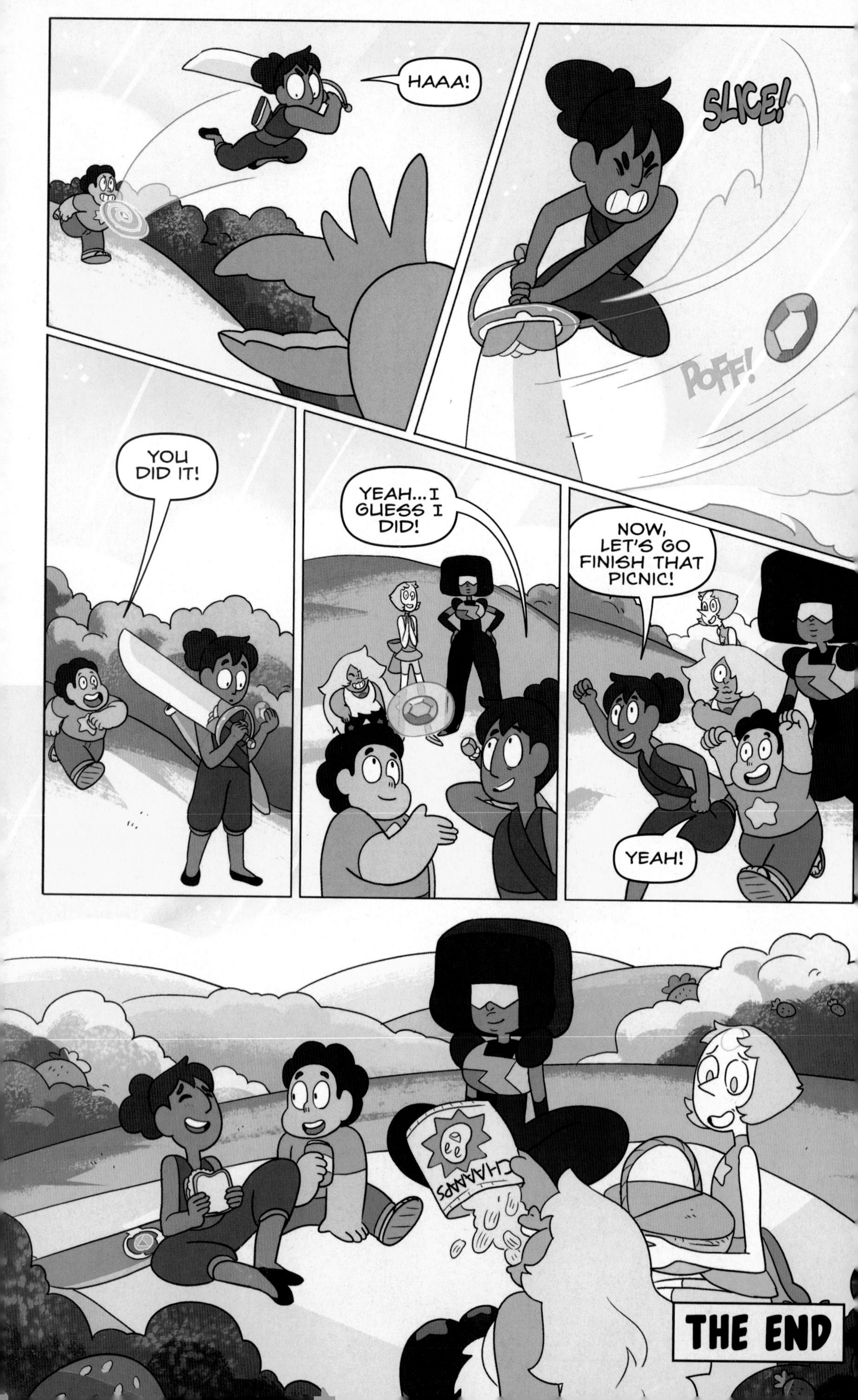
HAAA!
SLICE!
POFF!
YOU DID IT!
YEAH... I GUESS I DID!
NOW, LET'S GO FINISH THAT PICNIC!
YEAH!
CHAAAPS
THE END

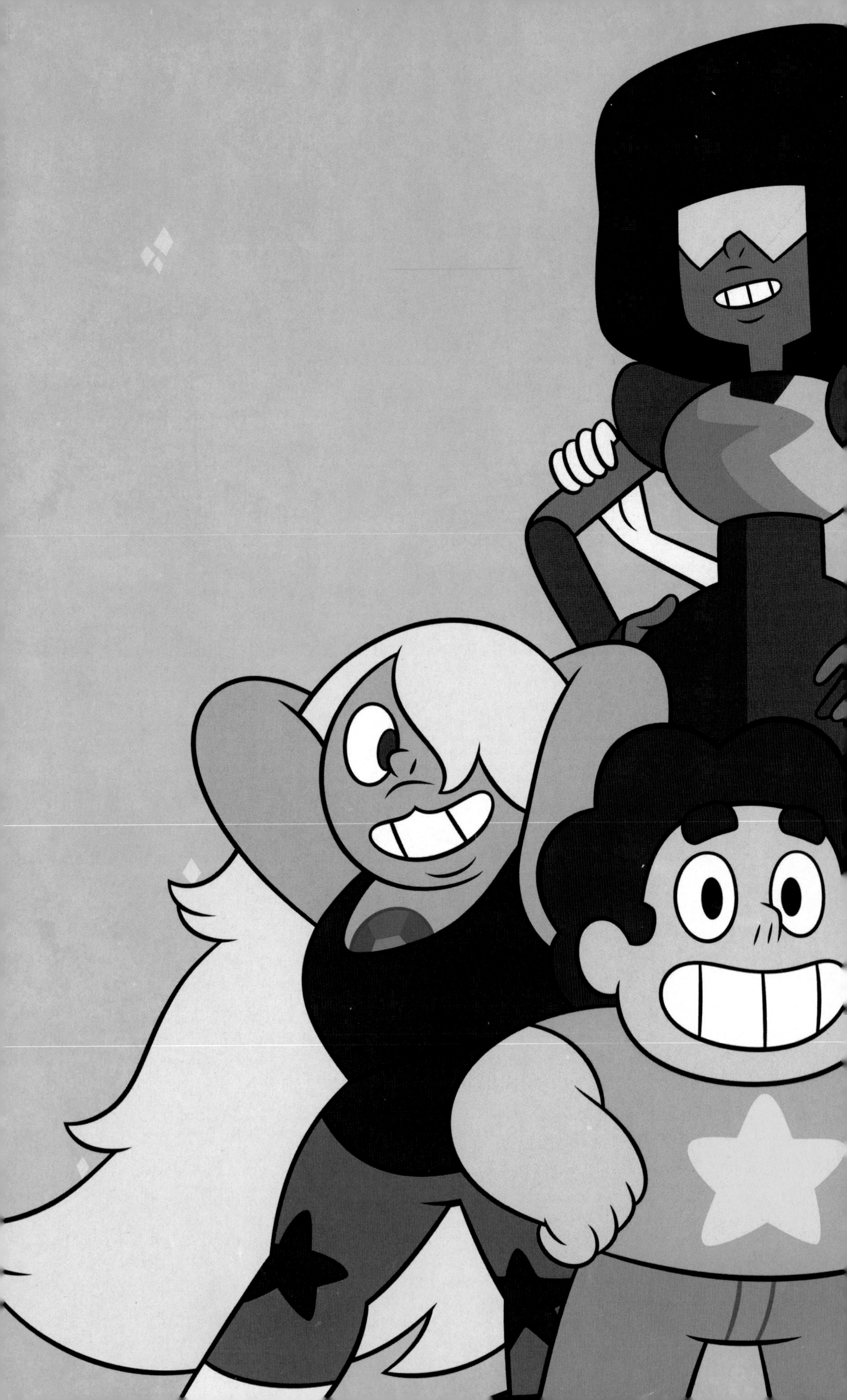

COVER GALLERY

issue seventeen main cover

MISSY PEÑA

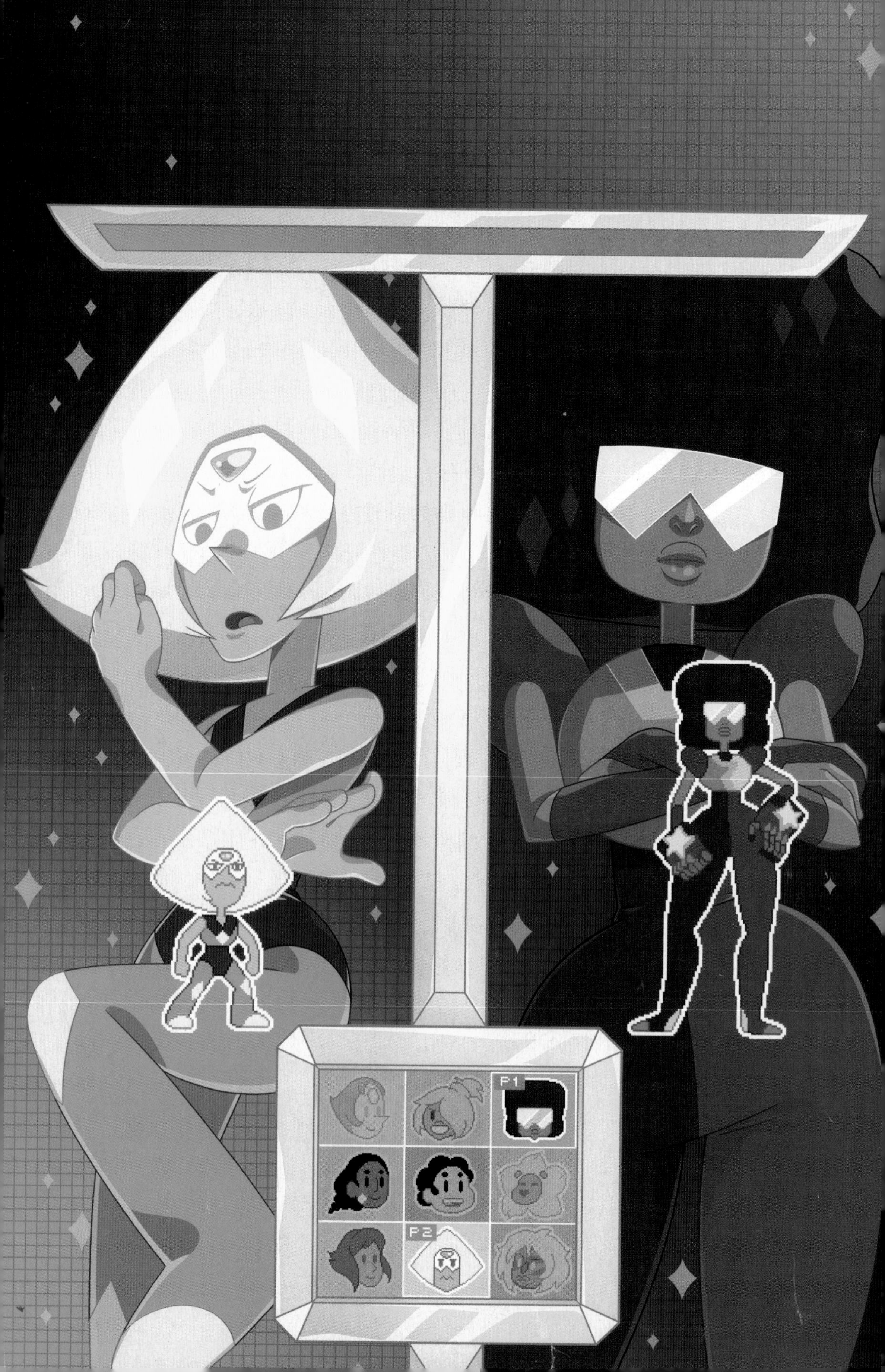

P1
P2

issue seventeen subscription cover
MEG OMAC

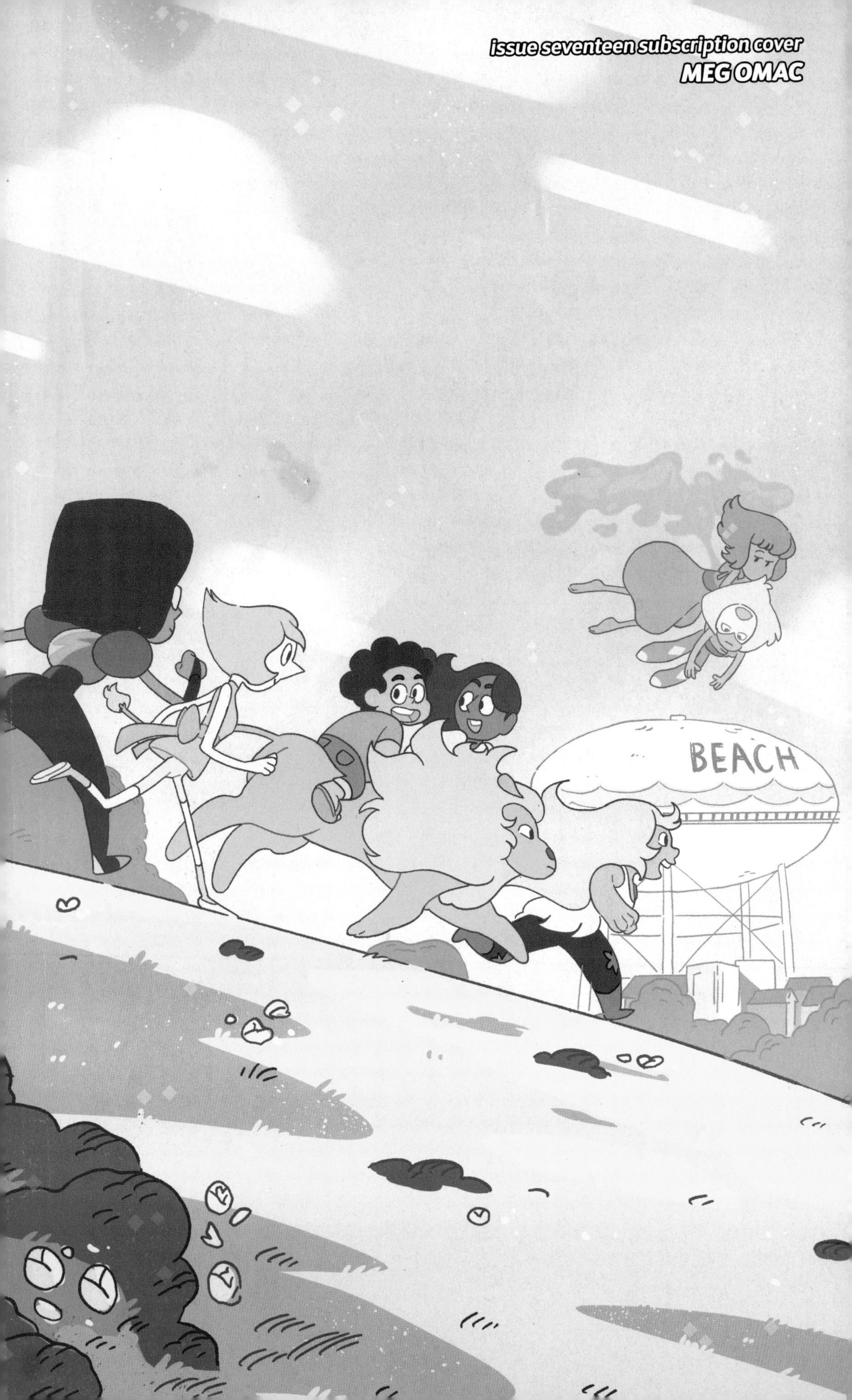
BEACH

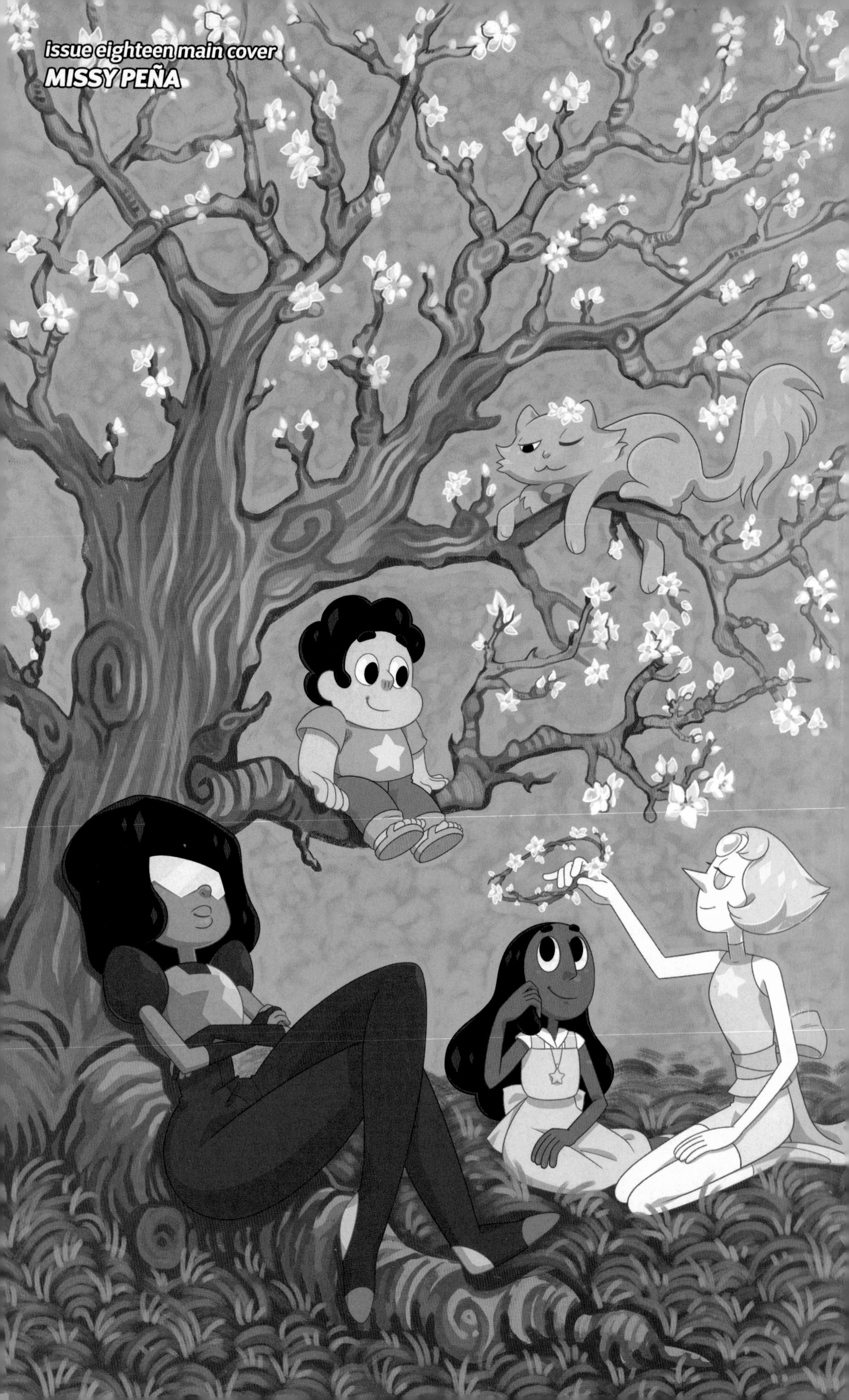

issue eighteen main cover
MISSY PEÑA

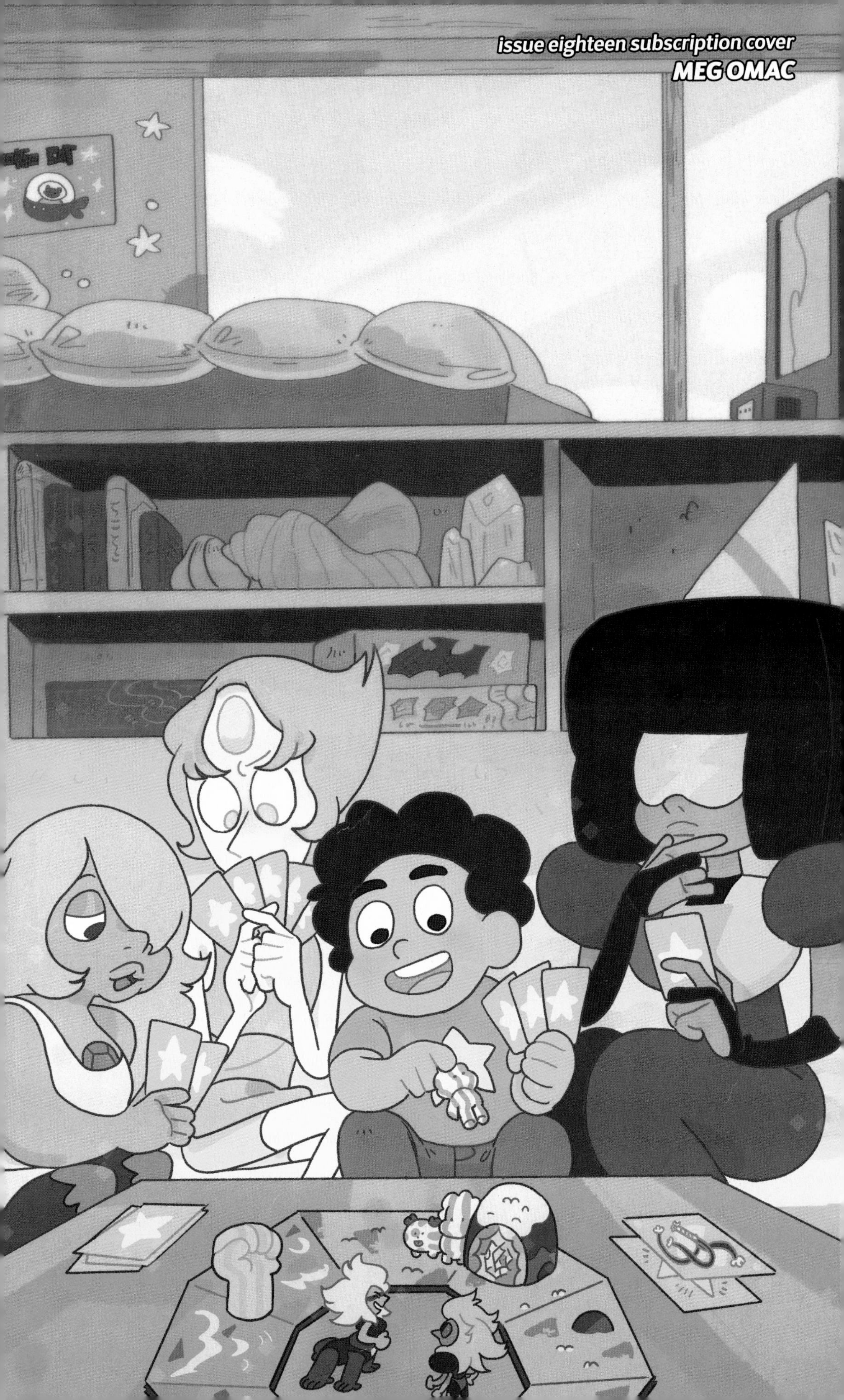

issue eighteen subscription cover
MEG OMAC

issue nineteen main cover
MISSY PEÑA

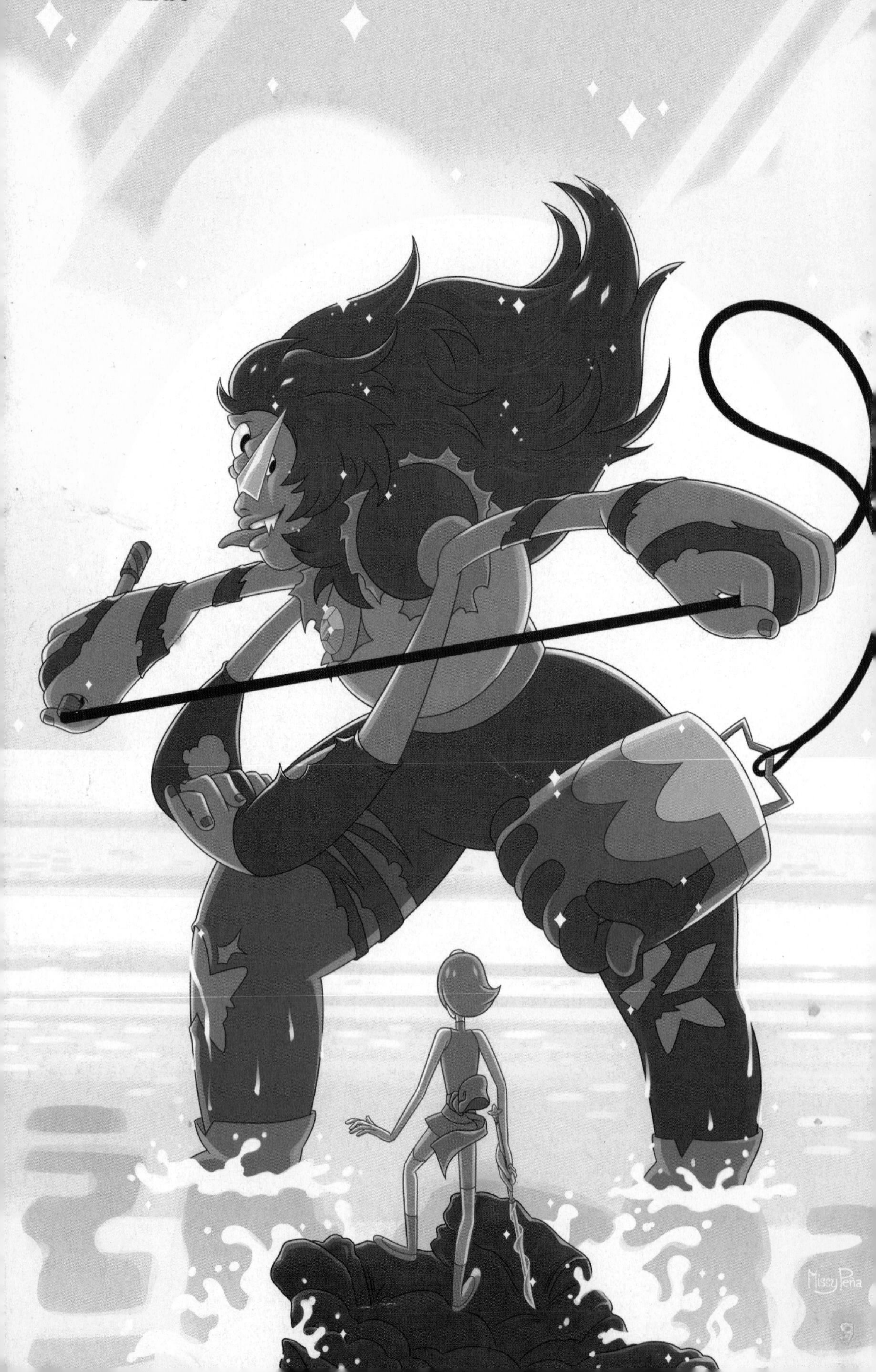
Missy Peña

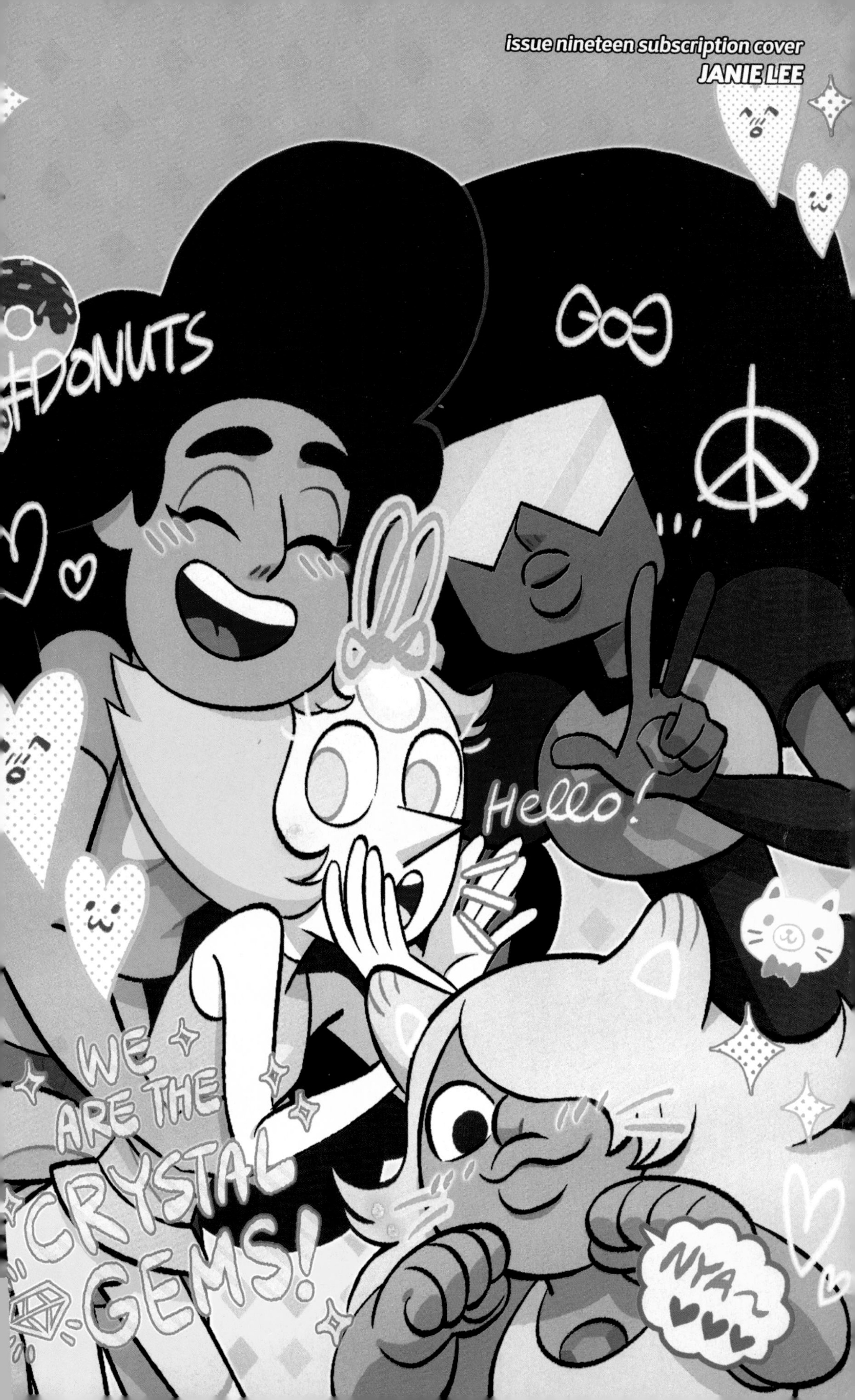
#DONUTS
Hello!
WE ARE THE CRYSTAL GEMS!
NYA~ ♥♥♥

issue nineteen subscription cover
JANIE LEE

issue twenty main cover
MISSY PEÑA

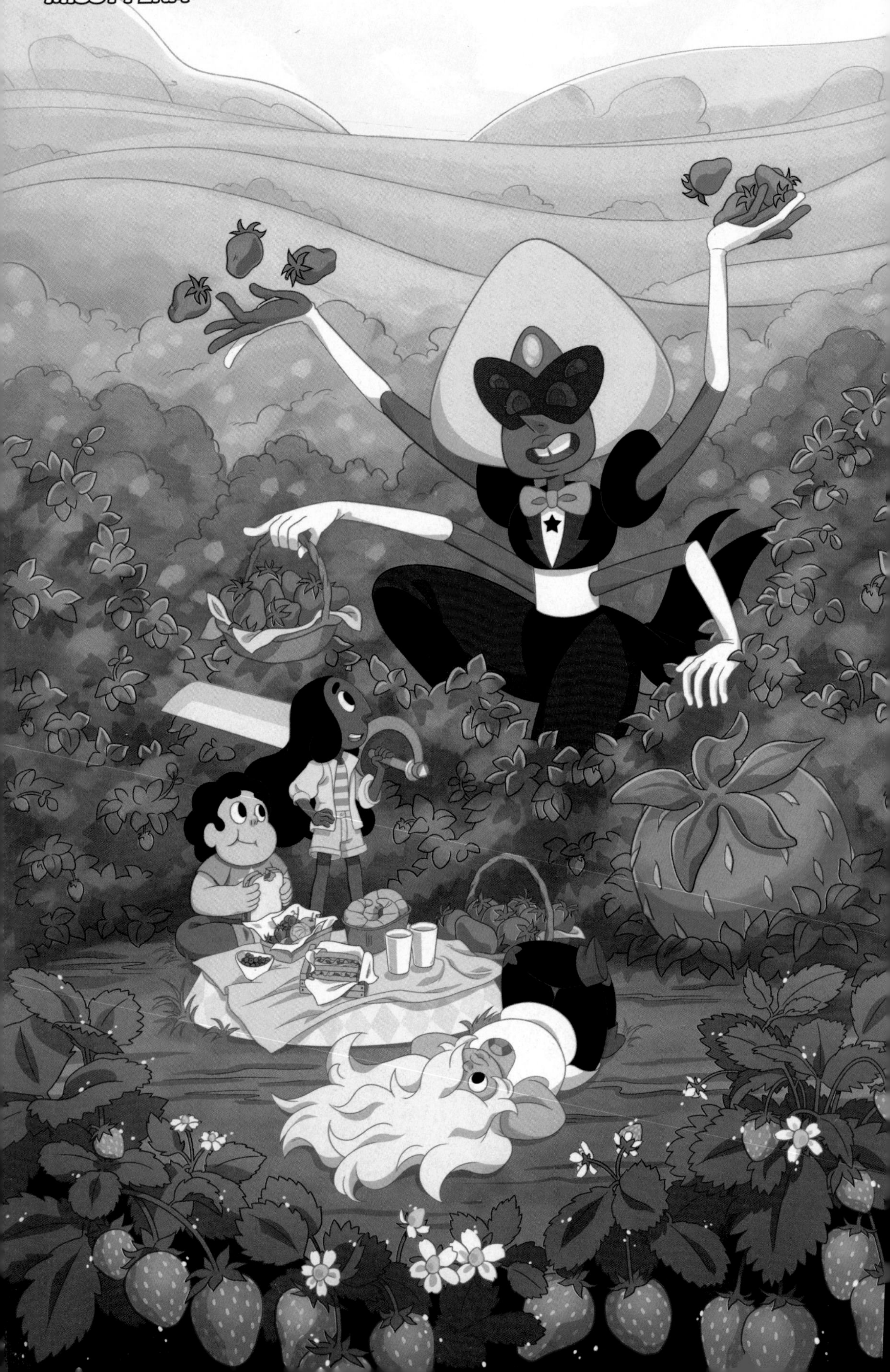

issue twenty subscription cover
CAITLYN KURILICH

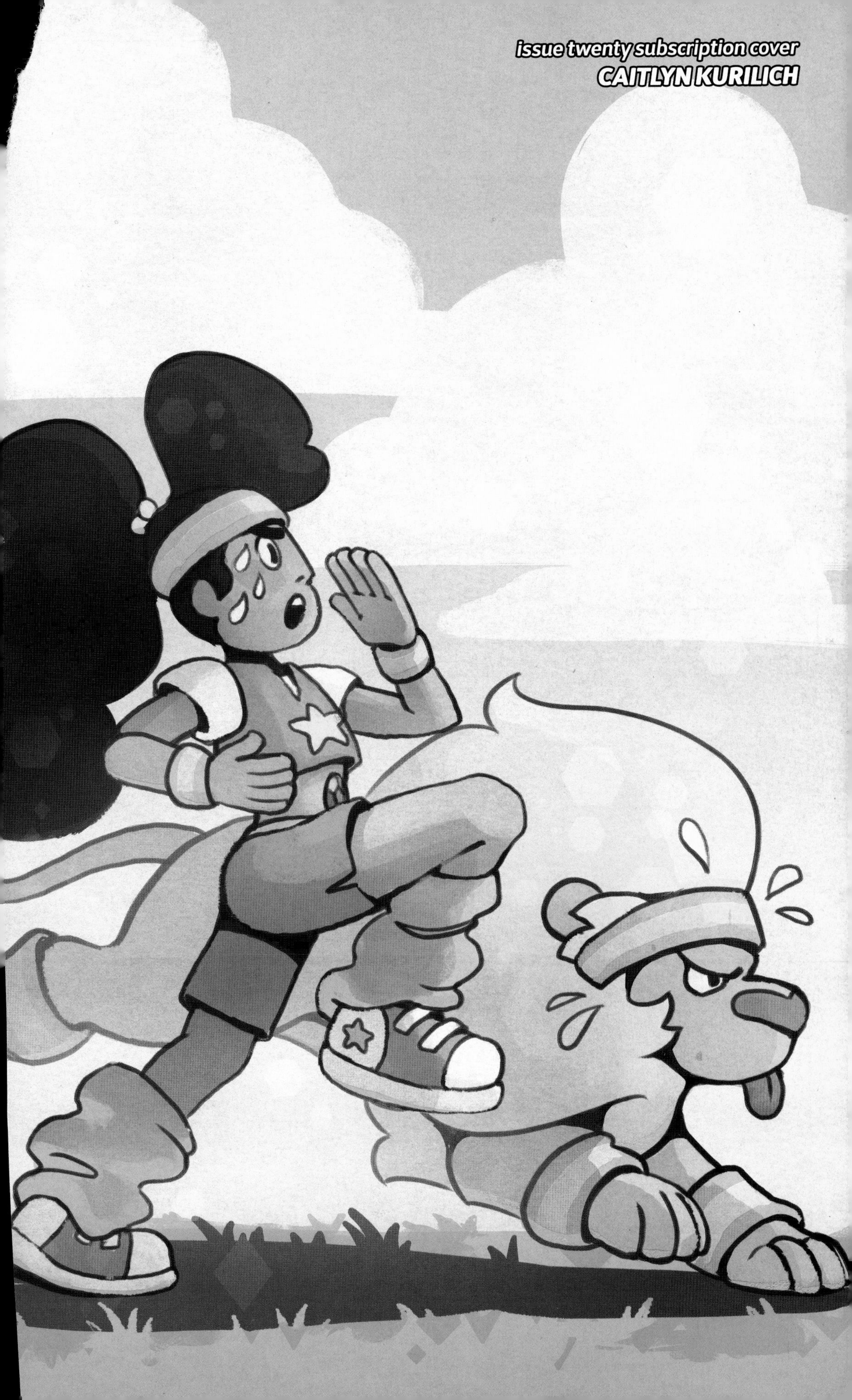

DISCOVER
EXPLOSIVE NEW WORLDS

ADVENTURE TIME

Sam Sykes · Selina Espiritu · Sarah Stern
Brave Chef Brianna

KELLY THOMPSON BRIANNE DROUHARD M. VICTORIA ROBADO
MEGA PRINCESS

THE NOT-SO SECRET SOCIETY
DALEY · CRAFTS · CLARK · BRUNI

OVER THE GARDEN WALL

STEVEN UNIVERSE
VOLUME ONE

Adventure Time
Pendleton Ward and Others
Volume 1
ISBN: 978-1-60886-280-1 | $14.99 US
Volume 2
ISBN: 978-1-60886-323-5 | $14.99 US
Adventure Time: Islands
ISBN: 978-1-60886-972-5 | $9.99 US

The Amazing World of Gumball
Ben Bocquelet and Others
Volume 1
ISBN: 978-1-60886-488-1 | $14.99 US
Volume 2
ISBN: 978-1-60886-793-6 | $14.99 US

Brave Chef Brianna
Sam Sykes, Selina Espiritu
ISBN: 978-1-68415-050-2 | $14.99 US

Mega Princess
Kelly Thompson, Brianne Drouhard
ISBN: 978-1-68415-007-6 | $14.99 US

The Not-So Secret Society
Matthew Daley, Arlene Daley, Wook Jin Clark
ISBN: 978-1-60886-997-8 | $9.99 US

Over the Garden Wall
Patrick McHale, Jim Campbell and Others
Volume 1
ISBN: 978-1-60886-940-4 | $14.99 US
Volume 2
ISBN: 978-1-68415-006-9 | $14.99 US

Steven Universe
Rebecca Sugar and Others
Volume 1
ISBN: 978-1-60886-706-6 | $14.99 US
Volume 2
ISBN: 978-1-60886-796-7 | $14.99 US

Steven Universe & The Crystal Gems
ISBN: 978-1-60886-921-3 | $14.99 US

Steven Universe: Too Cool for School
ISBN: 978-1-60886-771-4 | $14.99 US

kaboom!™

AVAILABLE AT YOUR LOCAL COMICS SHOP AND BOOKSTORE
To find a comics shop in your area, visit www.comicshoplocator.com
WWW.**BOOM-STUDIOS**.COM

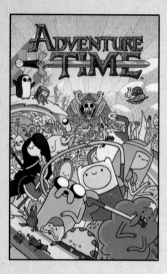

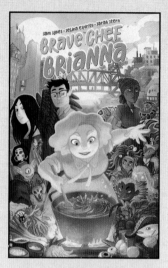

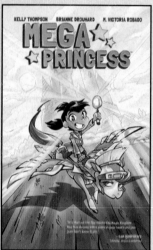

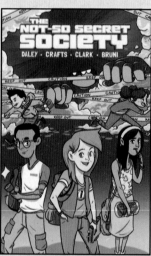

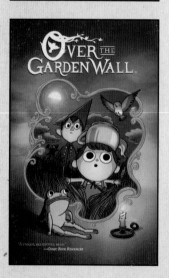

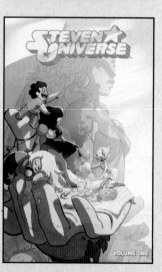

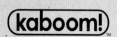